Leave Yesterday Behind

ALEXA ASTON

OLIVER
HEBER
BOOKS
SNARLY WOOL PUBLISHING
EST. 2001

Prologue

THE REALIZATION CAME *to him instantly. He'd had enough practice. He looked over at the girl, her eyes large with fear as she watched him cross the room and remove a can of beer from the mini-fridge. It hissed gently as he popped the top and took a swig. Then another. The cold brew slid down his throat, burning as it went.*

Practice made you perfect. That was the rule. His mother became the perfect whore, thanks to all her years of practice, men traipsing in and out of their ever-changing address. She died because of all those men—the never-ending line—and the booze that she used to make herself forget that same, endless parade.

And of course, the one man that bashed her face in until there wasn't a face left. That had been the kicker.

When no suspect surfaced, the authorities blamed him, an angry teen with a string of petty thefts and no good role model to influence him. Six years in the detention center and he'd learned, through trial and error, to be the model prisoner. He knew what to say to make them think he felt remorse over a crime he'd never committed— even though he wished he would have. He kept his nose clean and didn't associate with anyone. A spotless record that couldn't be beat.

And they let him out a year ago because he'd trained himself to fit in with a society that had never wanted him. Never acknowledged him. He still fit in, going to his boring job in the automotive store in Brooklyn every day, cheerfully working overtime, a smile pasted on his features, despite customer complaints over the smallest of issues. Visiting his parole officer every week, then every two weeks, and now only once a month—all because he was judged to be a reformed man. He pretended to enjoy the visits. Rehearsed what he would say so the underpaid idiot with a worthless degree in social work would think him normal.

But he'd practiced on what was important all along.

The girl tied spread-eagle to the table in the corner was proof of his due diligence.

He stood and slowly walked toward her, his eye roving up and down her naked body. She was young and ripe.

And blond.

They always had to be blond. Or else it wouldn't count.

Like a proud father, he took in how this one favored Jessica so much. He always tried to come close, but her resemblance to Jessica was quite remarkable. Why, given a chance, she might have been the next rising TV star herself. At least that's what he'd told her in the bar last night and she'd beamed at the compliment as she downed the tequila shots he paid for.

Although no one could truly hold a candle to his Jessica.

He tilted the beer above her slightly, allowing a small amount to spill onto her flat stomach. She flinched as the cold liquid hit its target. He leaned down and licked it *from her bellybutton, dragging his tongue around it in circles that grew wider and wider.*

She began to whimper behind the gag.

"Shush," he told her, as he brushed his palm across her forehead, pushing the hair back that had fallen into her eyes. She cringed at his touch.

That angered him.

He backhanded her across the cheek, a move quick in speed and fluidity that showed the hours he'd invested in the martial arts. That, along with other skills perfected through repetition, gave him the confidence it would take to accomplish his mission.

Both of them, actually.

He poured more beer across the trembling girl's breasts and watched as silent tears leaked from her eyes. As he bent, he pretended they were drips from an ice cream cone and licked them away.

He removed the knife from his pocket and laid it between her breasts as he drained the can and tossed it aside, the empty cling *echoing in the small, windowless room.*

"I need to put something on you," he explained.

He did this every time. It was part of the ritual. The ritual soothed him. He knew when the time came and it really counted, he wouldn't have the privacy he had become accustomed to. Jessica was never alone. She was older and would never want to come with him as all the others had before. No, when her time came, it would have to be different from the others he practiced with.

But the end result would be the same.

He removed a tube of lipstick from his shirt pocket and opened it, rotating the bottom until the color peeked above the gold rim.

"I would like you to wear this. It's Jessica's favorite."

The girl's confusion didn't matter. Only the ritual did.

3

"You must be very still and quiet. I'll put it on and you'll be very pretty. Even beautiful." He shook his head sadly. "But not as beautiful as Jessica, I'm afraid."

His knife cut through the cloth handkerchief that had kept her fairly silent after the Rohypnol wore off. He pulled it away, taking time to dab her lips with it before he dropped it to the floor. He hoped the knife atop her was intimidation enough. She shouldn't speak through this part. Silence was important.

He brought the lipstick to her mouth and concentrated as he brushed it across one side of her upper lip, then the other. As he began to trace her lower one with the vibrant color, she gagged.

"Be still," he warned. "It has to be perfect in order for me to release you."

He always tried to give them a glimmer of hope.

But the blond choked until a spew of vomit roared from her and landed directly onto his shirt. His favorite shirt.

He glanced down and studied the trail running down him, the smell of last night's tequila overwhelming. With lightning speed, he took the knife and plunged it into her stomach. The comforting, tinny scent of blood assaulted him.

He knew he would be all right.

Yanking the blade from her, he repeated the action several times until her gasps subsided. Until the blood bubbled up and spilled out around her. Until the look of horror was frozen in place for all time.

He frowned. "You ruined my last practice session, bitch," he complained to the college coed who had only wanted a few free drinks, served with a dash of compliments on the side.

Still, he took the knife and cut a large lock of hair from her head. He would add it to his growing collection.

He sighed. He was ready.
Jessica would be his.
Soon...

Chapter One

AT THIRTY-TWO, Jessica Filch Karris Richmond Faulkner Morrison Taylor had been married six times. Five if you counted one husband married twice in a row. She'd divorced a foreign race car driver; an egotistical actor; a temperamental chef; and a stodgy banker. She was now the recent widow of a renowned art dealer more than double her age that she swore was the love of her life.

Like all the rest had been.

Callie Chennault had given up trying to understand Jessica. After ten years, she was tired.

And beginning not to care.

"Callie? Hustle, girl! You're late again. Marvin is shitting bricks."

She pushed up her sunglasses to rest atop her head and grinned wickedly at Sandra, her favorite makeup artist. Sandra grabbed her arm and pulled her along the narrow corridor to her dressing room. She passed Husband Number Three and blew him a kiss. Ricardo was about to marry an heiress that was secretly conducting an affair with her son's best friend. Jessica knew all about it and was going to tell Ricardo later today.

That is, if she could pull herself together enough to do so.

Sandra removed Callie's sunglasses and pulled the navy T-shirt over her head and gave her a push. Callie landed in a chair. Sandra immediately grabbed Callie's yoga bag from her shoulder and tossed it and her purse onto the sofa. Margaret, their best hairdresser, began to comb Callie's long, honeyed locks with a brisk motion, twisting sections and clipping them atop her head.

"Hey, take it easy," she complained good-naturedly.

Margaret made eye contact with her in the mirror. "If you'd been here half an hour ago, things might be different, hon."

Sandra already had her palette in front of her and began slathering on the thick foundation that the TV cameras required. Callie knew she was in good hands. She closed her eyes, thinking about how Jessica would approach Ricardo today with her news about his heiress and her illicit affair, one which could land the woman in jail, considering the age of her young lover.

Jessica had never quite gotten over Ricardo. She'd even shared a one-night fling with her ex-husband during her marriage to the boring banker. Callie thought their chemistry was too good to limit the affair to a single session of fierce lovemaking, but the actor who portrayed Ricardo came down with walking pneumonia and looked like hell for six weeks. Why would Jessica be interested in a man who resembled death warmed over when she could have any man in Sumner Falls?

Still, Callie understood why Jessica felt the need to share such sizzling news with her former husband and lover. The naughty heiress was about to lose all her money to the IRS and Ricardo needed a lot of cash to keep his new restaurant afloat. Without his new wife's fortune, the moody chef would have no need of her. He was much too good-looking to be stuck with her when she had money, let alone if she were broke and jail-bound.

Besides, Jessica was a meddler. She thrived on manipulating the lives of those around her, just like Jane Austen's Emma Woodhouse. That part Callie deeply understood. She herself grew up in a small town, where everyone knew everybody's business. She'd gotten involved in the personal lives and loves of too many people in Aurora and could empathize with Jessica's need to stick her nose into the brewing storm.

"Finished, doll," Sandra said, patting her shoulder.

Callie opened her eyes and studied her image in the mirror. Her honeyed mane was swept into a chic chignon, her skin dewy, her mouth a sinful red. She smiled and stood.

She was almost Jessica.

She slipped off her soccer sandals and yoga pants. Sandra spritzed her with Jessica's signature fragrance while Margaret fastened a pearl necklace around her neck. She eased into a royal purple silk blouse and slim black cigarette pants. Sandra fastened the faux diamond bracelet around her wrist as Margaret held out the three-inch black stilettos that would put her at an even six feet.

She looked into the mirror again and smiled.

Now she was Jessica.

She took her time walking down the hall. Jessica wouldn't mind keeping people waiting. She ran on her own schedule, which was interrupted by unscheduled romps of wild sex. She was fickle and flirty and a bit snobbish at times.

In other words, Jessica was the total opposite of Callie.

Callie favored jeans and sneakers, a light gloss or lip stain as her only makeup, and was friendly and outgoing and always on time. She'd been in only two serious relationships in her twenties, but nothing came of either. She hadn't had sex in almost two years, making her thirties tame. Her friends considered her too finicky when it came to her taste in men. Besides, Callie wouldn't know how to flirt if her life depended upon it.

But Jessica did. Sometimes Callie thought of her alter ego as *The Evil Twin.* Yet primetime soap fans loved the bad girl who sometimes showed glimpses of vulnerability. At any rate, the role had kept Callie in a steady job for just over a decade. Unfortunately, she'd finally hit the point where portraying Jessica had her bored stiff. She yearned for more of a challenge. She thought Jessica needed to grow up finally. Change. Develop some lasting relationships with her family and one man.

Nope. Not according to the head writer of *Sumner Falls.* Jessica was much too interesting as she was, flitting from bed to bed, meddling in everyone's business. Even *TV Today* agreed, naming Jessica the most watchable character on primetime television for seven years in a row. Why would Callie want to mess with a good thing?

Jessica arrived on the set. A quiet descended. The gentle buzz of a moment ago stopped abruptly at her entrance. It was funny how even the cast and crew had come to think that she *was* Jessica. They spoke to her in a different way when she was ordinary Callie Chennault in no makeup, her hair in its customary ponytail. They would tease with her, joke with her, and even tell her about their families.

But whenever she came out all done-up in the Jessica duds, things changed. Confidences were no longer shared. From the gaffer to the cameraman, everyone gave her a wide berth.

Frankly, she was tired of it. She wondered if she had it in her to play another role after being identified for so long with one character. Many actors left television with a dream to work in film. Most came crawling back within a year or two, broke and scared. Sometimes, fans accepted their return; other times, they became has-beens, waiting tables or modeling shoes in industrial films, their brush with fame gone.

She didn't care. She missed the live theater of her high school and college days. She would love the chance to tackle a small, meaty role in some indie film. Anything, as long as it was far-removed from Jessica Filch Karris Richmond Faulkner Morrison Taylor.

Her contract was up in another month. She'd put off her agent regarding renegotiations. Harry assumed she would be bucking for a hefty raise and told her she would get it. He promised he'd pull off a sweetheart deal, where she'd work for several weeks at a time when involved in a major storyline and then get a stretch of weeks off in which to vacation or even pursue another acting job.

If she could find one. She didn't want to be typecast as Jessica 2.0 for the rest of her career.

'If we can't find a film for you, you could think about made-for-cable movies, like on Lifetime. Or even jump to a streaming series on Netflix or Hulu. Maybe something off-Broadway. You could step into a long-running show for a limited guest run. When *All My Children* was on the air years ago, the famed La Lucci did other things. She even had a nightclub act and did some spots with Regis Philbin." Her agent had eyed her appraisingly. "You don't sing, do ya?"

She assured him she didn't unless it was in the shower and her dog, Wolf, was her audience of one.

She walked across the set and sat in a gold brocaded chair and glanced up so she could see her director in the control room. Marvin rarely kept his temper contained, reaming out actors left and right, but he usually exercised caution when Jessica arrived. If she were Callie, she would have apologized to him for her tardiness and explained how her washer flooded her apartment and the one next to it this morning, else she never would have kept the crew waiting like this.

Jessica simply raised her chin a notch and coolly awaited her instructions. Not that Marvin really told her what to do anymore. She'd been Jessica long before he came onboard *Sumner Falls*. Besides, the writers understood how she turned a phrase and wrote accordingly for her. Callie knew instinctively when to pause, when to arch her brow, when to turn up the heat—and when to freeze someone out.

She was good. Four Emmys said so. Marvin earned three, riding her coattails.

"Let's go," the director said brusquely.

All vestiges of Callie Chennault vanished. Jessica picked up the phone, moistened her lips and said breathily, "I need to see you, Ricardo. No. It can't wait. Now. My place."

* * *

Callie dried her face with a fluffy towel and hung it back up. She loosened the tight chignon, which often gave her a headache and shook out her hair, combing her fingers through it as it fell about her shoulders. She picked up a tinted lip balm and smoothed it over her lips. They were always dry after she scrubbed away *Ravenous Red*, the flaming color that was Jessica's trademark and available for purchase at finer department stores. She slipped back into her street clothes and grabbed her yoga backpack.

Sandra popped her head into the dressing room. "Tomorrow's script, Cal. Lotta lines for you, girl. Beth stopped by earlier and highlighted them for you." She tucked the pages into Callie's messenger bag. "She said do not, do not, be late to yoga. Or she'll never forgive you. *Ever.* That is a direct quote."

She chuckled. Beth got her into yoga three years ago and they both were totally addicted. Callie lived for the seven o'clock twice-weekly class they attended and used a yoga fitness app once she arrived home other nights. Yoga helped her maintain her sanity in the crazy, stress-filled world of television dramas.

"Anything promising? Or did you actually not read ahead for once?"

The make-up artist shrugged. "All I'll say is that you and Ricardo end in a clinch, romance-cover style."

She grinned. "I suppose our next scene I'll be given the choice to eat him up, spit him out, or push him away. I know you know. Dating one of the show's writers does have some perks."

Sandra drew a line across her lips and tossed away an imaginary key. "I like it better when you don't know what's coming. Besides, it depends upon if you re-sign. Like that wouldn't happen." Sandra rolled her eyes. "See you tomorrow, Cal."

She nodded, picking up her bag and backpack. Good old Callie. Always predictable. The good girl who did what everyone expected and would naturally roll over her contract for another two years, no questions asked. Harry was bucking to set things up for three. She knew it was so he could buy that weekend place on the beach his wife always nagged him about.

Yet, why did she feel so unhappy? She was still fairly young. Single. Rich. Beautiful. She had one of the highest *Q* ratings around. What more could she want? Especially today, with so many network TV series biting the dust, replaced by reality or talk shows, which were more cost-effective. *Sumner Falls* was the second-longest running drama on primetime television. It was safe because it was a huge moneymaker for the network and had a rabid fan base.

Why would she even toy with the idea of not re-upping? For an actor to have a steady gig, much less one so successful and lucrative, was pretty much unheard of. No one in her right mind would opt out for the unknown.

Or would they?

She headed out of the studio. Only three fans awaited her outside tonight. She posed for selfies with them and signed autographs for everyone, even scrawling her name across a tennis shoe. That was a first. She started down the Midtown street at a rapid pace. Her class began in less than ten minutes. She couldn't afford to be late. She needed every minute of that deep breathing to cleanse away all the mess that was Jessica.

* * *

"I love you, Jessica," the man whispered under his breath as he watched her from across the busy lanes of traffic. He fell into step, matching her stride for stride. It was the fifty-ninth time he'd followed her to her yoga class.

He planned for it to be the last.

Chapter Two

CALLIE TOOK a last swallow of her chai tea and stretched lazily. She glanced around the coffeehouse and was surprised to find how few people remained.

"It's already after nine," she exclaimed. "I am dead meat." She began grabbing her things, standing to throw the yoga bag over one shoulder as she reached for her purse.

Beth laughed as she gathered her items. "Only TV folks would understand why you're in a tizzy, Cal."

"People think we lead such glamorous lives. Little do they know we have zero social life. Come home, learn your lines, hit the sack. Repeat." She sighed. "I can't remember the last time I was awake to see the eleven o'clock news, much less Kimmel or Fallon. If they're even still on."

They walked toward the door and Beth added, "I do believe you got in a yoga class and had a wonderful hour of gossip tonight. Isn't that worth getting home a little later than usual?"

Callie groaned. "You're the one that highlighted my lines for me, Beth. There's gotta be a ton. Jessica and Ricardo are alone at her place when we open tomorrow."

Her friend sniffed. "Thank God she's spilling the beans to him about Little Miss Rich Heiress. I just hate that two-timing bitch."

She laughed. "You hate her because she always took up all the dressing room with her crap thrown around."

Beth said, "Cal, it's been years since you had to share space with another actress. That woman was like a fifteen-year-old. Her stuff was always everywhere. And she would take *my* makeup and *my* designer clothes and dump them on the floor and push them under the sofa. She is the reason I left *Sumner Falls*."

Callie pushed open the coffeehouse door. The cool March night had turned windy. She zipped up her jacket and gave Beth a knowing glance.

"You chucked *Sumner Falls* when Mr. Right came along and you know it."

"Speaking of Mr. Right. Are we still on for this weekend?"

She grimaced. "Blind dates are not my idea of fun, Beth. You know that."

"It's a freakin' dinner party, Cal. Lots of people around. It's not as if you'll be stuck with Ted all night." Her friend grinned. "Besides, he's single, a plastic surgeon, and hot. Emphasis on the hot part. I think you'll be a terrific match."

"Then why hasn't Saint Ted, *the-appointed-hot-one*, already been snagged? Maybe I just have a suspicious nature but you're making him sound too good to be true."

A loud boom of thunder echoed through the dark night.

"I won't take no for an answer." Beth turned her eyes toward the sky. "I think it's about to pour. I'm going to catch a cab." She smiled at Callie. "The faster I can get home, the sooner I can send out an e-blast to all

Callie Chennault Fan Club members to be sure and tune in for a fatal showdown with Ricardo coming up in the near future."

She laughed. "Yeah, right, Ms. President. And here I thought you were just good at helping me with my lines and answering my fan mail."

Beth hugged her and then raised a hand to hail a passing cab. "Wear the red dress on Saturday night. You'll knock Saint Ted's eyes from their sockets."

"Great, a true blind date," she quipped.

Beth flipped her the bird and jumped into the taxi that pulled up.

Callie waved goodbye as the cab pulled away from the curb. She didn't know what she'd do without Beth's friendship.

Except for this dating thing.

Her friend was extremely happy, with a toddler and a loving husband, and she wanted Callie to be just as satisfied. She'd lost count of the number of times Beth set her up with acquaintances from church, Mark's hospital, various cousins, neighbors, and even a guy from Beth's dog's obedience class. She played along gamely. Half of her secretly hoped she would find her Prince Charming this way. The other half just wished Beth would wave the white flag of surrender and leave her in peace.

Because when it came down to it, what man wanted a woman who worked long hours, came home and stuck her nose in a script, mumbled to herself as she memorized lines, and then dropped into bed before ten every night? The men who wandered into her life for a short while found out how boring her regimented life was and left the relationship without a backward glance.

She hitched her yoga bag higher and started walking as a light mist began to fall. Hey, she was still single.

Would this set-up guy think something might be wrong with her? Maybe Dr. Ted, *the-appointed-hot-one*, had as many misgivings about Saturday night as she did. Maybe he would think she'd been married half a dozen times like Jessica. Most people did. Or maybe he would be one of twelve men left in America with no clue as to who she was.

She doubted it.

"Forget about it," she muttered to herself.

She had more important things to worry about, such as calling Aunt Callandra when she got home. Her great-aunt couldn't seem to shake this flu going around. Callie worried about her. She wasn't getting any younger at eighty-two.

Then a strange feeling washed over her, a sense of foreboding so strong that she quickly turned and glanced around to see if someone followed her. A man brushed by, jarring her without a word of apology. A couple in their mid-forties was about thirty yards behind her, turning the corner away from her. No one else shared her sidewalk. It was a late, dark, and rainy weekday night. In this neighborhood, all sensible people had already found their way home.

Spooked, Callie pulled up her hood and clutched her purse and bag more tightly as the mist turned to a steady rain. She couldn't help but shake the feeling that someone still watched her so she picked up her pace.

Maybe she should take a cab home. But her subway station was only a block and half away. It would be foolish to stand out in a downpour after nine at night when she could duck inside and be on her way downtown in a couple of minutes. She liked that people left her alone on the subway. A few sometimes stared at her and frowned, wondering if they'd ever seen her before. Most turned away, not quite able to place her.

After all, she left Jessica behind at the studio every day. No chic clothes, Ravenous Red mouth, or fancy hairstyle. She didn't often get recognized in real life unless it was a die-hard fan. Even then, most New Yorkers were cool about it and simply ignored her, while the *paparazzi* had lost interest in her years ago. The press declared her boring and turned their attention to other stars who liked to stir the pot.

The weird feeling washed over her again.

Chill out. Just move.

She took a few steps and stopped when her foot hit gum. "Great. That's what you get when you're not watching where you go, Cal." She stopped and lifted her shoe for inspection, swearing softly under her breath.

"Jessica?"

She turned automatically and thought it was sad that she answered to two names as she saw a man standing behind her. He was probably the reason she'd had the feeling of being followed. He seemed a little out of breath, as if he'd raced to reach her. It had happened before. She knew it would happen again.

And always with this type.

He was non-descript in every way—average height, average build, brown hair, glasses. Harmless looking. Dopey grin on his face, like he'd hit the lottery because he'd actually had the balls to speak to the crush of his daydreams. She knew enough to be firm. Give him a brief little personal moment, a smiling selfie, and her signature on something so she could get back to her life.

Then a quick flash of John Lennon signing an autograph for Mark David Chapman zipped through her brain. *He'd been average, too.*

And he'd killed Lennon hours after someone snapped a photograph of them together.

"You don't look like Jessica up close." His voice was

silky, almost caressing, yet the tone was definitely disappointed.

Her pulse quickened. She took a step back to put a little distance between them and brushed against a brick wall.

"I like to give my skin a rest away from the studio. All that heavy make-up and hairspray can cause a girl some damage. I like to let my skin breathe." She kept her tone calm and friendly as she glanced over the man's shoulder.

No one was in sight.

"I want to see Jessica." His mouth turned into a pout that would put Ricardo to shame. "She's my favorite, you know."

He pulled something from his pocket and held it up. "Put this on. It'll help. It's the perfect shade." He smiled shyly. "I'll even let you do it. You're the expert." He reached out and grabbed her wrist and laid the item in her hand before letting go.

Chills ran through her as she opened her palm. In it lay a gold tube of Jessica's signature *Ravenous Red*. This one meant business.

"I'm afraid I can't without a—"

A knife appeared, clutched in his left hand. Her heart beat erratically for a moment. Her words died in her throat.

"Don't worry," he said softly. "You know how to be Jessica whenever you want to."

Her palms grew damp. The lipstick almost slipped from her hand.

"Jessica always likes to be seen wearing this color. Put it on. Now." His voice was quiet but the underlying threat hung in the air all the same.

Callie brought a shaking hand to her mouth and realized the lid was still on. She removed it and twisted a few turns before she lifted the lipstick close again.

Oh, God, she was so nervous. She stroked color onto her upper lip and then across the bottom. Her hand slipped, though, and a searing red line jutted across her lower cheek.

"You made a mistake. Wipe it off and do it again. It has to be perfect." The tone was deadly calm.

"I'll need some cold cream. Red stains pretty badly." She gulped air, trying to calm herself. She couldn't let this guy see how rattled she was. "And I know you want this to be perfect. So do I."

"I can fix it."

She watched him pull a tissue from his jacket pocket. He gave it a lick and then stroked it down her cheek to her jaw several times.

"That's better," he said, dreamily smiling as he inspected his work. "Now, try again."

Her eyes met his and Callie prayed her hands would stop shaking enough for her to get it right this time.

Why me? her brained screamed.

She'd never seen the need to use any type of bodyguard. For God's sake, she was just a television actress. Usually, TV fans were always friendly. They didn't really treat you like a movie star because you came into their homes every week. They thought they knew you. Fans considered you family.

But fan was short for fanatic. She knew she'd just run into the motherfucker of all fans.

Do not cry, she told herself, wondering what would work to get away from this creep with a knife.

He said he wanted Jessica—so Callie would unleash her alter ego's persona in all her glory. Maybe Jessica could get her out of this situation.

Immediately, her posture changed. With confidence,

she applied the lipstick, tilting her head slightly as she pressed her lips together, sealing the color. The Jessica juices began to flow through her. The flirtiness. The sexiness. The pout.

"You are a very interesting man." She ran a slender hand along the arm without the knife. *Don't think about the knife.* "I'm convinced we need to get to know one another a little better," she said huskily. Whenever Jessica wanted something, she turned on all her charm. "What's your name? I want to know all about you."

She observed the uncertainty flash in his eyes. He'd been calling the shots a moment ago. Yet in the space of seconds, Jessica was now in charge. This jerk may have thought he wanted Jessica but he had a tiger by the tail.

"Simon," he whispered.

"Oh, I just love that name. Simon," she purred. "It sounds so strong. So masculine. So *sexy*." She ran a manicured nail slowly down his chest. He flushed and shuffled uncomfortably.

Good. She'd hit the right button. She was in Jessica's element. She couldn't worry about not having a script. Flying by the seat of her pants with some knife-wielding fanatic. She was in full-blown character. *Be charming. Stay in control. Keep in the zone.*

Be Jessica.

She moved into him, away from the wall. She became the aggressor, the one wanting something, the tables turned. He was the nervous one now.

"I'm glad we ran into one another, Simon. Would you like to get a drink? I'm mad for whiskey sours these days. They make me... lose control."

"No," he said unsteadily. He stepped back but Jessica moved right back into his space.

She placed a hand on his arm. "Then what do you

want to do, sugar?" She ran the back of her other hand along his cheek.

"K-k-kiss you," he stuttered.

The thought revolted her but she realized the hand with the knife had totally gone limp, as if he'd forgotten it was there. *Keep going with the flow.*

But without a script, who knew where this train wreck was headed?

She bit her lip and studied him a moment. It's not as if they'd start having sex on the street. She'd just suck it up and kiss the bastard. Then somehow she'd get away. Maybe she could knee him in the groin to disable him. Or lightning would strike Stupid Simon dead. Really, really dead.

"We barely know each other, Simon. Don't you want to go somewhere quiet? Out of the rain. We could talk a while."

He frowned. "You barely knew Alec or Ricardo. That never stopped you before, Jessica."

She smiled seductively as she played with his lapel. "You know so much about me. I don't know a thing about you."

"Would it make a difference?" he asked, a sad look haunting his eyes.

She let Jessica consider his question. "Sometimes," she answered. "I'm awfully fond of money. I won't hide that fact, Simon. Power. Knowledge. Position. I like a man with all those things."

"I can take care of you," he said earnestly. "I want to. I can do it better than anyone because I love you more than all the others ever did. Let me love you." He put a hand along her nape and pulled her close.

Warning bells blasted in her head. The survival instinct of fight or flight kicked in, pouring adrenaline into her bloodstream as if she'd just snorted cocaine. She willed herself to keep improvising. She'd done something like this a thousand times before in acting class. On the set. She could do this.

He lowered his head and she automatically shut her eyes.

Don't think. Just do.

He smelled of spearmint gum and Old Spice. She didn't know they still made that. Her dad had worn the cheap aftershave for years. The scent threw her for a moment. Then his lips touched hers. They were dry. She tightened her mouth as he clamped his arms around her.

Where the hell was a cop in New York when you needed one?

And then he pulled away. She didn't realize she'd been holding her breath until she gulped at the air.

"No. No. This isn't right," he said to himself, as if she wasn't there. "It's not supposed to be this way. I need to feel your love. I need to feel you."

Callie popped off, "It's not like we can do the dirty right here on the street."

Immediately, she knew it was a mistake. She could tell by the shock on his face that she'd blown it. She'd had him believing for a few minutes that she was Jessica. Then big-mouth Callie Chennault blurted out from nowhere and ruined everything.

She licked her lips and stepped smoothly back into Jessica. "We could go somewhere more private, Simon. I love a bed with satin sheets."

A hard look crossed his bland features. The non-descript little fan turned angry. Very, very angry.

She knew all about angry. She'd run more times than she knew when this same light came into her father's eyes.

Callie took off without thinking, automatically letting things slide from her shoulders to hit the pavement behind her, hoping they would trip him up.

"Bitch!" he roared above the rain.

She ran no more than fifteen yards when he caught her. His hand locked on her upper arm as he swung her around and smacked her hard. Her cheekbone exploded in pain. Before she could call out, he'd punched her hard in the gut, knocking the wind from her.

He was dragging her. She was aware enough to feel her hip bumping along the pavement. Her eye had begun to swell but she saw they'd entered an alleyway. They went a few yards into it before he lifted her, slamming her into the wall.

Panic flooded her as he pressed against her, holding her wrists as he forced his tongue inside her mouth.

She gagged and began to struggle but her claustrophobia kicked in. She couldn't breathe. The dark, tight space enveloped her. She thought she might pass out.

The stinging was almost incidental. An afterthought in the back of her mind. Something was terribly wrong but a break in her synapses wouldn't let her brain process the information.

Suddenly, her legs went rubbery. She slid down the wall. Simon moved away from her and the cool of the night hit her. Her butt hit the concrete and her vision started to blur as a burning sensation began along her side.

"You're like all the rest. You're not really Jessica. You just pretend to be Jessica. You aren't perfect at all."

She recognized the contempt in his voice as he walked away, his hand swinging by his side, the knife dripping. She was confused. It was blood. Her blood. It hit her. He'd stabbed her. More than once.

She reached up a hand and touched herself. Blood flowed. Sticky. Messy. She needed help. Callie had never been more helpless—alone, in the dark, the thunder rumbling angrily as the rain continued to come down now in sheets. She could hear the rats scrambling through the garbage behind her.

She couldn't die. She wouldn't die. She had too much left to do.

Things began to fade to black. Not good. She needed to move where she would be seen. Could she stand?

She tried and almost passed out. Okay, standing's out. But she could crawl. She pushed herself to the alley's entrance and then collapsed on the sidewalk. She was so tired. So cold. The warmth of Sun Burst pose no longer flowed through her. Every breath hurt and she had to force herself to do it. Breathe. Breathe. In. Out. In. Out.

She could hear the voice of the instructor from her yoga app, encouraging her in his quiet tone. Breathe in. Breathe out. Follow the movement of your breath.

But it hurt like hell. Bet he never tried to practice yoga while bleeding profusely. She couldn't inhale deeply. Instead, the air came in shallow spurts, like a panting dog in the sweltering heat of a Louisiana summer.

She quit struggling. She knew it didn't matter anymore. She wouldn't make it. And it pissed her off to think that every obituary would shout that *Jessica Had Died.*" Not Callie Chennault. Every picture accompanying every article would be of Jessica. Not her. She'd lost her identity in a character so long ago that no one knew the real her anymore.

Even if someone passed by on foot, they wouldn't stop for a bloody, limp Callie. She was a stranger, not the sophisticated beauty on the cover of *In Style* or *En-*

tertainment Weekly, the cool blond with the fiery lips and temperamental attitude.

No, she would die alone on a New York sidewalk. A no one.

Callie took one last, painful breath and gave up.

Chapter Three

NICK STRETCHED and rubbed his eyes. He'd been at it all night but he was through now.

She was dead.

He hated killing someone, particularly a pretty blond, but he had no choice. To get where he wanted, she had to be eliminated.

He'd planned it from the start. It still didn't make him happy, though. Death never did. Especially this late in the game. He could hear the fans protesting now.

He pushed out of his seat. His eye caught his image in the mirror.

He looked like hell. All thirty-five years and then some.

The combination of death and no sleep caused the look. It was a far cry from his glory days when the money rolled in easily for what was in truth very little effort. He had natural talent; the right people always paid for it. He'd enjoyed being a player.

What he did now didn't always come easily. And each murder had to top the last one.

But he'd gotten good. Very good. Almost too good. Sometimes, it scared him how the ideas flowed. How could one man be so cruel, inventing that many sadistic ways to off unsuspecting fools?

He stumbled down the hallway and through his bedroom, not remembering the last time he'd slept in the unmade bed. He entered the bathroom off the main suite and turned on the shower faucet. A hot shower would wash away his evil doings. It would separate him from the sin.

Nick stood and let the spray hit him for a long time as he tried to force the images of death from his mind. This murder had been harder on him than any before. He wasn't sure why. Maybe because she'd been so well loved. She had a lot of years ahead of her before he cut her life short.

Yet, he'd do it again in a heartbeat. The rush was too great.

He stepped from the shower and toweled off. Once he shaved, brushed his teeth, and combed his thick, dark hair, he felt almost human again. Murder usually put him into a funk. It was over now, though. Behind him. He would start a new chapter and put it behind him.

He always did.

Chapter Four

CALLIE DREAMED she was having the mother of all hangovers. Her head cracked into pieces. Her mouth parched. Her stomach roiling queasily. And it was hard to breathe.

Hard to breathe?

No hangover ever hurt this much.

She opened her eyes to end the dream and get on with her day. She couldn't remember learning her lines yet. Didn't she have a lot of pages for today's shooting?

It was really weird. Her eyes wouldn't open. She'd had dreams like this before, where she really wanted to wake up but her body wasn't ready to. Once she'd been having sex with the latest *People* Sexiest Man of the Year but he'd turned into her high school calculus teacher right before she climaxed. Talk about a double nightmare. She'd screamed in the dream that she would wake up but Mr. Finney calmly explained to her that shouting in class meant a double detention—especially if you were having sex with a married teacher while you did it.

That had been enough to arouse her from the horrifying vision. But this? This was... different. No movie ran in her head so she figured the dream had to be over.

The credits should've come up by now. Sleepy time was over.

She should be able to open her eyes. Wake up.

"I think she's trying to come around, Doctor."

Doctor?

She hadn't dreamed anything about being sick so why was a doctor making an appearance? Besides, she was never sick in real life. She was a nut about taking her vitamins and getting a flu shot and drinking plenty of fluids, year-round. She refused to believe she could be sick. This was just more of the crazy, unending nightmare.

Hell, she'd wait it out. Nothing could ever be worse than thinking about having sex with Mr. Finney.

Unless...

A flash of a scene came and went, quick as lightning brightening a darkened room. It was there and then gone, faster than she could figure out what she witnessed. But it gave her a very uneasy feeling.

Simon...

Where did that name come from? The only Simon she knew was from Alvin and the Chipmunks and she only thought about them at Christmas when she heard them chirping on the radio for a plane that looped the loop.

The flash came again. This time longer. A face appeared. A very ordinary face. She sucked in a quick breath. Why was such a normal face causing her heart to race?

Moreover, why couldn't she get a solid breath? She hurt everywhere. She needed to figure out why. She struggled to open her eyes again. This time she succeeded getting one to cooperate.

Definitely a hospital room. Dim. Door open. That's where most of the light spilled in from. A rotund nurse in faded blue scrubs stood next to her bed. A white-coated man with a dark, bushy mustache frowning at a clipboard was parked right next to the nurse.

"My eye feels like it's super-glued shut," she croaked.

The pair frowned at her, surprise written on both their faces. Oh, this wasn't good. It was like she was Frankenstein coming to life for the first time. No, they seemed more astonished than that. Maybe Frankenstein talking in full sentences? Yeah, that captured the mood in the antiseptic-smelling room. She'd always hated that smell. Ever since Mama died.

"I heard her voice. She's finally coming around, huh?"

Callie turned her head slightly, to exploding pain. She took a quick breath in and it hurt like someone had stabbed her.

Stabbed her. Simon! Oh, God. Was she dead?

"No," the doctor said, turning away toward the man who'd spoken. "She's just awakened. I need to examine her."

"And I need to find out who left her for dead," rumbled the deep voice.

She'd learned from her previous mistake. This time she kept her head still and only cut her eyes in the direction the voice came from. He was a mix of an older looking Jimmy McNulty from *The Wire* wearing a rumpled trench coat that maybe Lenny from *Law & Order* repeats had owned at one point. Gray at the temples. Circles under his eyes. World-weary air about him.

"I want... to talk. To him," she rasped.

Everyone turned and looked at her as if she were crazy. Maybe she was. Maybe she had died and gone to hell and this scene would be played over and over again. Oh and *It's a Small World* would be constantly sung in the background. Yep, definitely her idea of hell.

"Let me speak with her first," the doctor said in a clipped, professional tone. "I want to see if she's coherent enough for you to question her. She may remember very little of the trauma at this point."

"And *she* is right *here*, Mr. Medical Man," Callie spat out. It hurt her to speak up but she wanted their attention. She needed some answers. "Talk *to* me. Not about me."

The nurse rolled her little pig eyes. Callie could see *The National Enquirer's* headline tomorrow: *SUMNER FALLS STAR A PRIMA DONNA UNTIL THE END.* Old Nancy Nurse here would be their source, spouting off about how demanding Callie Chennault was, right up until she expired.

Well, who cared? She wiggled her toes. She was definitely alive. Not paralyzed. Ready to find the son of a bitch who did this to her—whatever *this* was.

The physician cleared his throat. "I am Dr. Maxwell, Miss Chennault."

"You pronounce it *Shuh-No*. It's French Cajun." Funny how a little detail like that mattered to her at the moment.

"All right. Miss Chennault."

She managed a half-smile of approval at his pronunciation.

"You were brought in last night by ambulance a little before ten." He glanced at his watch. "Almost twenty-four hours ago to the minute."

Okay. She'd lost a day. She nodded and was hit with another flash of hurt all over.

"A young man found you and called 9-1-1. He almost stumbled over you lying on the sidewalk. It was very dark and rainy. Do you remember that?"

She thought a moment. "I remember the rain. Enough weather recap, Doc. What's wrong with me?"

She bit her lip. The pain was really, really bad now. And growing.

"You'd been stabbed. Repeatedly. You lost quite a bit of blood. You're not a common blood type, Miss Chennault. AB-negative. Just about used up our supply on hand."

Well, when she felt better, she would march on down and be a one-woman blood drive. Callie wished she had the energy to say all that but she thought better of conserving her energy and kept her mouth shut.

"You went into surgery. Came through easily. You're in very good health, you know."

"Yoga," she whispered.

"Mmm." The doctor frowned and glanced at her chart again. "You had a concussion, as well. Skull cracked. One eye swollen shut, probably from a heavy blow. Overall, though, you'll be fit as a fiddle in several months."

"Months?"

What would the show do without her? And what would she do sitting on her ass for months with nothing to do? That thought frightened her more than the litany of injuries he'd described.

"Rest is imperative. But with lots of it and a thorough rehabilitation program, you'll be able to function in a normal manner. You're a very lucky woman, Miss Chennault."

She smiled weakly. At least, she thought it was a smile. It was hard to tell with her eye all screwed up. It made her whole face feel off-balance.

The doctor turned to the detective. She assumed he was a detective. Those were the ones who always investigated homicides and attempted murders on TV. Jessica had almost married a homicide detective years ago but the actor hadn't renewed his contract after an extended salary negotiation. Instead, he'd been pushed off a cliff by the serial killer he was hunting. Jessica almost married the killer, too, but she wound up killing him before he got her. It had been one of her favorite storylines. The bad-assness of it rocked.

"She seems to have her wits about her. I think you could speak with her for a few minutes. However, don't press her. She may not remember many details or even the incident itself."

"But it could come back to her?"

Dr. Maxwell shrugged. "It's a crapshoot, Detective. We'll see." He signaled the nurse to follow him and they exited the room, closing the door behind them.

The policeman moved closer. Callie caught a whiff of pipe tobacco clinging to him. The subtle smell comforted her. "There's another plainclothesman right outside the door. Gotta take your safety seriously. After all, you're a national treasure."

He smiled and his words let her know he, unlike Dr. Maxwell, knew exactly who she was.

"So, what did the headlines say this morning? *'JESSICA GETS HER JUST DESERTS?'*"

"Nah." He pulled up a chair and sat. She was grateful she didn't have to strain to look up at him anymore. "My little girl started watching you when you came on the show. What, ten years ago? Must've been because she's nineteen now and she was just nine when she demanded to start watching TV beyond cutesy comedies. I argued with my wife that she was too young for the kinds of things that happened on *Sumner Falls,* but my kid thought you hung the moon. Wanted to grow up beautiful and smart and not take shit off nobody, just like Jessica. My kid knows everything now, at nineteen. We all think we do at that age."

He gave her hand a squeeze. "I'm Paul Waggoner, Callie. Can I call you Callie?"

She gave a bare nod. Anything else hurt too much.

"Well, Callie, I need to know anything you remember. I'll tell you, we already spoke to your friend Beth so we know what time you left the coffeehouse. She also has your dog, by the way, and told me to tell you not to worry about him."

He reached into his pocket and pulled out his phone. He scrolled a moment and then held it up to her. "Beth made me take Wolf's picture and promise to show it to you the minute you woke up. He's as big as the side of a barn but a friendly thing."

The sight of her beloved dog made everything seem better. "That's good. Wolf likes Beth. I guess he'll be staying with her awhile."

"After the coffeehouse. You walked, even though the rain started. Beth says you like to ride the subway and your station was nearby. Did someone approached you on the street? That sound about right?"

She swallowed. "He called me Jessica." She sighed. "I turned around anyway. I always do."

The detective nodded. "He say anything else?"

She thought. Waited. "He had a knife. Left hand. Wanted me to put on..." She paused as she tried to remember. "Lipstick," she finally recalled. "Some lipstick."

She sensed the stillness that came over him.

"But you know that, don't you, Detective?"

He nodded. "Was it *Ravenous Red*?"

"Yes." Her voice sounded faint to her. "He said I..." Her voice trailed off. She squinted, trying to recall the rest. "Something about how I wasn't perfect after all."

Her head began to pound, so loudly she couldn't

41

hear herself think anymore. The effort to talk became too great.

"Can't... anymore. Maybe later..."

She closed her good eye. Detective Waggoner continued to hold her hand as she drifted off.

She thought she heard him say, "We'll get the bastard, Callie. We will get him. For you. And the others."

Chapter Five

CALLIE AWOKE TO AN EMPTY ROOM.

Although her door was closed, she could hear muffled sounds coming from the hallway. A squeaky noise probably came from a meal cart wobbling down the hall. Voices drifted by and then faded.

She eyed the TV remote, wondering if she had the strength to reach it. She pushed out a hand and leaned in the channel changer's direction, only to immediately realize her mistake. A searing pain rippled from under her arm down to her hip. She knew this area must contain a zillion stitches from the stab wounds she'd suffered.

Okay, not such a good idea. Still, she wanted to turn on the news. She rarely watched TV. Instead, she memorized script lines, read, played with Wolf, and worked with victims of domestic violence at a local shelter. She didn't need to watch the news. She couldn't change the world anyway. She'd never used her celebrity regarding politics. In fact, she was pretty apathetic about politics. She didn't believe one vote mattered, which would crush her high school civics teacher. It was a change from high school, where she'd been all gung ho, Miss Secretary in the Student Government, back in the day. And as an adult, she turned out to be apolitical. Go figure.

The world of primetime television was political enough. She had all the backstabbing politics and behind-the-scenes wheeling and dealing in the small, incestuous community of series that filmed in New York City.

All the news she ever wanted to hear could be found on The Weather Channel. She didn't need to go surfing the internet to read about what ailed the world. And while she'd once been a football and basketball fan growing up, tuning in for scores all around the country, she'd lost touch with teams and players' records long ago. Catching the occasional Knicks game in person satisfied her now.

But something Detective Waggoner said stayed with her as she slept. There were others who had been attacked. She wasn't the first. A compelling urge to tune into the local news station to find out what was going on overwhelmed her.

She wondered if she would become a news junkie in the months it would take to heal. Would this be how her brush with death might change her? She hadn't done the near-death experience thing. No rushing through a tunnel or beautiful sunlight cascading feelings of peace over her. The last she remembered was lying on a wet sidewalk, knowing she would die. Not exactly the warm fuzzy stuff they spotlighted on *GMA* feel-good segments.

A soft knock startled her. Callie called out, "Come in," and realized how weak her voice still was.

Beth entered, worry written over her face and in every line of her body, though she smiled at Callie as if she hadn't a care in the world. Her best friend carried a bouquet of springtime flowers and some magazines, which she placed on a tall cabinet by the window.

"Want to meet the guy who saved your ass?" Beth asked as she walked over to stand next to the bed.

Callie shook her head slightly, ignoring the pain. "What a greeting. No 'How are you, Cal? Heard you almost died.'" She smiled, though. Beth always lifted her spirits, even in the worst of times.

"Yes, I would like to meet him and gush appropriately. Hey—is he single? Maybe this is the new way to get a date. We'd have lots to talk about. On the plus side, he's seen me at my absolute worst."

Beth made a face. "Well, they won't let the little hero in. They won't let anyone in, Cal. People are going nuts. Miz Head Writer Deirdre's dying. She claims all storyboards are now ruined for the rest of this season and next, as well. She's got the writers pulling an all-nighter tonight. And Marvin swears you're trying to get him fired. He's afraid he'll never direct again unless it's straight-to-DVD shit. I think he's behind the rumors that you aren't really hurt."

"Guess you learn who your real friends are when a homicidal maniac stabs you." Callie kept her tone light but she was curious. "Seriously, I didn't know anyone wanted to get in. Why would the police keep out my friends?"

Beth pulled up a chair and sat. "I talked to Waggoner, the guy in charge of the case. Nice enough guy. Seemed protective of you. I'm sure it's just a precaution."

Beth reached over and poured some ice water into a glass and slipped a straw into it. "You look parched, girlfriend. Let me buy you a drink."

She brought the glass to Callie's mouth. She found

herself greedily sucking the life out of the straw and drained the entire glass.

"Best drink I ever had. Do they have Happy Hour here? I could go for a two-for-one."

Beth studied her a moment. "How bad are you, Cal? You're cracking jokes as usual but you look awful. I know how long you were in surgery. I wore a groove into the linoleum from pacing so much. Not to mention the network is worried. Without you? The ratings will tank."

"Then they need to let someone else step in and play Jessica for a while. It's been done before. There were two Daarios on *Game of Thrones*. Number Two Daario was way hotter than Original Daario."

Beth sniffed. "That has only happened a handful of times. The suits cannot replace the famous Jessica and not expect the fans to grumble and ratings to tank."

"Well, some actresses get away with pregnancy leaves by having their characters take an extended vacation," she offered. "Like a sudden honeymoon. Or they cling to life after a car wreck and stay in an induced coma. Whatever. They always come back. Jessica could, too, in her own sweet time."

But did she really want to return? Had what happened in real life actually been fortuitous? Could she finally make a break from Jessica? She had plenty of money socked away. Which was good, since she couldn't work for months anyway, according to old doom and gloom Dr. Maxwell.

If she weren't working, that might be the break she needed from being so strongly identified with Jessica.

Where could she go? Get away from everything here?

Especially the left-handed psycho with the knife.

Home. I want to go home, she realized with a sweet

ache. Back to Louisiana. It was the only place that appealed to her. Sure, she loved the hustle and bustle of New York and even the house she rented sometimes out on Long Island, but Aurora was what she needed. Mama was long gone but Great-Aunt Callandra was still there. She could rest. Heal. Decide what she wanted to do. Professionally and personally.

She opened her mouth to share her decision with Beth, only to be interrupted by a solid knocking on her door. It opened before she could reply.

In walked Detective Waggoner and another man, slender, with a neatly trimmed black beard. Carrying an iPad.

The detective nodded at Beth but immediately turned his attention to Callie.

"This is Frank. He's our best sketch artist."

She watched the man take a seat and power up his tablet. He smiled at her reassuringly.

"I know. Different from the old days but a lot faster. Waggoner tells me you might be fuzzy about details but I want to capture whatever you can remember before anything fades."

Beth stood. "I'll excuse myself and let you get down to business. Cal, what should I do? The phone calls. The emails pouring in like crazy?"

Waggoner interjected, "Say Miss Chennault is resting comfortably. Period. No info beyond that. Nothing about her injuries or what she remembers. Nothing. I've told the network PR people the same thing."

Beth nodded. "Got it." She bent and kissed Callie's cheek. "I'll stop by later."

Frank asked, "Are you ready?"

"I guess so."

She closed her eyes, trying to picture Simon.

Nothing came. Then a quick flash seared into her conscience, which caused her to gasp because it was so real. Her stomach flip-flopped as if on the downward slide of a roller coaster. She forced down the palatable fear to concentrate on the memory. She wanted to get it right.

"He's close to my height. I'm five-nine. Maybe an inch or so taller. Probably mid- to late-twenties. Brown hair. Brown eyes."

"Anything about the shape of his face? Hairstyle? Bushy brows?"

Callie squeezed her eyes tightly, hoping to remember more. "It was raining. His hair was short. Julius Caesar bangs plastered to his forehead. No skin problems. No moles or scars."

She balled her fists together in frustration and opened her eyes. "He was the male version of a Plain Jane. Just an average Joe. Non-threatening, to tell the truth. Regular eyebrows, regular lips. Not thin or thick. No jewelry. Tan jacket. I think he had on jeans, but I'm not sure."

She licked her lips and frowned. "Nothing else is coming. I'm sorry. I just don't remember."

"Hey, you had a concussion. But this is a definite start." Frank's fingers flew over the keyboard. "I'm putting in very generic guidelines. We'll see what you think."

He turned the screen around for her to view. She studied the image. "No, the eyes were a little closer together. The chin a little sharper."

"Good," Frank murmured. "See, you remember more than you give yourself credit for."

They worked for another ten minutes and got what the artist said was a solid picture they could release to the media.

"I'm sorry," she apologized again. "I wish it could be more detailed."

"Don't be," Frank told her. "This is more than we've had before now. No one has ever seen this guy." He stood. "Thanks for your time." He looked over at the older man. "I'll have these printed out for you at the station and emailed to law enforcement across the five boroughs and state."

Waggoner nodded as Frank left.

Callie studied the detective. "I'm guessing there have been more attacks. I didn't know. I don't watch the news. I only take the paper for the comics. I recycle the rest. I can't start my day without *Crankshaft* or *One Big Happy*."

The cop smiled. "How about *Rose is Rose*? I love when she turns into the motorcycle mama. I'm also partial to *Zits*. Reminds me of my daughter a few years back. Never much talked to the wife or me. Thought we were the ultimate in embarrassment."

She laughed. It hurt, yet at the same time it felt good to have something to laugh about. "Lots of teenagers are like that. She your only one?"

"Yeah. Took a lot of years of trying but she was worth it. Bet your folks think the same about you." He smiled shyly at her.

Callie shrugged. "My mom, for sure. We were pretty close. She died when I was twelve. Breast cancer. My great-aunt raised me. Dad... wasn't in the picture. Off somewhere chasing skirts and beating them half-silly when he caught them. At least, we got away."

Waggoner gave her a sympathetic look but he didn't say anything. She liked that.

"Am I a vic? Is that what you call me? Or a survivor? I need to know."

She watched him make a decision. "Survivor," he

said. "Definitely. There have been four others. All dead. All younger than you. Most in their early twenties. But the same physical appearance—your hair color and cut, your eyes, skin tone. Not so much the same height. Guess that's hard to tell from TV."

It dawned on her what he was saying. "You think he's been killing women that resemble me?" The thought brought a chill.

"Didn't think so until he butchered the attempt on you." He blushed. "Sorry. Wrong word choice."

"It's okay. Go on."

"They all resemble you. Or actually the gal you play on *Sumner Falls*. Not so much you. What decided it was the lipstick. Same color on all the vics. None survived but we didn't think it was a coincidence, them all looking alike and wearing the same distinctive shade of lipstick."

Callie thought on his words. "It's Jessica's trademark shade. It would be an easy Google. And he called me by her name. He must be obsessed with the character in some way."

He took out a thick notebook and flipped it open. "You get any crazy letters lately? Anyone threatening you?"

She laughed. "I'm on what basically is a nighttime soap opera, Detective. I play a character the audience has a love/hate relationship with. I get all kinds of letters. Inmates want to marry me or plain fuck me—and believe me—they get pretty graphic on how and where. Old ladies write to tell me I'm ruining the youth of America by setting such a bad example. Housewives love that I live out their fantasies. I get every kind of letter imaginable."

She thought a moment. "Beth's head of my fan club. She and a staff member weed through all the snail mail and email. Check with her. Something might stand out more than others."

He made a notation. "I will." He studied her a moment. "Don't get offended, Callie but I guess I just don't get why you're not dead, too."

She dreaded asking but she had to know. "How were the other women killed?"

He shrugged. "Every victim was abducted. Most were missing three, four days before the bodies were discovered."

"Missing that long... were they raped? Or tortured?"

"The first three were sexually assaulted. The killer used a knife in imaginative ways." He shuddered. "The last one? I think he got bored. She'd just been reported missing when the body was found dumped near Central Park Zoo. No signs of sexual assault." He paused and stared out the window.

"But what?"

Waggoner rubbed his eyes. "Brutal knife wounds but he didn't take his time with her like he did in the past."

Her stomach lurched. Her skin grew clammy. *Sexual assault. Knife in imaginative ways.* It could have been the same with her. She realized how lucky she'd been. The others hadn't made it, while she was still alive.

He turned back to her. "I think that he was working up to you. Probably thought he'd had enough practice through substitutes and was ready to go for the real deal."

She frowned. "He didn't try to take me anywhere. He didn't have a car or van waiting. He just approached me on the street." She frowned. "I think I intimidated him."

Waggoner leaned forward. "Why do you say that?"

"I was scared shitless but I thought if he wanted Jessica, I'd give her to him. I don't know how much you know about the character, Detective, but Jessica has yet to meet a man she's afraid of. So, I slipped into what's like a second skin to me and starting pushing him, like she would. He backed off physically. I could tell it threw him."

The policeman nodded. "He's a control freak who was no longer in control. Jessica was. That makes sense."

Callie's hand flew to her forehead. "Shit. I remember I broke character when he wanted to kiss me. Feel me, he said. I mouthed off in a very un-Jessica-like way and that seemed to bring him back from La-La Land. He was going to take control again and I instinctively knew it. I ran from him and his knife. The danger just felt too great to stick around."

Waggoner doodled aimlessly on his notepad as he spoke. "You threw him off his game. Then angered him. He chased you down and acted quickly. Didn't stick around to see if he'd finished the job. Damn..."

"What?" She sensed something terribly wrong.

The detective stared mournfully at her with his sad eyes. "He'll be disappointed in himself. It probably means another girl will go missing soon. He'll have to act out with her what he wanted to do with you."

Tears sprang to her eyes. "Then that means I'm respon—"

"Don't!" Waggoner barked at her. "He's a sick bastard. It has nothing to do with you. Profilers say all this crap goes back to childhood. Something like you resembled his mom and he hated her and how he wants to kill women that look like her. Be in control—unlike he was as a kid. That kind of thing. We don't know the tie-in to you yet. But we will. You're the link. Or Jessica is. We'll find out why. And when we do, we'll get the creep."

"You think he'll try with me again, don't you?

That's why the plainclothesman is outside. That's why you haven't allowed visitors or the press."

She brushed a tear from her cheek. "I can't live my entire life in fear. I can't."

He placed a reassuring hand over hers. "We'll catch him."

Callie bit her lip. "I'm a wimp, Waggoner. I'm not brave enough like some action movie chick. I can't—I won't—be bait for this guy."

He laughed softly. "We never ask that kind of thing in real life, Callie. That's only in books and the movies."

She placed her hand atop his and squeezed. "Well, I feel like running. As far away from the city as possible."

"I don't blame you, kid."

"I need to go home. To Louisiana."

Chapter Six

"**WHAT DO YOU MEAN**, I can't go home? They actually have medical professionals in Louisiana, Dr. Maxwell. It isn't the backwater bayou you seem to think it is. Why, they even have color TV and cable, I'm told. And they might get the internet any day now."

Her physician looked down his patrician nose at her, ignoring Callie's flippant remarks. "You must remain in the New York City area for a few weeks, Miss Chennault. Travel would be quite difficult for you." He cleared his throat, which she found to be only one of his many annoying habits. "Besides, you have the best medical care available to you right here in Manhattan. Why would you even consider going anywhere else?"

She had never liked him. Not since she opened her eyes and found him hovering. Callie couldn't believe this idiot wasn't going to let her go home. She needed to go back to Aurora. She couldn't explain it to this tight-ass but she didn't want to remain in New York any longer.

Not with Lefty still at large.

She'd given her attacker that nickname. The whole Lipstick Larry thing left her cold. That's what the press had labeled the nut job. She liked Lefty better. It didn't threaten her as much.

And she felt she was hanging on to her sanity by a slender thread as it was.

"Miss Chennault?"

Callie shook her head and rejoined reality. "A brown out, doc. I had them all the time before the attack. Sorry. What did you say?"

"That in a few months, if you still feel this urge to return to your... roots, we can surely accommodate your request. I will make inquiries. We will see you wind up in suitable hands. When the time is appropriate."

She frowned. "When can I leave here? Go back to my apartment? I have cabin fever. I'm tired of scratchy white sheets and constantly being awakened just to give me a sleeping pill so I can sleep. You've poked and prodded me enough. I want my own bed. And my dog in that bed. That would be the best medicine of all."

Dr. Maxwell fiddled with the chart in his hands, his nose crinkling in disgust. "I suppose we could send you home tomorrow but you will need around-the-clock care. You are very weak, Miss Chennault. Much weaker than you realize."

Score one for the doc. Callie knew he was right about that. She couldn't even swing out of bed and make a quick bathroom run alone. It turned into a major ordeal every time she had to pee. It made her thankful she had a strong bladder since it meant fewer trips now that the catheter was out.

"Then I'll hire someone. Just let me go home. Please."

"I have the perfect person," a voice said.

She looked over Maxwell's shoulders and spotted Waggoner. "Detective. What a surprise."

Actually, she was glad to see him. He'd stopped by

every day for a week. Kept her posted on the news conference he held and updated her on more than he probably should have. If she could've picked a father, she would've wanted one like Waggoner—a little gruff, funny, and with a tender heart.

He stepped into the room. "My niece, by marriage, is an RN. A petite, redheaded spitfire. Used to do hospice care but it killed her marriage. Phil, my wife's nephew, said she got too involved with her patients, which made his life an emotional roller coaster. Divorced her after a couple of years."

"You can't mean Gretchen Monroe?" Dr. Maxwell asked, a look of horror on his face.

Waggoner smiled. "Yeah. You know her?"

Maxwell sniffed. "She is very unorthodox. I don't know if Miss Chennault needs that kind of disorder in her life."

Callie grinned. "She sounds perfect." Anyone the doc didn't like would be right up her alley. She glanced at Waggoner. "How can I get in touch with her?"

The detective returned her smile. "I can have her here in less than an hour. She was coming over to have coffee with my wife this morning."

He pulled out his cell and punched it once. "Hey, babe. Gretchen still there? Uh-huh? Put her on." He cupped the phone. "My wife and I still see her. Phil? We sorta gave up custody of him."

Waggoner removed his hand. "Hey, Gretchen. I know you're between jobs. I found one for you. You'll like her a lot. Uh-huh. Yeah. She's one of my cases. We're... uh-huh. Right. Okay. Room 642. Come on over. I'll give your name to the guard posted outside."

He slipped the phone inside his jacket pocket. "She'll be here soon."

The physician snorted. His blatant disgust amused Callie. She put on Jessica's sweetest smile.

"Would you meet personally with us to go over any instructions, Doctor?"

Maxwell glared at her. "I have other patients to see. I'll get back here when I can."

She knew he would keep them waiting but she smiled all the same. "Thank you so much."

The doctor strode from the room. Waggoner came closer and pulled up a chair. "Guess we ticked off Mighty Doc."

She laughed and held her side. "Don't be funny, Detective. I will not forgive you if I split these stitches. I refuse to be held hostage here another day."

"You might split them anyway." Waggoner leaned forward in the chair, his countenance serious. "We got him."

His words stunned her. "You... you..." She couldn't spit anything out, her mind going numb.

He nodded. "The picture we released based on your completed description brought a flurry of activity. It usually does. Ninety-nine percent of the time, it's a wash. But this time, we hit pay dirt pretty quickly. Five of the first seven calls logged sent us looking in the same direction. Two knew the guy's name. Worked with him in a hardware store in the Bronx. The others were all customers who'd been waited on by the creep."

He sat up, his face more serious now. "Except the one call from his P.O., that is. We nabbed the guy in the middle of his bi-weekly check-in. He lawyered up fast but we have him in custody. Apartment's already been swept. More than enough evidence that ties him to your attack. He even had your purse with your cell phone inside, though it was shut off. You can relax, Callie. We got him."

She began to cry and couldn't stop. The floodgates opened and Niagara Falls spilled over. Waggoner came and sat on the bed. He wrapped his arms around her and let her dump a river down his shirtfront.

Relief was a big part of it. She realized she'd been tense ever since she'd awakened in the hospital. Fear would come and go in uncontrollable waves. Even knowing she was safe in a public facility with an armed guard stationed only a few feet away, she still had bouts of terror. Nightmares, too, came and went.

Lefty had been caught. She was safe. That is, if the legal system could scrape together the proof in the proper manner and convince twelve citizens to lock her attacker away forever.

Her crying subsided and she leaned back into the pillows, spent. Waggoner pulled a few tissues from the box beside the bed and handed them to her. She blew gently, as any pressure caused her entire right side to throb. She wiped her eyes and then smiled at her new savior.

"Thank you." Her voice quavered slightly.

"That's my job, Callie. Getting the bad guys." He squeezed her shoulder affectionately. "Even better, I've matched you and Gretchen up, too. It's a great day all around."

He stood. "You need some time to be alone and process all this. I'll let you soak it in."

"You'll come by tomorrow? Or better yet—I'm going home. Would you mind... I mean... could you stop by my apartment?"

"Sure, kid." He smiled. "I'll do you one better. I'll be your ride home. How about that?"

Callie spirits soared at him. "Can we use the siren? I've always wanted to do that."

He laughed. "Whatever you say. You're the famous

Callie Chennault. Your wish'll be my command." He rested his hand on the door handle. "We'll keep the police detail in place until you're discharged tomorrow. I'll see you then."

Callie raised a hand in goodbye as he opened the door and left.

She took a deep breath and realized how utterly exhausted she was. She closed her eyes.

She was finally safe.

* * *

Callie stretched lazily as she awoke. She sucked in her breath quickly as the pain rocked along her side in ripples.

"Hurts like hell, doesn't it?"

She opened her eyes to find a beautiful redhead with large blue eyes and creamy skin sitting next to her bed.

"You must be Gretchen."

"The one and only."

The woman stood and took Callie's wrist in a professional manner, studying her watch. She nodded to herself, a satisfied smile playing about her lips.

"I talked to the girls at the nursing station. Between them and reading your chart, I'm pretty much up to speed." She took her seat again.

Callie nodded. "We're supposed to meet with my doctor sometime later today. What time is it?"

"A little after three." Gretchen sighed. "I heard you have Hannibal the Horrible. Maxwell's nickname, you know."

She shuddered. "He is a world-class jerk. He doesn't want to let me go home to Louisiana. He seems to think it's locked in the Middle Ages. Or worse."

Gretchen studied her. "Hmm. You're a Southern

gal. No accent, though. Although I've heard Jessica lay on a Southern one before."

"That was eons ago. When she... oh, don't tell me you're a *Sumner Falls* fan."

The nurse laughed. "Wasn't until I started hospice care. You wouldn't believe how many sick and dying people watch TV. I guess they like escaping from their own problems. Sure, they enjoy watching their game shows or even the news programs but they love night-time dramas. *Sumner* Falls always crops up as a favorite, and you in particular."

"Seriously? Jessica can be a real bitch sometimes."

"But a vulnerable one. That makes a difference. I had a patient once—Henry Greenley. Admitted to seventy-five but I think he was well into his eighties. Diagnosed with inoperable cancer. We spent his last six weeks together. He wouldn't miss a day of you. We started with the first season you arrived and watched every season available on Netflix. Twice. Even at the end, when he was in and out, I'd make sure the TV was playing *Sumner Falls* episodes so he could hear your voice."

Gretchen stood, her arms wrapped around her. "Remember the moody chef you married?"

Callie cocked an eyebrow. "One never forgets marrying a moody chef, no matter how long ago it was."

"Well, Henry was pissed that you two were together. It was just before he died and he hadn't been able to follow much of anything. He slept more and more. But he opened his eyes wide and clutched my hand and asked me if Jessica and that temperamental chef were really going to tie the knot."

Gretchen laughed. "I told him yes, that the moron proposed to you. Henry said that Jessica was too good for that bastard because he'd never treat her right." She looked down at Callie. "Those were his last words before he slipped into a coma."

Callie's throat grew tight. Tears filled her eyes.

"Yeah, Henry knew that egomaniac of a chef wasn't the one for Jessica. Despite all her bravado, Jessica's got that lost little girl side. People want to protect her. People like her, deep down. They may love to hate her at times because she's got so much and she causes so much trouble and makes so many mistakes—but that's why they always keep forgiving her and taking her back. She's a very human character, Callie. You should be proud of the work you've done over the years."

"Thank you." It came out a whisper. She felt raw, almost as much as she had when she'd awakened from Lefty's attack.

"Well, Dr. Horrible will give us a boatload of instructions, but you and I will pretty much piece together what's best for you. I'll cook for you and help you in all your personal matters. Get you to your medical appointments. And as soon as we can, we'll start some physical therapy."

Gretchen pulled out a notepad and a pen from her purse. "Let's get some basics down first. I don't think you'll have a restricted diet. Your injuries wouldn't prevent you from eating what you wanted. I'm sure after being in the hospital this long, you've been dreaming of plenty of things you'd like to scarf down."

The pretty nurse studied her a moment. "You look a little on the skinny side. What presses your buttons? Pizza? Ice cream? Chocolate?"

Callie moaned. "You just named my three favorite food groups. What I wouldn't give for a Dove Bar and a pizza with all the works."

"Anything you don't like?"

"Liver. Anchovies. Beets. And English peas. Yuck to

the max. I love tuna casserole but I pick out all the peas in it."

'Okay. I'll go over to your apartment later and throw out what needs to go from the fridge. Poke around and get some ideas of what you might want me to stock up on."

'I use Sam's in the Village for my groceries and sundries. I'm on account there."

Gretchen made a note. "That'll be helpful. I'll also straighten up, change the sheets, make everything nice and cozy for your return. I'll go through your messages and make a list of who's called and what about. Once we get home, you might want to let me know who you have to talk to, who gets the 'wait until she's stronger' line, and which ones I need to dump."

Callie smiled. "You're so organized. It sounds like we're going to get along great. Besides the fact that Dr. Horrible didn't want me to hire you. That told me right away that we'd click." She thought a moment. "Are you allergic to dogs?"

'No. Do you have one? Who's been feeding and walking it?"

'My best friend, Beth Mitchell, has graciously taken in Wolf."

'Romy? Romy de Shoenberg? Oh, all my patients were so sorry when she died in that avalanche, escaping from a serial killer. She was a real favorite."

Callie smiled. "She did go out in a pretty spectacular way. She told the writers to make it big and make sure she'd never be able to come back. She was getting married and wanted to stay home and have kids. She didn't want any temptations whispering in her ear to come back to the show. She wanted a clean break."

'She could always come back as her evil twin. It's been done to death but the fans would love that. Maybe she and Jessica could be best friends and cat fight over—"

"Whoa. Slow down, girl. Jessica is on the shelf for now. That's one thing I'll need to talk to my agent and the showrunners about."

Gretchen's eyes widened. "No more Jessica? Then *Sumner Falls* might as well throw in the towel."

"No guilt trips, Gretchen. It's something I've been thinking about even before this mess happened. I think Jessica needs to go off on an extended European vacation. For a year at least." Callie massaged her stiff neck. "I need some time to think about what I want to do. I've spent my entire adult life playing Jessica. My entire twenties and into my thirties. I might need to see what else is out there."

"Okay. Shall I set up a meeting with your agent? Would you rather it be over the phone or in person?"

She thought a moment. "I think face-to-face. Harry's been good to me. I'll be going home tomorrow. Make it for the day after that. All my numbers are in the address book next to my landline and also programmed into my cell. Beth took it back to my apartment so I'm sure it'll be easy to spot. I'll write down my passcode and a few key names for you and who they are."

Using Gretchen's notepad, Callie scribbled away, including a few instructions the nurse would need.

"I'll also call my management team and be sure you're given full access. Would you see that Beth is there when we get home tomorrow? I'd love if she would bring Wolf home."

Gretchen smiled. "He'll be the best medicine for you. Don't worry, I'll walk him and everything. I'm crazy about dogs. My ex hated them. And I spend so much time with my patients, I never thought it was fair to have one."

"You'll love Wolf. He's an Akita, a Japanese breed. Bigger than a German shepherd. Fluffiest white coat you've ever run your fingers through. He's also the only dog I've ever had that didn't have chronic bad breath."

"He sounds adorable."

A sharp rap on the door startled them both.

A look of mischief crossed Gretchen's face. "It's *The Hannibal Show*, now playing in Room 642. I guess we better get this over."

Callie smiled at her fellow conspirator. "Come in," she called.

Chapter Seven

CALLIE WATCHED the scenery rolling by, excitement building within her. As they passed the lush, green trees that lined the Louisiana highway, she knew she was almost home.

Home.

Though she wanted to leave New York immediately, it took a few months of intense physical therapy before she actually felt strong enough to make the trip. She didn't want to arrive at Aunt C's as an invalid. She wanted to be able to walk out the back door down to the lake and stroll peacefully, feeding the ducks. Not like a stiff Frankenstein, a patient that needed to be coddled and cajoled.

She was better now. Not a hundred percent by a long shot, but definitely on the road to recovery. She needed the open spaces that Noble Oaks would provide both inside and out. Claustrophobia crept upon her like a cat silently stalking a mouse. It seized her at moments that brought sheer terror. Her apartment, while spacious by New York City standards, seemed to grow smaller and smaller, as if she were a caged bird who yearned to spread her wings. She needed room—and lots of it—if she were going to heal. Mentally, that is.

Callie spotted the mileage sign and pointed it out to Gretchen. "Look—Aurora's just a few minutes down the road."

"I can't believe we're almost to Hicksville. Driving to the moon would've been faster, Callie Chennault. If I colored my hair, I'd have needed to use two more boxes by now."

"You're the one that wanted us to drive," she noted. "See the U.S., eat at local diners, and keep Wolf from being crated on the plane ride down. Sound familiar?"

Gretchen groaned. "So, I might've made a mistake. After all, the most I've ever seen is upstate New York and the Jersey Shore. I thought a road trip would be a ton of fun." She glanced at Callie. "You have to admit the food has been pretty amazing. It's just taken. *For. Ever.*"

Callie shrugged. "You're the one who wanted us to take our time. Not put too big a strain on me."

The redhead snorted. "That's before you took over the music. Before I knew you had this obsession with Frank Sinatra and Glenn Miller. How does a twenty-first century woman even know about these guys? And women like... like..."

"Billie Holiday?"

"That's the one. Boy, she has a set of pipes on her, but it's so depressing listening to her sad songs."

"Well, I like her. Once we get settled, I'll drag you into New Orleans. We'll hear some real blues, live and in person. Preferably with a couple of hurricanes in hand."

Gretchen gave her a sideways glance. "How far is civilization?"

Callie laughed. "Aurora is civilized. It's up to about thirteen thousand now. It's got a diner and a bakery with a few tables and chairs. You can sit and schmooze with the locals in the morning while you drink your coffee."

"No Starbucks. No bookstore. No frank and soda carts. No nightlife. I may go out of my mind, Callie. You'll be putting me on a plane to New York this time tomorrow."

"No," she said firmly. "You'll love it. Aurora's got a rhythm all its own, and New Orleans is only about a half-hour away. We'll make plenty of time to go into town and shop. Eat. Eat. Eat. Eat some more. Drink a little."

"Pick up men?" Gretchen asked hopefully. "I think it's time I got back into circulation."

Callie sniffed. "Wolf is about all the man I want in my life right now."

At his name, the dog stuck his head over the seat. She swore he smiled as both women automatically rubbed him, one scratching between his ears while the other patted his massive chest.

"I plan on getting you into tip-top shape, Miss Chennault," Gretchen threatened. "Then we'll go bar hopping in the Big Easy in sparkly spandex and stilettos."

"I didn't pack anything remotely like that." She chuckled. "Actually, I've never bought anything like that."

"Well, you brought everything except your bath-room sink. The kitchen one did make the trip, I think," Gretchen quipped. "You need to compliment me again on my wonderful driving with that little trailer fishtailing behind us all the way from lower Manhattan."

Callie laughed. "You've done an excellent job, Nurse Ratched."

Her friend cranked up the air conditioning another notch. "Why is it so steaming hot here?"

"Because we're arriving in mid-August. I'll admit, not the best time of year. But you'll really like it, Gretchen. I promise. And you know I wouldn't have come home without you."

It was true. She and Gretchen had formed a firm friendship over the last few months. The nurse accompanied her to every doctor's appointment. She'd rallied Callie's spirits when they were low, giving her both a mental and physical boost. Gretchen even sat in on every meeting connected with the show, including the nightmare of talking with the producer and writers regarding her future on *Sumner Falls*.

In the end, though, Gretchen helped Callie stand up and get the leave of absence from the network she so richly needed. The attack left her frazzled. Unable to focus—much less learn pages and pages of complicated dialogue while working endless hours. Gretchen laid it on the line to everyone involved. Callie needed rest. Callie needed absolutely no worries. If she wanted to come back to *Sumner Falls*, she needed to know that opportunity was available. If she didn't, Gretchen pointed out the many years Callie had put in, making the show number one in the ratings.

Gretchen wound up negotiating a deal with the suits that even amazed Harry, Callie's agent.

Most importantly, it gave her the freedom to go home. No one there expected Jessica. She could simply be Callie Chennault, private citizen. She couldn't wait to arrive.

She sighed. "I am so ready for us to sink our teeth into some jambalaya and Mississippi Mud and—"

"Whoa! Stop right there." Gretchen wrinkled her nose. "What's this mud stuff you're pushing? I didn't even try mud pies when I played in my sandbox many moons ago."

'It's absolutely the most heavenly chocolate mess you'll ever put in your mouth."

Gretchen smiled. 'Okay. Chocolate? I'm on board with that." She ran a hand through her hair. 'This humidity, though, leaves much to be desired."

She took in Gretchen's hair. The usual, loose curls had gone haywire in Louisiana's humidity. 'It gives you a wild, sexy look." She playfully ruffled Gretchen's hair.

'As long as the men here think I'm hot. Hell, everyone'll be hot down here. What am I babbling about?"

'Gretchen, once the guys get a look at you in those shorts, they will fall at your feet."

Her friend grinned. 'I *do* have great legs."

Callie glanced down at her own legs in khaki capris. Several scars ran from her right hip down the side of her thigh. She hadn't been brave enough to put on a pair of shorts all summer. Not even in the privacy of her apartment. She didn't think she'd be slipping into cutoffs— or a bikini—anytime soon.

'Okay. You need to slow down."

'Not another little blip on the map," complained Gretchen. 'Every five minutes, it's go from sixty to thirty in the blink of an eye or get a ticket."

'Well, this time it's Aurora. And Essie promised me she'd have shrimp gumbo and hot French bread and something sinfully sweet waiting for us. I don't want anything like getting a ticket to slow us down."

'Thank God for small favors." Gretchen slowed the vehicle as they entered the town's limits.

Callie's eyes grew unexpectedly moist. She'd visited Aurora a few times over the years during breaks from the show, but this time she treasured the fact that she had *this* place to go. Maybe she was running away, leaving all kinds of problems in the city, but she yearned to smell the magnolias and hear the cicadas. Feel the sultry breeze coming off the lake.

"We're coming up on the square.".

Her excitement grew. Despite the air conditioning blowing on high, the sun's heat permeated the car. She spotted the center of town, a mixture of old buildings blending with the new. Barrels of flowers in a rainbow of colors dotted the sidewalks in front of stores.

"There's Robineaux's Grocery and The Sweet Shoppe. Best ice cream this side of the Mississippi. And look at all the antique stores that have sprung up. I can't wait to check all this out."

A siren suddenly sounded behind them.

"Great. Welcome to the sticks," Gretchen mumbled. She pulled over in front of The Feed Bag.

"Relax, you weren't doing anything wrong. And if you were," Callie advised, "flirt. It's the national pastime of the South. You can get away with all kinds of things if you perfect the art of flirting."

"Gotcha." Gretchen rolled down the automatic windows and turned off the engine. She moistened her lips and turned to greet the policeman who approached.

He leaned down, mirrored shades covering his eyes, his firm jaw set, a frown on his face.

Gretchen immediately winced. Callie knew Gretchen would go into New York overdrive.

Which she did.

"I am sorry, Officer, well, I guess not really sorry, because I don't think I was doing a single thing wrong. I have gone the limit or at least mostly the speed limit from New York City to here. Now, is that about a thousand miles of law-abiding driving or what? I have not hit any stray cows. I haven't run a single stop sign. And I surely never—"

The uniformed man broke out into a smile. "I'm sure y'all're doing everything y'all need to. I just wanted to say hey to Callie." He glanced to the passenger seat and removed his sunglasses.

Callie grinned. "Well, hey, Eric. I hear you're the new sheriff these days."

He nodded. "Good news travels fast—and bad even faster." He rested his arm on the SUV. "Miz Callandra told me you'd be coming in about now. I've been watching for the past hour. I told her if y'all needed an escort home, I'd be happy to provide it."

"Only if you use the siren, hon. My friend, Gretchen, is from New York proper. It'll take at least that much to impress her."

She watched Gretchen's lashes flutter. She took in Eric studying the feisty nurse in a way that caused Gretchen to blush.

"Well, ma'am, I have all kinds of ways to impress the ladies. The siren is the least of them." He smiled lazily at her.

Gretchen licked her lips again. "I'll bet you do, Mr. Chief of Police."

"Say, are you going to be hanging around with Callie for a while?"

Callie shifted in her seat. "Gretchen is not only my friend, Eric. She's my nurse. I'm still doing a little physical therapy. After... you know."

He turned his attention back to her. His brow creased. "Everyone knows what happened to you, sweetheart. Those damned tabloids had a field day with it. But I promise—as a friend and a lawman—nothing remotely funny's going to happen to you again. You're home now, girl. You're safe."

He slid his sunglasses back into place. "Come on, now. Let's get you home before Miz C's calling me up again." He sighed. "As it is, we've been chatting about two minutes. I'm sure she's already taken her third call telling her you've hit the square and will be home in less than five."

Eric returned to his squad car and pulled alongside them. "Follow me, ma'am," he told Gretchen as he fired up the lights. "It's just a couple of minutes down the road."

Gretchen started the car up. "My. Oh, my. Do they grow all of them down here that delicious?" She glanced at Callie. "Did you see the biceps on that man? And that massive chest? And that swagger? God, I love a man in uniform who can swagger."

"Just drive," Callie said, with an eye roll. "I'll let you be the judge of the current male crop. Once it gets out that I brought home a drop-dead gorgeous, petite little redhead, half the parish will be paying us a visit."

Gretchen smiled mischievously. "I think Aurora is showing real promise."

Chapter Eight

NICK TURNED OFF THE RADIO, tired of the pounding rock music. He was close to home and wanted to savor his return after a long week in New York. Minna insisted he come up this time to discuss his finished novel and ideas for his upcoming story. As an agent, she was part protective mama bear and part bear in pursuit of dinner, namely the best book deal she could negotiate. He enjoyed spending time with her so he was happy to comply. While he was there, his publishing house gave a party kicking off his third book's release, already shipped as a bestseller. Without him in attendance, as usual. He didn't want anyone knowing who he was and he had no interest schmoozing with the literary crowd.

Funny, in his playing days—and especially his hard partying days—New York seemed like the center of the universe. The best restaurants. The best women. The best clubs. The best coke—next to L.A., of course. He'd cut his teeth on the L.A. party circuit, the golden boy Dodger and Cy Young winner in only his second season with the club. Doors opened magically to brooding, successful athletes. Access to anyone, anywhere, anytime became the norm.

Until his mother straightened him out. Nick still felt a rush of gratitude every time he saw his mom, knowing she'd been the one person in the world who'd gotten through to him, letting him know in no uncertain terms that he was wasting his God-given talent on booze and bitches. He'd pulled his act together and concentrated on his pitching, stopping cold turkey with the recreational drugs.

It had been a turning point for him, one of several in the last decade. With a failed marriage behind him, he thanked his lucky stars that he had a place like Aurora to come home to.

If he could only make it home in time for dinner. He'd called Miz Callandra to let her know he'd be arriving home tonight. She worried about him almost as much as she did that TV star niece of hers, the one too good to make it home the last couple of years for any kind of holiday. Nick had been living in the guest cottage on the Noble Oaks estate for two and a half years now and Callandra's famous relative had yet to make an appearance.

Not that Miz C pined away for the girl. With Nick to boss around and half the town beating a path to her door every day for advice, gossip, and some of Essie's double fudge brownies and mint iced tea, the grande dame found plenty to keep her busy. She'd been sick, too, back in the spring. A terrible flu that turned into pneumonia overnight. He'd rushed her to the hospital, thinking the worst but hoping for the best. He'd been ready to call that flighty actress to hightail it home when Essie got the word of the stalker's attack.

Nick decided to keep the knowledge from Callandra at the time. He didn't know if she was strong enough to learn about it and try to hang on to life herself. Only after the doctor discharged her from the hospital and she was ensconced in her own bed did Nick reveal what little they knew about the incident.

Since then, Callie was never far from Callandra's thoughts and her conversations. He grew sick of hearing about her wonderful great-niece and all the woman had accomplished. When Callandra went off on one of her Callie tangents, he simply retreated into plotting mode, moving his characters around in his head as he wove together his next book. He could smile, nod occasionally, and 'um-hmm' a few times and Miz C was happy as a clam.

Until he'd been scheduled to go to New York. He finished his last manuscript back in the spring, but he'd stuck with his usual pattern of putting it away for a couple of months before he took a hard copy out of his drawer and began re-reading it for pacing, flaws, and whatever else might crop up during a fresh, objective read. He played around with the manuscript, punching up the dialogue and repairing plot holes, polishing it to perfection. He'd completed it last week and figured he might as well hand-deliver it to his publisher before the launch party for his latest hardcover.

While he was in New York, Callandra wanted him to drop in on Callie and check up on what she deemed *her precious angel*. Nick said he would if time allowed but he hadn't bothered to call, much less run by Callie's place. Callandra would be royally pissed at him. Nick didn't care. They bickered like an old married couple, despite the fact they weren't married and almost fifty years stood between them.

Still, Callandra was good to him. He should've made the effort to at least touch base with Callie instead of haunting his favorite bookstores and small jazz clubs.

Great, a case of the guilts already in full swing, and this was before he'd seen Callandra and had her harp on him. At least he hadn't made any excuses to her. She'd been out when he called from La Guardia to let her know about his departure time. Essie said she would relay the message and that Nick better get himself there in time for dinner. She had made chocolate pralines for dessert, and his flight better not be delayed. Essie wouldn't guarantee there'd be any left for him otherwise.

He turned off the main highway and soon was pulling through the center of town. He waved at his cousin Pam, the high school speech and drama teacher, and at Wally Windell, one of Aurora's patrolmen, walking on foot along the square. Despite the heat, he cut the air and rolled down his windows for those last few blocks. He breathed in the heavy scent of magnolia and knew he was almost home.

He pulled into the drive at Noble Oaks, surprised to see a squad car there. Parked behind it sat an SUV with a small trailer attached. His cousin Eric stood on the porch with suitcases in both hands. Two women and one very large dog made their way up the porch steps. All three peered over their shoulders as his convertible turned into the drive and he cut the engine.

"Mr. Celebrity!" Eric placed a suitcase next to him and waved. "Glad you made it. Must've smelled Essie's gumbo from the airport."

The dog came bounding down the steps straight for Nick as he got out of the car. He could've sworn the animal wore a large, slobbery smile.

"Wolf! No! Come back here," one of the women shouted. He watched as she clutched the porch rail, coming gingerly down the steps.

Wolf had no intention of listening to his mistress.

He ran straight to Nick, pulling up less than a foot in front of him, tongue dangling, breathing hard. He laughed and bent to ruffle the dog's coat and scratch him behind the ears.

"You'll never get rid of him now. He'll magically see the word *Sucker* plastered on your forehead each time he sees you. Just be sure you don't feed him or he'll want to move in with you. Unfortunately, the IRS won't let you claim him as a dependent, no matter how much he eats."

"Thanks for the warning."

He looked up from petting the dog and his heart slammed hard against his ribs. In front of him stood the ponytailed girl he had a crush on years and years ago, walking up as if from his memory. They'd spent a few hours together one summer evening half a lifetime ago but Nick never forgot her easy manner and sweet smile.

He visited Aurora for a couple of weeks each summer with his mother. That last time he'd been seventeen and pitched in the town's annual Fourth of July softball game. Afterward, Pam introduced him to one of her new friends and somehow they wound up together at the carnival on the green. They rode a few rides, ate sticky cotton candy, and then sat on the cool grass during the band's concert under the stars.

He'd opened up to the girl, younger than he was by three years, but she'd been so easy to talk with and seemed wise beyond her years. He told her of his dreams of playing professional baseball and of his favorite books, as the music played softly in the background. Afterward, he'd walked her back to Pam's because she was sleeping over. He gave her a kiss that somehow, as the years passed, grew sweeter with memory.

Over time, he hadn't remembered the girl's name and he'd been drafted out of high school the next summer, heading straight to the minor leagues. Many years passed since that long-ago July in Aurora, but Nick had never forgotten the innocent beauty. Only her name. He thought it foolish to ask Pam about her when he'd returned to live here a couple of years ago after so many years of being absent.

But he'd searched for her in town—at the diner, the post office—everywhere his path crossed others. He never set eyes on her again and assumed her long gone, married, with kids and a husband and a dog.

Now, she stood in front of him once again, the long, honey-blond hair still pulled back into the familiar ponytail. The emerald green eyes sparkled with interest and just a bit of mischief. The dewy skin and sweet smile and patrician nose. It was as if she stepped from yesterday, only she was older now, her beauty still achingly fresh, but matured.

Nick rose to his feet, drinking her in, the dream from long ago now reality standing before him.

"Thanks for the warning. I think I'll let you retain ownership. I'm Nick."

He held out a hand to her over the dog's head. The color drained from her face as her smile quickly faded. He wondered what was wrong with her, the friendliness and humor turned off as suddenly as a faucet.

Eric ambled over and gave the woman's shoulders a friendly squeeze.

"Guess you may not know this little lady, Nick. This here's Aurora's claim to fame. I doubt you ever met her when you visited. She's Pam's age, and you mostly hung out with us older guys."

It hit him just as Eric smiled and said, "Meet Callie Chennault, Miz C's great-niece and the famous Jessica."

84

Chapter Nine

SHOCK RAN through Callie as Nick's hand grasped hers and she met his midnight blue eyes. They seemed so familiar. She must know him but she didn't know from where. He wasn't an Aurora boy. He wasn't in the business, though he easily could have been. The hooded, bedroom eyes and chiseled cheeks alone might have opened modeling doors for him, yet she didn't remember him from any ad campaigns.

She pulled away her hand and focused her attention on Wolf. It had become habit, this withdrawing from men. Gretchen gently chided her for it. So did Beth. She couldn't escape her feelings, though. The formerly outgoing, confident Callie Chennault—the woman with a tendency to be a little too independent and who found it difficult to accept help from others—had changed.

The stalker had done the damage.

Overnight, she became afraid of tight spaces with no exits, well beyond her original case of claustrophobia. Other things that had never bothered her before—crowds, storms—made her chest grow tight. She found her eyes always roaming during the few attempts she'd made to go out in public. Searching for *him*.

She knew Lefty was in custody. She appeared at his preliminary hearing. She would also face him in court when he went to trial early next year. It didn't matter. She panicked at the oddest times. The city scared her, its noises and throngs of strangers.

Worst, though, was her deep fear of men. Just when she thought she might get over it? Zap. It would strike out of the blue. She hated even being in the same room with a man once the feelings washed over her. It didn't matter if it were her long-time agent or the pizza delivery guy. Her heart began to race. Her mouth went dry. A panic attack would begin.

That's why she'd needed to come back home. Back to Aurora. Aurora meant safety.

Just nonchalantly greeting Eric, whom she'd known since she was ten, felt better. Normal. They'd teased. She felt relaxed in his presence. It was the beginning of a new start. She knew she could heal here.

Until this man had showed up.

Her fingers tightened in Wolf's coat. The ease with which she greeted this stranger ended abruptly with the simple physical contact of shaking hands. He made her instantly uncomfortable. Knowing and yet not knowing him at the same time.

Eric and Gretchen strolled toward them. Wolf broke away and began to run in circles, barking excitedly. Callie stood. Her side pained her because she rose too quickly. The long row of fresh scars caught fire but her training kicked in. Anyone looking at her would see only a bland look on her face, never knowing the agony she experienced.

Eric slapped the man on the back and shook his hand.

'Ladies, I'd like to introduce you to my worthless

excuse for a cousin, Nick La Chappelle. Cal, you might have met him when he visited with his mom."

The minute she heard his full name, Callie realized who he was.

He was *the guy from that summer*.

She'd been a gawky teen, who hadn't yet blossomed into the beauty who started in commercials at age twenty. No way would he recognize her.

She remembered hearing through the school grapevine that the Dodgers drafted him straight out of high school. Pam passed along that Nick had been sent to the farm leagues for seasoning. Callie assumed he eventually made it to the majors. Baseball had never interested her, though, and by that time her acting career had taken off.

She viewed Nick with full recognition now, as Gretchen gushed.

'I am such a huge fan, Mr. La Chappelle. That Game Seven of your last World Series was nothing short of amazing. You deserved every Cy Young you won and maybe should've gotten a few more. What are you up to these days since you left—"

'Miz Callandra says to bring this party inside. She's tired of waiting on you young folks and wants her dinner."

Callie smiled at the sound of Essie's familiar voice. She returned to the porch and gave the cook a hug.

'Girl, you ain't been eatin' right, have you? I'm gonna fatten you up like I did when you was a little girl."

'It's good to know you'll have a mission in life, Essie. I've bragged non-stop about your cooking to my friend Gretchen."

The group headed up the steps, Wolf trotting along

behind them. She looked over her shoulder and saw Nick following them inside. Why was he here? And coming in as if he belonged?

Callandra Lesueur Chennault sat in a wheelchair inside the foyer, ready to greet her guests in a pastel blue suit and pearls. Callie rushed to her side and embraced her great-aunt. The smell of *White Shoulders* enveloped her, familiar, comforting.

This house and Callandra meant refuge from all the world's woes—her daddy beating on her and her mom, the moving from town to town, never having enough to eat. When her daddy died in a barroom brawl, thanks to his quick temper, Callie and her mother returned for good to Aurora, the place of her parents' birth.

Because of that, Aurora always meant security in her mind. She hugged Callandra tightly and then pulled away.

"You're too thin," nagged her great-aunt.

"I could say the same thing about you," she retorted. "And this wheelchair. Why didn't you tell me?"

Callandra stroked her hair, making Callie feel all of ten years old again.

"Why worry you? You had enough on your plate. Besides, it's more of a convenience. At my age, the stairs are beyond me these days. I don't ever want to work that hard again. Besides, people are just so darn nice to me now."

Eric laughed. "Yeah. Miz C rolls right up to the front of the line at the post office. The grocery store. Communion. You name it. Between that chair and her superior Chennault look, nobody messes with Miz C now. Not that they ever did before."

"Tsk-tsk, Eric. I'm not some demanding monster. Merely an impassioned senior citizen." Callandra waved her hand in a grand gesture and then erupted in laughter. "Oh, let's be honest. I've always gotten my way. We Chennaults usually do.

"Let's eat." She glanced over at Callie. "I want to hear all about your drive down and Nick's trip to New York."

Callandra turned an appraising eye to the former baseball star. "I suppose you didn't get a chance to look my Callie up before she left to drive down here."

Callie noticed Nick flushed as he shook his head no. He lowered his eyes to his shoes like a scolded schoolboy.

"Gretchen, dear. Come sit by me. You're even lovelier than your phone voice revealed. It was so thoughtful to keep me updated on Callie's progress. Eric, you're invited to stay but I know you'll say you're on duty."

Callandra turned and smiled at her cook. "Essie, slip some gumbo in a Tupperware bowl for our sheriff. He can eat in the car while he keeps the streets of Aurora safe."

Eric tipped his hat. "Thanks, Miz C. Well, I'm off." He glanced at Nick. "Catch up tomorrow?"

They moved into the dining room, and once again, Callie felt a rush of warmth seeing the table set with the beautiful Lenox china and tall, white, flickering tapers casting a glow across the room.

"We might not dress up as in earlier times," Callandra informed Gretchen, "but I still know how to set a magnificent table."

They took their seats. Callie found herself across from Nick. She avoided his eyes as she unfolded her napkin and placed it in her lap and then fiddled with her silverware. As she took a sip of iced tea, she could sense his gaze on her.

"This is so refreshing, Aunt C," she said. "I've always loved a hint of mint in my tea."

Callandra patted her hand. "It's good to have you home, dear. I want to keep you here as long as I can. Isn't that a good idea, Nick?"

She turned her gaze back across the table. Those penetrating blue eyes still focused on her. They were a stormy, volatile blue. She shuddered involuntarily, wondering why he was here. She decided to find out.

"I assume as a professional player you made quite a bundle, Mr. La Chappelle. Have you retired to Aurora so your millions will stretch farther?"

Anger sparked in his eyes. He opened his mouth to comment when Callandra chuckled and said, "I see that Magic Gumbo has arrived."

Essie served each of them a generous portion. The aroma did seem magical to Callie.

"This was my favorite dish when I moved here," she explained to Gretchen. "I called it Magic Gumbo."

With her first bite, Gretchen closed her eyes and moaned. "It's delicious. I can see why. I am really going to have to watch my waistline here." She took another bite before turning her attention to Nick.

"What does an ex-professional athlete do in such a small town?" Gretchen batted her lashes daintily. Callie decided her friend would do quite nicely in Aurora.

"I live in the caretaker's cottage around back," Nick said, a frown creasing his brow.

He was Aunt C's caretaker?

"I maintain the lawns. Try to follow orders on the gardens. Miz C supervises each snip of every vine."

"It seems like a large estate," Gretchen commented. "I suppose it's... interesting work."

Callie could see her friend was just as curious about Nick's existence at Noble Oaks as she was.

He shrugged. "I enjoy working with my hands. I destroyed enough teams with them. It's nice to create a little something nowadays."

Callandra snorted. "Nick, you are getting too busy to play at being my gardener. I intend to hire someone full-time."

"Why?" Callie asked. "What has you so busy nowadays?"

"My writing career is taking off," he replied. "Still, Miz C, I don't mind. When I work the soil, I work out my plotting ideas. But I can vacate the cottage at any time. Just let me know when you need me gone."

"Oh, no, my boy," Callandra said. "I love having you close. I wouldn't dream of asking you to move. Day help can come in. Eric will know whom to hire. He has his finger on the pulse of the community."

"Then at least let me give up the free rent."

His casual words shocked Callie. What was a superstar millionaire doing living rent-free on Noble Oaks?

"I hope you haven't taken advantage of Aunt C's generosity," she fired off.

He laughed. "I have earned every penny of that so-called free rent. Just look at the yard. The shrubs. The flower beds."

Callandra nodded while giving Callie a questioning glance. "Nick definitely earned his keep in the lean times." She paused and called out, "Essie. Would you please bring in the crawfish étouffée?"

Callie concentrated on eating as her aunt pumped Gretchen for information about herself.

"I'm just a Jersey girl. I lived at the shore summers, trying to work on my tan but only getting freckles in return. I became a nurse and did critical care. Went into hospice work eventually."

"An attractive girl like you must have lots of beaux," Callandra pointed out.

"Well, I married one of them. It didn't work out." Gretchen smiled at Nick. "Maybe Aurora will have some better prospects."

Nick didn't acknowledge her comment, buttering another piece of cornbread in response.

"Despite Aurora being a small community, it has grown in the last several years. More than I would have liked to see, but that's another story." Callandra winked at Gretchen. "There are some lovely single gentlemen I will introduce you to. You, too, Callie."

Callie dabbed her mouth with a linen napkin. "No men for now. I've sworn off them. That's what a knife-wielding stalker will do for you."

She'd meant to make light of it, but an awkward silence fell around the dinner table. After a moment, Callandra broke it.

"Perhaps we're all ready for a little dessert."

* * *

Nick thanked Callandra for dinner and went to his car. He drove it around back and brought his luggage inside the two-bedroom cottage. He'd save unpacking for later. He needed to work now.

Grabbing his laptop, he pulled up his latest cast of characters and goal/motivation/conflict sheet. He stared at it without inspiration coming so he closed the program and opened his plot outline. It was the barest of bones now. He started half a dozen times typing out ideas that came to him but he deleted every one of them.

Restless, he shut down the computer and began pacing the small living room. Suddenly, he wanted a drink. He hadn't wanted one in a long time. Then again, he hadn't been this uncomfortable in a long time.

Callie Chennault did that to him.

Why had she come, just as he was settling into a routine? He asked why the sweet, lovely girl he'd known for one brief night had turned into a superficial phony.

He'd learned all about shallow from Vanessa. The one basic principle that stayed with him was that all actresses were lower than pond scum. Their beautiful shell only contained a dark, manipulative soul.

No exceptions to this hard-and-fast rule.

Nick felt sorry that Callandra had such a slimy relative. The old woman had become a sweet grandma, sage mentor, and advice-giving friend, all rolled into one.

It hit him that their relationship might be in jeopardy. Callandra worshipped her great-niece. With Callie around all the time, he'd probably never have a single conversation with Miz C without the actress lurking in the background.

That is, for as long as she stayed. He didn't give the New Yorker two weeks before boredom crept in. She would hightail it back to the Big Apple. Let her and her man-hungry friend go home and gobble up all the fresh meat in Manhattan for all he cared.

Nick would make sure Aurora would stay safe from these two. For now, though, he needed to retreat into his characters. If he could jumpstart this plot, the next month would fly by. Callie Chennault and her companion would barely register a blip on his radar. When his writing flourished, Aurora didn't exist. He would be caught up in a world of his own making.

Nick realized he was a perfectionist. He placed high expectations on himself and others. He often felt let down when others didn't come through as he expected. But he was finally learning to excuse their faults, their mistakes. Instead, he now concentrated on the people he could control—his people, the characters he brought to life. He enjoyed being their boss and controlling every aspect of their lives.

If only he could forgive himself and his own failures.

HE WAS TOO LATE. *She was gone. It was bad enough another almost beat him to his final goal. He couldn't believe the news reports that Lipstick Larry had struck again, this time attacking the famous television actress Callie Chennault, Jessica from Sumner Falls.*

He was Lipstick Larry—though he despised the moniker the press hung upon him. Only he found women that resembled Jessica and punished them accordingly.

Jessica was meant for him, not some dollar store knock-off. It appalled him to see the man's capture, his sniveling—his cowardice—for all to see on network newscasts. Everyone would mistakenly believe this wimp masterminded all those loving attacks on the series of young blonds. What sacrilege!

Despite his indignation, he realized this could work to his advantage. The authorities assumed they had the right man in custody. His trial would occur several months from now.

That left him free... free to do his true work. In peace. With no one suspecting he still roamed unseen, unknown. He'd been careful to tamp down the compelling urge to keep in practice. It would be safe for him to remain in anonymity. For now.

It rankled him, though, that another would receive credit for his painstaking work. Already, he heard rumors that the little moron was starting to deny involvement in the other murders that they believed he'd been responsible for. Looking at living life behind bars might do that.

But it would be a long time before the idiots in charge figured out they had the wrong man—if they ever did. The fool accosting Jessica on the street and forcing her to use Ravenous Red only proclaimed his guilt to the media and public, in turn.

Still, if the shitty little copycat continued his protests, he would be taken care of. All in good time.

Unfortunately, fate had torn Jessica from him, keeping them apart yet again.

He tried to get to her when she was at her most vulnerable, but the hospital had crawled with security. The fact he'd been clever enough to even gain access to the floor she was on showed his true superiority. Yet no opportunity could be taken with the bulldogs constantly at her door. She went home to recuperate without a sweet, nocturnal visit from him.

She'd left her apartment on a few rare occasions, always in the company of her watchdog, the redhead he assumed was her caregiver. He only witnessed two separate efforts but he suspected she may have kept a few more doctors' appointments. The haunted look in her eyes pleased him, obvious even from across the street.

Now, she'd vanished from his grasp. Not without a trace, though. When he thought to make a delivery to her co-op, her concierge explained he was authorized to sign for her packages, divulging only that she had left town on an extended visit. The concierge promised she would receive the item, before becoming distracted by two prissy *poodles who'd both stepped off different elevators at the same time. Rushing to break up their yapping brawl, he took the opportunity and quickly perused a leather-bound notebook behind the desk.*

Sure enough, a forwarding address was on the page containing her name. He recognized it from the official fan club website as some hole in the wall in Louisiana where she grew up.

It aggravated him about having to change his plans. But surprisingly enough, it would be even more convenient than he'd dreamed possible.

Because she'd run to the same town where Nick was from. Maybe he would kill them at the same time.

Wouldn't that be a ton of fun?

Chapter Eleven

CALLIE ROSE EARLY, as she did every morning, dressing in loose yoga clothes and rolling her mat out in the large bedroom from her childhood. Callandra had kept the sunny aspect of the room although new wallpaper and curtains graced the walls and windows since her last visit.

She eased onto the mat for her breathing exercises. Wolf opened one eye from the bed and seeing nothing interesting going on, he closed it and soon was softly snoring. She shook her head as she prepared her mind. Yoga calmed her like nothing could these days. As she breathed slowly, in and out, she lost herself from the world of worry, from the claustrophobia that nagged at her, from the shadow of a stranger that corrupted her life and changed her in unspeakable ways.

After several minutes she became lost in the very stretches themselves. Potted Palm and Downward Dog still brought her satisfaction. She did have trouble with certain poses she'd loved before, such as Cat Chaturanga and Cobra, even Sunburst. These were simply beyond her physically at this point.

Her side continued to ache. Lefty—she still

wouldn't dignify giving him the media's label—sliced and stabbed her right side from under her ribcage down to her upper thigh. She still found it hard to believe she'd survived his vicious attack.

Yet, she made what Gretchen termed amazing progress. The nurse altered each therapy session so they didn't become boring, knowing just how far to push Callie physically. Gretchen could be quiet when Callie needed it and knew instinctively when to joke her out of the gloom that descended from time to time. She was grateful Gretchen agreed to make this trip to Aurora. It might be a healing experience for them both.

A soft knock brought her back to the morning. Gretchen slipped into the room and smiled warmly.

"I thought you'd be up and hard at yoga." She cast her gaze around the space. "Your room is large enough that we can do your therapy sessions here if you'd like."

"Yes," Callie responded immediately. "I definitely want the privacy. I don't want Aunt C to think you're my nursemaid. She already wants to baby me. If she knew what bad shape I'm still in, she would hover as if I were a lost lamb. I can't have her worry that much."

Gretchen nodded in agreement. "I know you're down. But you've made—"

"Amazing progress," Callie finished for her. "I know. You've told me enough times. I might even start believing you some day." She gently rose to her knees and rolled up the yoga mat. Before the attack, she would have stood and stretched to do so. Maybe one day. Soon.

"Let's get started."

Gretchen left briefly and returned with her table and some hand weights and commenced with their session. An hour later, Callie had been massaged, stretched, and strained until sweat poured from her.

"You made great strides today. I'm pleased." Her

nurse grinned. "I also want to thank you for bringing me to Aurora. I know you've realized by now you could do these exercises on your own. You don't really need me anymore.

"I needed this break, though. Maybe I should move out of New York. Just the drive down, seeing new parts of the country. That was nice." Gretchen bit her lip.

"Let's face it. I blew it with Phil, even though I figured out he wasn't the Prince Charming I thought he was cracked up to be. But I've cut myself off from the world ever since we split by burying myself in work. I'm glad you talked me into this trip. That's all."

"It is beautiful here," Callie said. "The people are great. Southerners greet you with a smile. I promise we'll get out and see the area. Not just Aurora but New Orleans and beyond. We're going to have a great time here."

Gretchen nodded with approval. "I'm glad to hear you say this. You've seemed more relaxed since we've been here." She frowned. "Except around Nick La Chappelle. I sensed a little tension there, Cal."

She shivered. "You know how I've been about men. And frankly, I don't want him taking Aunt C for a ride. She's known throughout the parish for her generous hospitality."

"She is a gracious lady but did you catch what she said about Nick and the lean times? Maybe he did need her help."

Callie had picked up on the remark. It troubled her. Had Nick gambled away the fortune he must've made in sports? Was he like some topnotch athletes that drank and drugged their careers away? He sure didn't look like it. She remembered his muscled physique, the broad chest and shoulders that weren't hidden by the navy T-shirt he'd worn. She grew warm at the thought.

"I didn't see a ring, so he's available," Gretchen said. "I think I read in *Us* where he was married before. I guess she didn't last." She sighed. "Foolish girl to walk away from that much man."

Gretchen brushed back the hair from her face. "I flirted like crazy with him but he only had eyes for you, Callie. I don't think he took them off you the entire time at dinner last night. Maybe Mr. La Chappelle is the one who'll get you back on the right track."

Callie set her yoga mat in the corner. "You are crazy, Nurse Monroe. All that driving fried your brain. That man has no interest in me." She dismissed the thought with a wave of her hand. "I'm off to shower. By then, Essie will have breakfast ready."

Gretchen groaned softly at the thought. "I may need to take up yoga with you. Or jogging. Or something. If breakfast is anything as heavenly as dinner last night, it'll be like freshman year at college all over again."

Callie grinned. "They don't call it the Freshman Fifteen for nothing!"

* * *

Nick plowed through the rich-smelling earth with gloved hands. The sun beat down on his back in warm waves, lulling him as he worked. Part of him was right there in Miz C's garden but the secret part was in L.A. —the Hollywood Hills, to be exact. Detective Pete Wheeler was responding to a frantic call from *paparazzi* fav Amelia Blake, who'd come home to find her cat dead, his head sliced cleanly off and resting dead-center on the doormat to the entrance of her fabulous mansion.

Amelia had recently been investigated for her husband Parker's murder. The film studio chief had been murdered only last month while swimming laps early one morning. All fingers pointed to Amelia, but Wheeler had cleared her. No arrests had been made. That meant the killer was still out there.

Amelia had now come home to find Rupert, her loving Siamese cat, dead. This despite all the beefed up security she'd set into motion after Parker's death. Pete, who'd had a crush on Amelia since her screen debut fifteen years earlier, knew it had to be the same killer toying with Amelia's head. He tried to reassure her, but the lady was in hysterics.

"Oh, I'm sorry."

Nick came out of his characters' world and returned to Aurora in a heartbeat. He whipped around to see Callie Chennault standing there with her dog by her side, dressed in a sleeveless shell pink blouse and white capris. Her blond hair was down today, tucked behind her ears. She wore only a light pink gloss on her lips. Her green eyes were large. Her skin flawless.

His pulse jumped at the sight of her simple beauty. She appeared fragile and very uncomfortable. He fought the sympathy that swam to the surface, remembering how she'd been attacked only months before. Despite her snappish words last night, he could see in the morning light that she wasn't running at a hundred percent. He decided he should at least try and be civil to her. If only for Miz C's sake.

"No, you didn't interrupt me. Well, actually you did, but I really didn't know what was going to happen next."

Damn. He sounded like a befuddled schoolboy. He watched her brow wrinkle in confusion and he shot to his feet.

"I'm sorry. When I'm with my characters, I tend to forget there's a real world still going on around me.

When I'm working with the flowers in particular, I play scenes in my head of the book I'm working on. One particular lady is in quite a bit of trouble and I'm not sure how I'm going to get her out of it. Or even if I want to." He grinned sheepishly, hoping he made some sense.

He must have, because a smile tugged at one corner of her luscious mouth. She nodded slowly.

'I do that some, too. Not exactly the same because I'm not writing the lines as you do, but I read through a scene and then I play it out in my head. Where am I standing? Will I move as I speak? How will I say that line—wistfully? Forcefully? Will I pause? Will I rush through and let the emotion speak more loudly than the words?"

She flushed, as if revealing that much of herself to him was a mistake.

He nodded, suddenly eager to extend the connection they'd made.

'I really understand what you mean." He laughed. 'I don't think most people would, though. Anyone listening in on this conversation might certify either of us for the psych ward."

Callie stood there, still as the breezeless morning, as if she contemplated how to leave without seeming rude. Nick realized he didn't want her to. He'd thought about her often over the years. Though she'd been a prickly pear last night, he didn't want her to go just yet.

He pointed to the bench sitting in the shade of a bald cypress. 'Want to sit for a spell? I was ready to take a break."

'From gardening? Or writing?" Her mouth twisted in amusement, but she went and sat on the wrought iron bench he'd indicated. Wolf trotted after her and sat at her feet.

108

'Both." He pulled off his work gloves and moved to sit on the ground, his back resting against the tree.

They sat in silence a few minutes. He hesitated to break it, for fear she would run like a startled deer. She was already perched as if ready for flight as her eyes darted around uneasily, her hands nervously twisting in her lap.

What could he do to put her at ease?

'I remember you," he blurted out. Probably the last thing he'd meant to say.

She started and then her emerald green eyes met his. 'It took me a few minutes but I remembered you, too."

'You were different from any girl I'd ever met," he said softly. 'I pretty much hung around nothing but guys. Didn't date much. Girls scared me to death back then."

'Guys scare me now."

Her words made him realize that the stalker's attack affected her more than physically. It had violated her soul.

'I'm sorry." He didn't want to acknowledge the depth of the stalker's influence in her life now.

Instead, he moved back to the past. 'You didn't scare me. Then. You were so... normal. Better than normal. All the guys I knew talked sports mostly. Nothing really personal. Like there was an unwritten code that men weren't manly if they went beyond a surface conversation." He paused and gazed into her eyes. 'You really listened to me."

She shrugged and stroked Wolf's fluffy coat. 'You were interesting. And you talked about things that interested me. Books and movies and reaching for something beyond... this." She pushed back and relaxed on the bench. The dog picked up on her mood and curled up on the ground. "You didn't treat me like a punky little teenager. You made me feel as if I had value."

He detected a struggle flit across her face, which spoke more loudly than words ever could. "You do have value. You've become a professional actress."

She grimaced. "Yeah. On what amounts to a night-time soap, which most actors belittle. Still, I wouldn't trade the experience I've had on *Sumner Falls*. The bond I've created with our audience over the last ten years."

"But you got out of Aurora. And you're good at what you do."

Her eyes grew hooded. "You got out, too. From wherever you lived in Texas. From what Gretchen said, it seems you made a real name for yourself. Cy Young. World Series. Even I know what those mean, despite not following baseball."

He put a hand on his heart, giving her a look of mock indignation. "I do remember you being a football, basketball kinda gal back then."

"Used to be," she said wistfully. "Not much time for anything else with what I do. Did."

"Well, you're here now." Nick sat up, his hands resting on his knees. "Maybe you never saw me play but you can see what I do now."

He stood. "You know the pace in Aurora is slower than snails. I have just the thing for you. Stay here. I'll be right back."

He sprinted to the cottage and regretted not being able to stay in the cool air conditioning. He grabbed a book off the shelf and raced back, half of him thinking Callie would be gone by the time he returned.

She was still there. Still looking a little lost. Pale. She twisted a loose strand of hair around a finger. It made him wish he could run his hands through the corn silk of her hair.

"Here." He walked up to her. "Maybe you'll never see my fastball or change-up, but you can see what I've been up to since then."

He handed her the book. She took it, a puzzled look on her face.

"You want me to read a Nick Van Sandt book? I've read all his previous books, including this one. I can't wait for—"

And then the look on her face told him she realized *he* was Nick Van Sandt.

Chapter Twelve

CALLIE FROZE. The gorgeous hunk right in front of her was a famous crime novelist who'd won an Edgar for his first effort?

She studied him, the piercing blue eyes, the chiseled cheeks, and blurted out, "No way. I picture Nick Van Sandt as a grizzled, scruffy, wear his pajamas around the house all day while he taps away on an old typewriter kind of guy. Or maybe even an urbane, tweed jacket type with a pipe in hand, scribbling on yellow legal tablets before he bothers touching a computer."

She shook her head. "You look like you just stepped off the pages of a Ralph Lauren ad." She wanted to say he looked like a David Beckham-wearing-underwear model, with his sleek, muscled physique, but even she knew when to hold her tongue.

Nick laughed. She liked the sound of it. The laugh came deep from his belly. Not the lightly amused, isn't-life-insane, bored chuckle of the New York artsy-fartsy crowd she'd grown tired of.

He squatted and leaned against the tree again. "It's me. All me. Sometimes I even surprise myself. I'll read something I wrote and wonder where the hell it came from. Or I'll start a scene headed in one direction, and the characters head off hell-bent in another. It's like Geppetto sitting back in astonishment when Pinocchio comes to life. Nothing the puppet master anticipated."

He sighed. "I feel like that. All the time." He raked his fingers through his hair, a slight look of wonder on his face that was extremely appealing to her. "My people do what they want all the time. Sometimes I think I'm just the typist getting it all down before they change their minds."

"Why a writer?" she asked. "I thought all athletes wanted to coach so they can stay in the game. Or the pretty boys go into broadcasting. Why didn't you?"

Nick's brows furrowed as he studied her. "You really don't know?" He chuckled. "I *was* in broadcasting. ESPN."

Warmth crawled up her neck to her cheeks. "Oh. I didn't know. I don't watch much TV."

He got a faraway look in his eyes. "I walked out in the middle of the season. They nearly crucified me for that."

Despite her initial reservations about him, his words fascinated her—and jumpstarted her curiosity about him and what he'd been doing for the last two decades. She was on the verge of chucking it all. Nick was someone who actually did it.

"Why? Walk away, I mean. Was the money not enough? The hours too odd? The travel get to you? Did you have personality problems with another broadcaster?"

He closed his eyes a moment before he opened them slowly and focused on her. A pleasant tingle rippled through her.

"No. The money was great. More than I think I was

worth. The hours? Not too bad. I got along with the talent in the booth. The crew. Everyone, really."

He ran a hand through his thick, dark hair again. "It flat-out didn't make me happy. I talked about the same stuff, over and over. I could close my eyes and see myself five years—fifteen years—down the road. Doing the same thing."

"But gray at the temples?" she interjected.

He nodded. "Definitely gray. But all over." His gaze held hers. "I wouldn't have contributed anything new. Challenged myself. Grown as a person. I had to move on. It was time. No one understood that. Except me."

An odd feeling trickled through her. She knew exactly what he meant. Everything Nick said paralleled her situation with *Sumner Falls*.

He stood, cracking his knuckles. "I always wanted to write. Even earned my English degree the hard way, since I was drafted right out of high school and never went to college. On the road, I wrote term papers and read novels for my online classes, while other guys wasted time watching TV and playing video games."

Callie cleared her throat with that comment, her eyebrows raised.

Nick winced. "Sorry. I never had time for that stuff. If I weren't working on a course, I would hole up and write."

"What?" Her curiosity grew enough to push away the strange feelings rushing through her.

He shrugged. "Anything. Everything. Short stories, poems, novellas. A few novels." He grimaced. "A few really bad novels."

He moved to sit next to her on the bench. Her heart jumped as his knee brushed against hers. Her throat tightened, the panic beginning to slowly hum with a man's nearness.

She glanced at him but he seemed oblivious to her rising terror. He stared out across the gardens, a myriad of rosebushes and magnolias, and finally spoke.

"But I learned from them. How to really plot. Create conflict. External conflict came easily to me, but internal conflict eluded me. I learned with every mistake. I worked hard at my craft."

He grew quiet. With his very nearness, Callie inhaled, smelling the dirt from the earth he'd been working, rising with a hint of subtle cologne. She was aware of his strong forearms resting on muscled thighs. His closeness. Right by her. Something stirred within her that she'd figured dead and long buried. It made her want to run—not from fear of him as a man but for the feelings it brought. Still, she hungered to continue their conversation.

"I can't believe no one knows it's you," she said, her voice a little shaky. "The public would eat it up. Former professional athlete becomes best-selling novelist."

Nick turned, a fierce look darkening his eyes. "I don't want them to know. Ever," he spit out. "I didn't want doors opened to me for the wrong reasons. I wanted to make this my own. I didn't want to be published because of my name recognition and have people buy a book they'd never read simply because my name graced the cover."

"You simply wanted the work to speak for itself," she observed.

"Yes," he said enthusiastically. "Exactly."

She thought a moment. "That's why there's never a photo on your jackets and sketchy bio info. It always says, 'Nick Van Sandt lives in a small town. He is the author of… however many books you've written.'"

He eyed her. "You know that by heart?"

"I pay attention. Especially if I like the work. Most

authors have web pages or at least e-mail addys for fans to contact them. Not you."

"Not Nick Van Sandt." He smiled.

Then an awkward silence rose between them, the kind where people who've shared certain intimacies didn't know where to go next or what to say.

Callie handed him the book he'd brought to her. "Since I've read it a few times, I'll let you keep your copy." She glanced away and shyly added, "Maybe you'll autograph mine for me sometime."

"Sure," he said softly.

She stood and Wolf did the same, sticking close to his mistress' leg. "I've got to go."

He rose. "I've got to get back to Miz C's flower beds."

"And your characters."

Nick smiled at her. Oh, God. It was one of those classic Robert Redford smiles. The kind that swept Barbra Streisand off her feet in *The Way We Were* and Glenn Close in *The Natural*. She couldn't breathe.

She mumbled, "Okay, then," and abruptly started off. She wanted to say something else, anything else, but she didn't know if her mouth could form words at the moment.

As she moved up the path, Wolf on her heels, she turned and looked over her shoulder. Their gazes met. Callie swallowed, frozen in place for a moment, then she hurriedly went back up the path to the house.

* * *

Nick let out a long breath that he hadn't realized he held. It was as if all the years in-between melted away. He'd spoken to Callie from his heart. It surprised him how much he'd revealed to her in a few minutes of conversation.

It had never been like that with anyone, especially Vanessa. She took no interest in his writing, even chided him for wasting his time on it when he could be working out or helping on one of her charity events.

Vanessa, with all her glitz and glamour, seemed the exact opposite of Callie.

That messed with his head.

Vanessa—and every actress he'd known in L.A.— was shallow. Self-centered. Selfish bitches. They expected the world to revolve around them and their needs. None of them—especially his own wife—really cared about him as a person or what he was interested in.

But in the space of a few minutes, he'd revealed things to Callie that he never spoke about. Maybe because she wasn't quite what he thought she would be. Hell, she probably thought he was totally insane to think about his characters the way he did, much less admit that sometimes he wasn't even in control of their actions. They were make-believe, and yet he knew them so well. Even better than real people.

Nick slipped his work gloves back on and picked up the trowel before he slammed it down in disgust.

"Oh, yeah, she must've loved the part about how I thought the guys wasted their time on the road watching TV. Way to go, Sherlock."

He glanced around, glad no one was there to hear him berate himself.

Curiosity began to gnaw at him. What had Callie done all these years? What series was she on? Was she really any good? Miz C always bragged on her, most of which he tuned out, because that lady would shower love on a flea on a dog.

He decided to abandon weeding for now in favor of Googling. He stood and stripped off his work gloves and went back to the cottage and fired up his laptop. A search for Callie hit a wealth of sites. He decided to focus first on her official fan club's offering and then go from there.

Two hours later, Nick was a Callie Chennault expert. He learned the backstory of her *Sumner Falls* character, Jessica, and had read recaps of every episode since she had joined the cast a decade earlier. It was obvious she was the character that the entire show revolved around, despite its large cast. She'd Jessica had been married numerous times and was related to practically every person in the town, by blood or marriage.

Callie also had won a slew of awards. Big ones, including Emmys, Golden Globes, and People's Choice Awards. He also read the message boards. Rabid fans wrote reams about her. Most voiced complimentary sentiments but some real nut cases logged in with wild accusations about Jessica's actions and what they'd do to her if they ran across her in real life. It was as if some people couldn't distinguish between fantasy and reality.

Nick had experienced his share of groupies who crossed the line. One in particular followed him from city to city for the better part of a season, always trying to hook up. Something in her eyes made him uncomfortable and he always tried to ease around her without stirring up trouble. She'd found out his home phone number and left a few messages that spooked him. After he'd changed the number, he came home from a road trip to find someone had broken in and trashed his place. He'd gotten a restraining order against her after that. Even dropped his landline and relied solely on his cell, giving very few people access to its number.

She disappeared on him for a while. He ran into her

in the middle of the next season in New York. She was on the arm of a player from the Yankees. He couldn't get out of the room fast enough for fear she'd see him and it would start up all over again. He now realized he was only at the tip of the iceberg with what Callie dealt with on a daily basis.

He also found a small piece written about her personal life. She donated both time and money to an abused women's shelter and the New York SPCA. She did yoga. She was best friends with some other actress who used to be on her show and now served as president of Callie's fan club. Nothing online mentioned anything about her family. Or if she was seeing anyone.

The official fan website was tastefully done. Gave the fans probably enough of what they wanted, while allowing Callie to maintain some sense of privacy.

He wondered how many times her stalker must have come to this site. As he wrote more and more crime novels, he'd begun to think like a criminal. He instinctively knew this guy visited her website many times. A fierce possessiveness flooded Nick. He found he wanted to break the guy's face.

As he closed the window on the site, he felt like someone punched him in the gut.

"No. No way. Not again."

Chapter Thirteen

HE WAS ALMOST THERE.

He tidied up all the loose ends in New York. Killed the nosy landlady, then told the neighbors she was heading down to Florida to see if it was all it was cracked up to be. He knew he would be believed because it was all the woman talked about for the last twenty years.

He said she left him to close up the place. He stopped the newspaper, the electricity, the phone service. He knew where she kept all her records. Besides, he was a whiz when it came to technology. He found all the info he needed.

He financed his trip by clearing out her safety deposit box. The old woman outlived three husbands, and they all left her set pretty well financially. He asked an estate agent to come appraise the furniture. Cleared another bundle that way. Pawned the silver and the few jewels he found.

Then he locked up the place. Told the neighbors he found another apartment in Queens. He would only sublet in case the old woman hated Florida and changed her mind and returned. He really loved her, he said, his eyes misting over.

Now the place stood empty. The basement still held

evidence that could easily convict him of murder. All that DNA shit these days. But he was smart. He covered his tracks as best as he could. He watched enough crime procedural shows on TV. They were paint-by-numbers in helping him commit his spree of terror.

He planned to do his business down south and take a vacation afterward. Go to some of the places he'd always wanted to see—Vegas, Disney World—stuff like that.

Then he'd slip back into New York and burn the brownstone to the ground. Bye-bye evidence. Sayonara. He'd be outta there.

Finally, free at last. From his mother. From Jessica.

And Nick. Especially from Nick.

Chapter Fourteen

CALLIE AWOKE from her daily afternoon nap feeling physically refreshed. Mentally was a whole different ballgame.

She'd dreamed of Nick, both then and now. She visualized the Nick of long ago, almost on the cusp of manhood.

What a man he'd become. Just looking at him caused her mouth to go dry. He was the whole package —intelligence, looks, accomplished, looks, a sense of humor—and had she mentioned looks?

Surprisingly, he was also sensitive. If she were having an expert put together the perfect man? He would look, talk, and be as beautiful as Nick La Chappelle.

Callie shivered involuntarily. It didn't matter if he seemed to be her fantasy man. She was too raw from the mid-March attack. She didn't want or need any man in her life. Without warning, she flashed back to the forced kiss with Simon. Bile rose in her throat. No, she might find Nick hot as hell, but she was still an emotional wreck. She couldn't afford to be interested in him—or anyone else—in her fragile state of mind.

She stepped into the bathroom and slipped off the

terrycloth robe she'd napped in. Gingerly, she removed her bra and panties and stood before the mirror.

Face it. What man would be interested in this?

Her eyes roamed over her injured body. The stitches were gone but angry, red scars ran from just under her right breast, along her side and down to the top of her right thigh.

Callie examined herself as an impartial observer. Her frame was too thin. As Essie would say, meat had fallen off her bones. She'd lost her appetite since the attack, but hopefully Essie's cooking would change that. Last night she'd cleaned her plate, the first time in months. The gumbo had been fresh and spicy, and she hadn't realized how much she'd missed Southern-style cuisine. Hopefully that problem might soon be solved.

She took another appraising glance. Her hair still had a nice sheen to it. Her skin remained clear and peach-like. Her eyebrows could stand a good waxing, though. Everything else seemed fine... until the scars. Dr. Maxwell said they'd fade in color during the next few years.

Years. And she'd still be left mutilated. She couldn't imagine ever showing her naked body to a man.

Especially one as sexy as Nick La Chappelle. Like that would ever happen.

She dressed hastily. A man that attractive would need to hire someone fulltime to beat the women off him with a stick. Or a cattle prod. A stick wouldn't keep some determined women far enough away. She doubted that even an electric jolt or two would affect the diehards.

As a professional athlete, Nick had probably done groupies in every city. A man with his looks and muscular body would have had his pick of the litter.

He would never want a reject like her.

Callie brushed her hair and wound it back into the familiar ponytail. Gretchen begged her to put it up in Jessica's elegant chignon once, but she refused. It was the only harsh words that had occurred between them. Callie wanted nothing to do with her alter ego. In a way, she blamed Jessica for the attack on her.

She opened the door and caught Essie about to knock.

"Gracious, Miss Callie, you startled me."

"Sorry, Essie. What's up?"

"Miz Callandra would like to see you. She's ready for a good, long chat."

She smiled. "Same here. Where is she?"

"In her bedroom, same as always. Mr. Nick knows how Miz Callandra loves her sanctuary. When the doctor let us know it would be the wheelchair from now on, Mr. Nick insisted we put in an elevator so Miz Callandra could still come upstairs. Paid for the whole thing himself." Essie laughed. "That boy. He's something."

Her mind whirled at Nick's thoughtfulness to her great-aunt. He wasn't the man she'd first believed him to be. She tucked that thought away as she focused on Essie.

"I'll be seeing you at dinner," the cook told her. "You did me proud last night. Thought you might've licked that gumbo bowl clean, but having company probably stopped you." Essie gave her a wicked grin.

Callie shook her head. "Just because I did that very thing twenty years ago..."

"You'll never live it down, girl." Essie grew serious. "I've loved you since you was that pint-sized peanut. We put you back together all those years ago, you and your mama. Miz Callandra and I'll fix you up fine again. You'll see."

Essie gave her a swift hug and stepped back. "I'm off to fix us something special. That Miss Gretchen's been bugging me about making mud pies."

Callie laughed. "She means *Mississippi* mud. I told her yours was the best."

"She's all right. For a Yankee. I'm gonna let her watch me work my magic. I'll be sure to give her all the local gossip while she's licking the bowls." Her eyes twinkled. "I'll make that gal a Southerner before you can say Mark Twain ten times."

Essie walked one way down the carpeted hall as Callie went in the opposite direction. She paused in front of her aunt's door and knocked.

"Come in, Callie." The voice was strong and clear.

She turned the doorknob and stepped into her favorite room in the house. It was the largest of all the bedrooms, two actually, since some Chennault had knocked down a few walls sometime around the turn of the century so his invalid wife would have a place to entertain her guests without having to go downstairs.

The room held so many memories. She gazed fondly at the canopied bed which she'd run to when the nightmares came. Aunt C never turned her away, always holding her close, making her secure. She'd curled up hundreds of times in the club chair by the marble fireplace, escaping to new lands and adventures in her books.

Her great-aunt was seated on a periwinkle blue sofa on the sun porch, an addition that had been made after Callie and her mother came to live at Noble Oaks. She would come up here each day after school, carrying her backpack filled with homework. Essie would follow, tray in hand, and leave her and Aunt C to talk over the school day. Callie's mom had been present in those early years, before breast cancer ended her life prematurely.

After that, it was only the two of them, sipping hot cocoa with plump marshmallows in the winter and ice-cold lemonade when the weather grew warm. Always with plenty of tea sandwiches and *petit fours* to accompany the gossip as each shared her day with the other.

Callie smiled and took a seat next to her aunt on the plush sofa. "You still enjoy spending time in the sunroom?"

Callandra smiled. "I have the best of both worlds here. I can laze about like a cat soaking up the hot sun, all the while letting the cool air-conditioned breeze whisper over me."

She indicated the tray on the table in front of them. "Essie brought both tea and lemonade. Would you like some? For old times' sake?"

"Yes. But let me pour." She filled two tall glasses with ice from a silver bucket and poured lemonade into each one.

Callie took a sip, the familiar sweet liquid tinged with a hint of sour, tart lemon. "Mmm. Still the best. Nothing in New York compares to anything Essie can make."

Callandra slipped a hand over hers. "But New York has much to offer an ambitious young woman, doesn't it?"

Their eyes met. Tears moistened both.

"It's been my whole world, Aunt C. I loved the pace, the excitement, the acting classes, the challenge. Then came the money and fame and awards. And then," she stopped for another sip, "came the itchy feet. Like it's time to move on."

"Oh, dear. Your father's bad genes coming out, I suppose?"

She shuddered. "I hope not. But... I don't know

how to explain it. It's everything I wanted. Everything I thought it would be. And yet..." Her voice trailed off.

"You want so much more." Callandra gave Callie one of her all-knowing looks. "You became so good at what you did, the challenge and fun fled. Routine became boring. You felt tied down to a role that you'd made all your own—but now that role is your prison."

"Yes. You say it so simply, and it's true. I owe everything to Jessica and the show, but it's not enough anymore. It hasn't been for a while now." She shifted, folding her legs under her.

"I had these thoughts months before the attack. I pondered moving on. Not renewing my contract. I'm not foolish enough to think I could jump directly to another hit primetime series or even movies, because all anyone would see is Jessica. But I could do regional theater. Maybe off-Broadway. Something. I want to quit going through the motions. I could be Jessica in my sleep at this point."

"Ah, the fragile and often misguided Jessica. I do love that girl." Callandra sighed. "Just when I think the poor child has taken too much, the bitch in her comes out and she roars back to life."

She leaned over and stroked Callie's cheek. "You've created a marvelous character, my dear. Full of flaws and surprises. I shall miss seeing her on screen."

Callie studied her aunt. "You act as if I'll never return to the show." She thought about it a moment. Cut all ties. Truly not go back.

"That scares me," she admitted. "It's as if Jessica's always been there, hovering in the shadows, watching my every move."

"All the more reason to move on." Callandra's tone grew serious. "You have great talent. Only the tip of it has been explored. I want to see you happy, Callie. If that means not returning to *Sumner Falls*, I shall support you. I love you as my own flesh and blood child, and I would see you settled before I pass."

Alarm whizzed through her. "You're all right, aren't you? Nothing's wrong?"

"Do you mean am I dying? Why, yes. We all are, I suppose. Nothing specific has been diagnosed but I am getting on in years. I sense my time draws near."

She buried her face in Callandra's lap. She couldn't imagine life without her aunt's wisdom. Slowly, she lifted her head.

"I need you, Aunt C. More than I ever did. I'm not just a mess about my career. I'm a mess inside."

Callandra pushed Callie's head gently back into her lap, stroking her hair as she had many years ago. "I know the attack changed you. You're sharper in tone. At least, you were to Nick."

Callie froze. Then she took a deep breath, trying to relax. "I'm not very comfortable in the company of any man right now."

She closed her eyes as her aunt rubbed her temples in slow, languid circles. "Nick is not very happy in the company of women. I suppose I have two wounded birds who've flown home to heal."

She sat up. "What's wrong with Nick? He seemed fine to me."

Callandra pursed her lips. "It's for Nick to share his story with you if he chooses. I'll simply say that his wife —his ex-wife—bruised his poet's soul." She looked at Callie steadily. "Much as a stranger hurt my girl."

She swallowed. "Will I ever have your wisdom, Aunt C? Your ability to calm someone and restore his confidence?"

"You're a Chennault, dear. What you seek has always been within you. You'll find it's there."

She grinned. "Then maybe I'll be able to hear it without cab drivers blaring their horns and construction crews' jackhammers, or street vendors hawking their wares.

"Maybe I'm like Dorothy, Aunt C. I'll find out there's no place like home."

Chapter Fifteen

"MISS PAM JUST CALLED," Essie told Callie. "She's coming by shortly."

Callie closed *Southern Living Magazine* and placed it on the coffee table. "Thanks, Essie."

Callandra's eyes left her embroidery a moment. "It'll do you good to see her. You girls were thicker than bees' honey back in high school."

"We still talk all the time. Usually texts and a monthly FaceTime. It's hard for either of us to be free at the same time with our schedules, but we've always stayed in touch."

"She still wants a child?"

Callie nodded. "Pretty badly. She had a third miscarriage back in the spring. I didn't know about it until summer because of... you know." She stood, feeling restless. "I think I'll go wait for her out on the porch."

"I'm sure you'll be out there half the night, so I'll say goodnight to you now. Be sure to look at Gretchen's latest flower arrangement. She's doing quite well."

Callie went and brushed a kiss on her aunt's paper-thin cheek. "Good night. Sleep well."

She walked out of the living room and into the foyer. A new arrangement of roses and day lilies stood on the entry table. Aunt C had taken Gretchen under her wing since they'd arrived a few days ago, helping her to learn the fine Southern art of arranging flowers. Under Callandra and Essie's tutelage, Gretchen believed she was well on her way to becoming a modern Southern belle.

Callie opened the front door and stepped out onto the wide porch. The evening heat washed gently over her, as did the smell of magnolias. She went to sit on the porch swing to wait.

Pam pulled up in her old Chevy minutes later. She swung her long legs out and hurried up the path, a wide grin on her round, freckled face.

Callie rose and they embraced, then she pulled away, her head cocked to one side. "When are you going to get another car? That sedan was ancient when we were in high school."

Pam laughed. "It's reliable. Still gets great mileage. I wouldn't trust it on a cross-country trip but for going from one end of the parish to the other, it suits me fine. Besides, what would you expect a poor public school teacher in Louisiana to drive? A Lexus?"

They took a seat on the porch swing. Pam studied her with a look of relief. "God, it's so good to see you in the flesh, Cal." She gripped Callie's hands in hers. "I miss you. I always do. You could've knocked me for a loop when I got back from my debate workshop at LSU and Eric told me you were back in town. Why didn't you let me know you were coming?"

She shrugged. "I didn't know if we'd actually make it all the way down here. I didn't want either of us to get our hopes up and then me not show."

Pam gave her a questioning look but Callie fell

silent. How could she explain to her oldest friend that she didn't know if she could be confined in a car that long? That tight spaces made her throat go dry. That there were a thousand times she fought to keep the words in her mouth for Gretchen to turn the car around and go back to New York. That she didn't think she could set foot on a plane because she might freak out somewhere over the Appalachians and be arrested by Homeland Security after the plane made a forced landing.

Pam squeezed her hands and then released them to ruffle her curly, short hair. "Well, girl, we are definitely going to celebrate your homecoming in style. I'm throwing a barbeque tomorrow night in your honor."

Callie's eyes widened. "I don't know if that's such a good idea, Pam."

Her friend frowned. "I sense reluctance here. Is the heat of August too much for my little New Yorker these days? I know this steam bath makes me tired and all wrung out. If that's the case, we can just send the men out to grill and eat indoors."

She swallowed. "Would... are you inviting lots of people?"

"Not really. Tom and me. And Eric is itching to bring your friend Gretchen. I can't wait to meet this gal. Eric is about as smitten as I've ever seen him." Pam laughed. "Wait until Sally runs into them. She still thinks Eric pines away for her. Dumb bitch," Pam grumbled. "I'm glad she's history.

"Oh, and Nick, of course," Pam continued. "But that would be it. Why?"

At the sound of Nick's name, that funny feeling washed over her, making her heart flutter and her pulse race.

Pam touched her arm. "Say yes, honey. We need to catch up and with school beginning in a couple of weeks, I won't have as much time as I do right now. That reminds me, would you like to be a guest speaker for my drama classes? They will go nuts hearing it straight from a real live star who's been there, done that, in style."

"I don't know, Pam," she said quietly. "That's a lot of people. A lot of strangers to talk in front of."

Shock painted Pam's face. "I have seen you roll around half-nekkid on TV with a dozen different men. Not at the same time, of course. But talking with your clothes on in front of a few hormonal teenagers should be a piece of cake for a pro like you."

Callie closed her eyes. "Seems like it would be. But..." She hesitated. "Pam, it's different now. I've... changed."

Pam reached for her hand. They sat silently for several minutes, only the creak of the swing making any noise.

"I remember how we sat here and talked about when I first got my period," Pam finally said. "It about freaked me out. I thought I had to be dying."

She smiled. "Your mom hadn't thought to tell you, having two boys ahead of you. Thank goodness Aunt C clued me in before it hit."

"Remember how we used to sit out here and make our plans? Talk about boys and life and everything?" Pam eyed her steadily. "We need to talk about what's wrong now. We're face-to-face. It's not e-mail or a text. Don't put me off, Cal." Pam put an arm about Callie's shoulder. "I want to help. In any way I can. You've got to trust me."

"I try to be normal," Callie started. "But it's hard. I get these panic attacks. I think... he's... following me again. I know it's incredibly stupid because he's in jail back in New York, but I still get paranoid. If it starts to storm, that scares me even more."

She broke off, her eyes searching Pam's face. "It was raining that night. I lay there bleeding on that dirty sidewalk as the thunder growled and the rain beat down on me, and I knew I was a goner." She sucked in a deep breath. "Being around people—men, really —upsets me."

Pam squeezed her shoulder. "It'll just be Tom and Eric. You've known them forever. And Nick. I forget you don't really know him much. But you'll like him. He's family."

"I don't want to like him," she said stubbornly.

Pam snorted. "He probably doesn't want to like you, either."

"Why?"

Pam faced her. "Nick had it rough. He retreated here, mostly because his mom had moved back to Aurora. It's complicated. Besides, it's not like I'm setting you up on some god-awful blind date with him. And he's here at Noble Oaks anyway. He and Miz C are tight. You're going to have to get used to him sometime. Might as well be with a medium-well cheeseburger in your hand."

Pam stood. "In fact, I'm going to go see him now and let him know about tomorrow night. He never has plans anyway." Her face softened. "Please come. Please. We'll make it like old times."

Callie bit her lip. "Okay. Only because it's you asking. I can't promise how long I'll stay, though."

Pam laughed and grabbed Callie's hands, pulling her to her feet. "Okay, your mission—which you'll now choose to accept—is to go sweet-talk Essie into sending

141

her world famous coleslaw along with you. I'll admit it, that's the only reason you're being asked to come. We're all hankering for Essie's slaw and couldn't figure out how to get it there without inviting you."

Pam kissed her cheek. "You be good now. Bye-bye."

As Callie watched her friend cut around the side of the house and head to Nick's cottage, she wrapped her arms around herself and whispered, "What have I gotten myself into?"

* * *

Nick had the lights low. Eric Clapton played softly in the background. His thoughts wandered, his writing pad close by in case he needed to capture something as he sat on the sofa.

Nothing came.

Nothing except Callie Chennault's image—fragile, vulnerable, constant.

He lowered his head to his knees and groaned. He refused to let it happen again. He'd fallen for one self-centered actress, the biggest mistake of his life—and he'd made several doozies in his thirty-five years. He would not let another one get under his skin.

Vanessa had played him like a master strumming a classical guitar. He believed every smile, every lie, until it was too late. She trapped him into marriage, something he didn't really believe in. Or so he told himself now.

She never really loved him. That's probably what hurt the most. Oh, she loved the nine thousand-square-foot house with every amenity available. Her designer clothes and Jimmy Choo shoes and diamonds too numerous to count. The first-class travel. The couple who took care of the house and the lawn crew. Having her own personal assistant at her beck and call.

But most of all, Vanessa had loved the status. How little Vannie Malone from Hicksville, Nowhere, had become the lethally seductive Vanessa La Chappelle. The fact that she hadn't made it as an actress didn't matter. Acting proved too much work, with all the early calls and learning lines. But she loved playing at being Mrs. Nick La Chappelle and seeing all the doors that name opened for her.

When Nick retired early due to rotator cuff problems, she'd been thrilled when he reluctantly accepted the network job she pushed him to take. It only improved her status among her in-crowd, having her husband in the ESPN booth.

When he became so miserable doing it that he didn't want to get out of bed anymore, he told her he couldn't stay in broadcasting. He wanted to get serious about his writing and return to his own small town roots. Aurora, in particular.

That's when the shit hit the fan. He could still hear her screaming now.

"Nick, you don't want to do that. Leave this? L.A.? This is our life, Nick. This is what makes us happy. I have my charity work but you're an athlete and an entertainer. You need the spotlight to thrive. Don't you realize that? How can you think to go back to some backwater bump in the road to be a fucking writer? Besides, I have a terrific chance to be on next season's Real Housewives of Beverly Hills.*"*

"No," he'd replied. *"You need the spotlight. You need the three-hundred-dollar massages and nine-hundred-dollar shoes and the stylist and limousine and paparazzi. Me? I need a life again. My life. Not this glitz and glamour fakery."*

"You dumb fuck, you can live it without me. I will never give up all of this. Never!"

"What about love?"

"Love?" She looked puzzled before her nose crinkled and her whole face turned into a giant sneer. *"What about it? It's just a fantasy, Nick. Love doesn't exist. It never has. Not for us. Not for anyone. Just face it. We used each other. I needed you to get out of the rattrap I was in. My career was headed straight into the toilet. You gave me instant name recognition and opened all the right doors so I could blossom into who I am today.* People Magazine *writes about which fashion shows I attend.* US *covers my charity events. I'm named to best-dressed lists. Even Oprah returns my calls."*

"How did I use you, Vanessa?"

She laughed. *"You needed a nursemaid, Nick. Someone to be sure your clothes matched. Someone to organize your leukemia foundation and keep your head out of the clouds with all that silly writing and be sure you showed up to games on time. You needed someone around so you wouldn't feel so lonely. Well, I did my part, babe, but I refuse to do it out in the sticks. I'll take you for every cent you have, down to your last cashmere pullover.*

"I never loved you, Nick. That's why it'll be easy for me to walk away."

That's why he couldn't fall for another shallow, self-consumed actress. Or really any woman. Women always had a hidden agenda. The few dates he'd been set up on since he'd come to Aurora proved it. They only went out with him for who he used to be, in order to brag about their time spent with a sports legend.

The one woman he thought was different ended things a month into their relationship when she realized he had no money—and what she decided were no prospects.

That made him give up on women. And romantic

feelings. He wouldn't be bothered by them anymore. He knew he'd never marry again. He was all right with that. As a writer, he was used to a solitary life. Besides, he still had his family.

And his characters.

That's where he created true, lasting love. Each of his novels had murder and mayhem in them since crime sold well, but every time, every novel, he built a romantic relationship between two main characters. Twice it had been between a cop and the heroine. Once the hero had been a journalist instead. But in his perfect world, he could create real, lasting emotions. He could give his people the love he craved that he knew didn't exist in real life.

He would not—under any circumstances—give in to this momentary infatuation with Callie Chennault. For God's sake, she was an actress who could probably fake every emotion on the planet. He could feel sorry for her because of the brutal attack she'd endured. He could even learn to get along with her while she resided at Noble Oaks. He would be friendly but keep his distance.

He knew not to get hung up on her, though. Because as an actress, she probably decided to milk this whole attack for publicity purposes. It probably hadn't been nearly as bad as reported. She'd even retreated to Aurora the public would keep guessing. Then she'd make the comeback of her career at twice her old salary, and the ratings of her stupid show would go through the roof. Plus, she'd probably win every award out there since she'd survived a crazy stalker's attack.

Nick would be one of the poor fools she practiced her story on. Glean a little sympathy. Play up to him like they had some things in common.

No, sir—he would *not* fall for her. Or her act. He would keep his distance and pray she returned home soon. Before he lost his willpower.

Because he wanted nothing better than to take Callie in his arms and kiss her senseless.

A brisk knock summoned him from his reverie. Nick went to the door, flipped on the porch light, and found his cousin standing on the porch.

"Hey, Pammie. Come on in." He stepped aside to let her inside. "How was your—"

"I'm here to invite you and your grilling skills to a barbecue tomorrow night. You are the best at chicken, hands down, and you give Eric a run for the money with your burgers."

He laughed. "Don't let him hear you say that. He'd disown you and punch out my lights."

"Nope. I'm making my molasses baked beans and potato salad, so he'll show up. Any starving bachelor would."

"What can I bring? Make it easy. Buns, maybe? Or I can pick up dessert from *The Sweet Shoppe*."

"Dessert is covered, so buns it is. That and Callie, and we'll see you around six-thirty." Pam started down the porch before her words hit him.

"Wait a minute, kid. Buns... and Callie?"

She grinned. "Yep. The barbeque is in her honor and since Eric is already picking up Gretchen, it falls to you to bring Callie."

"Why can't Eric—"

"Because he's taking Gretchen into New Orleans for the afternoon. On a date. They'll come straight from there. What's the big deal? You live right next to her."

"No big deal. We'll be there. Hot buns and all."

Pam reached around and pinched his butt. "You

have the amazing hot buns in this family, Cuz. See you tomorrow night."

She zipped down the drive with her usual, boundless energy. Nick closed the door thoughtfully.

His willpower would definitely be tested tomorrow night.

Chapter Sixteen

CALLIE CHECKED her appearance once more in the floor-length mirror, nerves flittering like raging butterflies in her stomach.

"Relax," she told the image in front of her. "It's just a few friends. Food. A little laughter. Gretchen'll be there. Pam."

And Nick...

She knew she was being foolish. Why should it bother her that some stupid ex-jock would be there? She would keep her distance, eat a little of the delicious food, and then hightail it out the minute she felt ill at ease.

Or better yet, she should simply stay home. She was already uncomfortable enough as it was. And it wasn't just being in the presence of more than two people.

It was being in sight of Nick. Her heart skipped a beat at the mere thought of him.

She gave a stern look in the mirror. "This is craziness, Callie Chennault. You are not fourteen years old. This is not a date. You don't want or need any man in your life. Period. You need to put on ten pounds. Get your head together. Find what you want to do with the rest of your life!"

Her hand gently stroked her right side as she spoke, aware of the scars hidden below her sky blue sleeveless blouse. A man had done that. She hadn't been able to stop him. She determined no man would ever hurt her again—either physically *or* emotionally.

She was strong. She was a Chennault. She would conquer her fears, and by golly, she'd enjoy tonight. Damn Nick La Chappelle and any other man that caused her to miss a step. She deserved a little fun. Gretchen told her that all the time.

Callie left her room with a tad more confidence than she'd mustered in weeks and headed down the stairs. She heard voices in the kitchen and turned in their direction. As she entered, her aunt and Essie were seated at the table in the breakfast nook, laughing and chatting over bowls of red beans and rice, accompanied by plates of hot, steaming cornbread. Wolf sat close by, an expectant look on his face in case anyone dropped something.

"I see you're ready for your outing," Callandra said, her eyes sparkling with approval.

Essie rose. "Let me get you that slaw, else Miz Pam'll make you turn around and come back. She is one bossy gal." The cook opened the refrigerator and took out a large glass bowl covered in Saran wrap and handed it to Callie.

"You have a nice time, hear?" Essie gently squeezed Callie's shoulder. "Eat something of everything for me."

"I'll do that. Bye now."

She left the kitchen and went to the foyer table. She slung her purse over her shoulder and grabbed the car keys to the SUV they'd rented and headed out the door.

"Better lock it."

She froze at the low, deep voice. She whipped around and found Nick seated on the porch swing, his long legs stretched out in front of him. A slight breeze ruffled his dark hair as those midnight blue eyes focused on her with intensity.

"You about made me drop this," she accused him, hugging the glass bowl tightly. "How dare you sneak up on people like that."

He stood as she stormed down the steps.

"Wait a minute," he called after her.

She stopped and watched him slip a key into the front door and turn the dead bolt before he moved down the steps with a grace that screamed his athletic roots.

"I told you to lock it," he said. "Miz C is careless about that. I tell her all the time that times have changed. It's a different world now than the one she grew up in."

He placed his palm against the small of her back. "Let's go."

Callie stiffened at the touch and turned to face him. "What are you talking about?"

"I'm your ride to Pam and Tom's." Nick paused a moment. "I thought Pam told you."

"No. She didn't." She took a deep yoga breath to calm her racing heart. "That's okay. I'll see you there." She turned to go.

"Wait." Nick took her elbow in his hand. She winced and he dropped his hand.

"We're going to the same place. We might as well go together."

She hesitated. "I... I might have to... leave early. I wouldn't want—"

"Then I'll leave early, too." He gave her a crooked smile. "I'm not much on get-togethers myself. You give me a sign when you want to leave. I'll do the same." He stuck out his hand. "Deal?"

Callie held the bowl close to her with her left hand and moved to place her right hand in his. "Deal."

He clasped her hand in his. Warmth flooded her at his touch. It felt... nice. Reluctantly, she pulled her hand from his. He reached and took the slaw from her.

"Come on. Pam's a-waiting."

He escorted her to his red convertible, which sat in the front drive. She was disappointed for a moment that the top was up. She hadn't ridden in a convertible in fifteen years and realized she'd missed the feeling of the wind blowing through her hair.

Nick opened the door for her. "Don't sit on the buns," he warned.

She located two packages of Mrs. Baird's hamburger buns in the passenger seat and picked them up before she slipped into the car. Nick handed her the bowl and closed the door as she fastened her seat belt.

The car smelled of its leather seats and Nick's cologne. Utterly male. Callie shivered. She didn't know if it was in fear or anticipation.

He backed out and headed toward town. He didn't attempt any small talk. Neither did she. Yet the silence between them wasn't strained. She felt a small victory when they pulled down the long driveway of Pam's rambling two-story. Her breathing was still normal. She hadn't panicked in Nick's presence or needed him to stop the car.

Maybe this night out would be good for her, after all.

Before she had unbuckled her seat belt, Nick was already out of the car and opening her door. He took the food items and gave her a hand to get out of the low-slung car. Once again, she experienced a feeling of security for the few moments her hand rested in his. As if everything was right with the world.

"Hey, guys."

She watched Pam's husband headed toward them. Tom hesitated a moment before he gave her a swift hug. Callie was certain Pam had told him of her feelings about men. But the hug was brief and she didn't feel like a trapped prisoner because it was over so quickly.

"How's the team this year?" she asked, glad to hear her voice sounded natural. "Pam said you made it to regionals last year."

Tom snorted. "This football team is headed all the way to state, honey. I have a quarterback with an arm on him that you haven't seen the likes of. The kid's six-three and still growing. Accurate as hell. And he reads defenses like a dream."

He smiled at her. "You'll have to come to a few games."

She returned the smile, relaxing in the presence of someone she'd known for many years. "I'll do that. It'll be odd, though, seeing you coaching on the sidelines instead of out there making tackles and forcing fumbles."

"You'll get used to it. Besides, it's the only place I get to boss anyone around." Tom winked at her.

"You aren't saying that you're henpecked, are you, Tom?" Nick asked, a teasing light in his eyes.

"I prefer to think of myself as a modern man. One who knows he pleases his wife and yet knows his place."

"I'd say your place is back at those coals, buster," Pam said. "Go nurse them so Nick can get things rolling. I'm starving."

Tom rolled his eyes dramatically. "It'll be another ten minutes, Nick. No need to rush back. I've got it covered." He headed toward the grill.

Pam hugged her. "Glad you're here. Elvis just called. He said to say hello."

"How are things going for our newest state legislator?"

Pam took the bowl of slaw and set it on a picnic table dressed in red-and-white gingham.

"You know Elvis. Politics is his life. It wasn't enough being Aurora's district attorney. He had to aim for the big leagues."

"I know you must miss him not being around. How is Eric taking it? I think it would be hard to be separated from your twin after so many years. I mean, they even roomed together in college. And married sisters from their same hometown."

"Elvis definitely got the better part of that deal. His wife is the sweetheart in that pathetic excuse for a family. Poor Eric got saddled with the Queen Bitch for what thankfully turned out to be a very short ride." Pam sighed. "But he's perked up, for sure. Gretchen's only been here for a few days. Even Elvis said that Eric sounded like a new man on the phone."

She nodded. "They are already thicker than thieves."

A dark sedan pulled up as they spoke. "Why, there's the devil himself, with an angel by his side," Pam said. They watched as the couple got out of the car and came up the drive, and Pam went to greet them.

Callie always thought Gretchen vivacious. She had a rich love for life written across her heart-shaped face. Yet this Gretchen seemed even more alive and vital than the woman Callie had lived with these past few months.

"He's smitten," muttered Nick under his breath, but she caught the comment all the same. She turned to him.

"Look at her. She seems pretty taken, too."

Nick frowned. "Yeah. After she made a play for me." He shrugged. "Redheads are supposed to be notoriously fickle."

"Gretchen is not fickle," she hissed between her teeth. "She's had a rough time of it. A man who never tried to understand her. A very messy divorce. She deserves a little happiness."

"Don't we all," he added sarcastically.

She chose to ignore him and walked over to her friend. "How was New Orleans?"

"Divine," Gretchen drawled in an imitation Southern accent. Eric came up beside her and draped an arm around her shoulder. She smiled up at him. "I couldn't have had a better tour guide."

Eric beamed. "This little lady can move." He shook his head. "Hey, Cal, do all you New Yorkers walk so fast? I had to about tie her ankles together to slow her down so she could actually see the sights and not race by everything."

She laughed. "Everyone is pretty much in a hurry in New York. Of course, down here the heat'll slow anyone to a crawl."

Gretchen collapsed on a nearby lawn chair. "You are not kidding me. I could use a cold one."

Callie had worried about standing around feeling useless. Now, she had a job. "I'll get you something. I'll get everyone something. Be right back."

She hurried into the kitchen, pleased that she'd made small talk and actually enjoyed it. She spied a pitcher of iced tea sitting on the counter, but she knew most people would want something a little stronger. As she opened the refrigerator, she heard the kitchen door open behind her. Thinking it was Pam, she said, "Go back and poll the guys if they want beer or wine. I know what you'll want."

"That so?"

She popped up her head and found Nick standing there. "I... thought you were Pam."

"Pam sent me in to help. She didn't think you should have to make so many trips. Don't worry. I know where everything is."

"I'm fine. You can go."

He stayed.

She pulled out several beers and a bottle of white wine and set them on the counter.

"I had you pegged as a white-wine kinda gal," he said.

She stiffened. "For your information, I don't drink wine. I don't drink. Period. My daddy did enough drinking for the entire family—and he turned mean when he did it. Mama and I got slapped around enough times because of it. I supposed I'd be prone to it, so I've never touched a drop."

She slammed the refrigerator for emphasis and crossed her arms protectively in front of her.

Why did she go blurt all that out?

She rarely mentioned her father to anyone, much less the abuse she and her mother endured. She kept opening up to this man at the oddest moments. For the life of her, she couldn't understand why.

Nick's brow creased. If Callie didn't know better, she might have thought it was in anger.

"I'm sorry," he said quietly.

She almost aimed another retort, but she recognized true sympathy on his features. Her heart did a back flip that would have made an Olympic gymnast proud.

"I'm not," she continued, her voice calming. "When he died, Mama and I came to Noble Oaks. I never felt as safe as I did that first night. I got more than enough to eat and I was always starving back then. Aunt C herself scrubbed me from head to toe that night and she read me a story from a fairy tale book. I fell asleep lying in a big bed with clean sheets and frilly curtains hanging around the windows. I thought I'd died and gone to Heaven."

"Noble Oaks has that effect on people." He acted as if he wanted to share a confidence, but he turned away and opened a cabinet instead. He took out several coozies and slipped the canned beers into them.

"What would you like to drink?" she asked, her anger evaporating.

"Iced tea would be great." He swallowed and said hesitantly, "I had a little drinking problem myself at one point. Drugs, too. My mom marched herself into her big league son's life and straightened me out but good." He smiled. "I don't even like to take aspirin nowadays."

He gathered the beers up in his arms and took them outside. Callie watched out the window as he distributed them to Gretchen, Eric, and Tom. She poured a glass of wine for Pam and two tall glasses of iced tea for herself and Nick as she reflected at his surprising candor.

As she reached the door, Nick came back. "Thanks." He took the glass from her and gulped a big swig. He turned and headed over to the grill, and he and Eric good-naturedly started teasing about who was the best grill master.

Callie took Pam her wine and then went and sat on a picnic bench.

There was a lot more to Nick La Chappelle than she'd first thought.

Chapter Seventeen

CALLIE VIEWED the group gathered around the picnic table. She had enjoyed the leisurely meal and the company. She couldn't remember the last time she'd been so relaxed and unguarded. Laughing as she listened to Eric's story about a couple of teenagers who'd taken a prank to embarrassing levels, and how he'd called their fathers rather than book them for being in the town square's public fountain without any attire.

"I seem to recall a streaking incident in your and Elvis' past," Tom said. "Your parents would've sooner killed you than come get you, I'd imagine."

"All the more reason to show a little compassion, Thomas," Eric said, grinning. "Hell, Mama's still bent out of shape about us getting suspended for spiking the tutti-frutti punch at the junior-senior prom. Best we not divulge anything about running around buck nekkid at the Sunday school's Fourth of July social."

Pam shook her head. "I still can't believe Mama didn't recognize either of you."

Eric laughed. "Never can say enough for a good Halloween mask and a fast pair of Nikes."

"To think you and Elvis are now considered up-standing, model citizens. Boy, this town is fooled by charm, I'll tell you," Nick added.

Pam stood. "The sun's about to go down. Let's clear away these dishes, girls. The guys can scrub the grill and gather up trash. Tom, be sure to light the citronellas before the mosquitoes declare open season on us and try to eat us alive." She started picking up empty cans. "Anyone need another beer or Coke? Tea? We've still got dessert coming."

A collective groan echoed around the table.

Callie began to gather silverware off the paper plates. She reached across the table, where her fingers brushed against Nick's as he handed over his fork and knife. She dropped what she had in her hands.

"Sorry," he said. "Just trying to help."

He eyed her steadily, and she knew the telltale blush racing up her neck and across her cheeks gave away that she wasn't as calm and collected as she let on.

"No, just me being clumsy. It's a good thing I got an acting gig pretty soon after arriving in New York, because I never would've made a living waiting tables."

Actually, she'd been thrown for a loop. When they shook hands earlier, her hand in his had seemed like a warm, fuzzy fit. Yet now the contact between them was the stuff she'd read about in books—sudden, instantaneous lightning that rocked her world. She decided it was time to leave.

But not with Nick.

She peered at Gretchen, who had gathered up the empty bowls of beans and slaw as she flirted with Eric. She couldn't ask Eric to run her home now. Not when Gretchen appeared so happy.

"We can leave right after dessert," Nick said, his

voice low enough so that no one could hear. "Just don't deny my sweet tooth." He crossed his heart. "I promise —three bites and we're outta here."

"No, I'm fine," she said quickly. She reached to pick up the scattered silverware.

"Are you sure?"

Her gaze met his. The stormy blue had warmed somewhat. They were now the cool blue of a summer pond in the fading light.

"Sure, I'm sure. Uh, I need to help now." She threw the cutlery into the empty potato salad bowl and scooped it up. Hurrying across the lawn and up the steps of the back porch, she entered the kitchen.

"Just set it in the sink," Pam instructed. "Run a little water in it to soak. The dishes can wait." Pam hugged her. "It's so good to have you back. Let's get dessert out there before the guys come looking for it."

Pam handed Callie a stack of colorful plastic bowls and spoons and a tub of Cool Whip. "Take those out for me. I'll bring the cobbler and then the ice cream. I'm sure Eric will be the only one who thinks he needs the Cool Whip."

They brought the items to the picnic table and Pam removed the foil from the oblong glass dish.

"Do I smell peach cobbler?" Tom slipped his arms around his wife's waist as he leaned over her shoulder to inhale the aroma wafting up. "My dear, you are a keeper." He kissed her neck and growled.

Eric looked around expectantly. "Any Blue Bell? I can't have hot cobbler without ice cream."

"It's in the kitchen," Callie said. "I'll get it." She walked back inside, a part of her heart aching for her friends. Pam and Tom were so good together, and they had wanted kids as long as they'd been married, close to ten years now. She was grateful they still seemed as much in love as ever, despite their infertility troubles.

She brought the ice cream and scoop to the table. Nick opened the carton and faced Gretchen.

He pointed the utensil at her for emphasis. "This is one of the best things you'll ever put in your mouth, Yankee Girl. Blue Bell Homemade Vanilla, from the little creamery in Brenham, Texas. Not far from where I grew up." He eyed the ice cream appreciatively. "I used to dream about this when I lived in L.A. I would've traded a good half-dozen strikeouts for a bowl of Blue Bell on any given day."

As Pam dished out the cobbler, Nick plopped scoops of ice cream on top of it. Only Eric dumped the whipped topping over both of those. Callie was glad Nick was making an effort to be nice to Gretchen, especially after his earlier comment on her fickleness. It was obvious to all present, though, that she and Eric already had strong feelings toward one another. Maybe Nick believed that it would only be right to welcome Gretchen into his cousin's life for the time she would be in Aurora, instead of causing trouble.

Callie stared at the full bowl Nick placed in front of her and her eyes widened. "I don't know how I'm going to eat all of this," she proclaimed.

"I'm a little full myself after two burgers and all the sides," he admitted. "Mind if we share?"

"Okay." She hoped her voice didn't betray her reluctance. Sharing food seemed intimate to her.

"Here, trade spots with me, Nick," Pam insisted. "It'll be easier than you leaning across the table."

The two swapped seats and Callie found Nick right next to her. His masculine scent invaded her space.

He reached to hold the bowl. "I'll keep it anchored

for us." He handed her a spoon and then dipped his own into the gooey mess.

Callie followed his lead. Yet it was hard for her to concentrate on eating when she tingled from head to toe. Her forearm brushed his each time she dipped her spoon into the bowl, causing an instant mass production of butterflies to bounce around on the walls of her insides.

"Enough for me," she finally proclaimed, too weary of not tasting a single bite of one of her favorite dishes.

"Fine by me." Nick continued to hold the bowl steady in front of her instead of bringing it to his center. This caused him to lean into her each time he dipped into the dessert. Their hips seemed joined, as did their thighs, on the crowded bench.

Callie took a deep, steadying breath and folded her hands in her lap, forcing herself not to wring them, one of her new nervous bad habits. She closed her eyes. She could get through this. She had to.

"Are you tired?" Gretchen asked.

She opened her eyes. "A little." Though it was due more to a relentlessly fast beating of her heart and Nick's nearness wearing her out than anything she'd done to exert herself.

"Eric, we need to take Callie home. Do you mind?"

"No, don't do that," Nick chimed in quickly. "I didn't hit my page quota today. As it is, I was going to have to leave early to burn up my keyboard until the wee hours. I can take Callie home with me now. No sense busting up your fun. Or Eric's second helping of his layered cobbler extravaganza."

Nick stood and stepped over the bench. His hand cupped Callie's elbow and helped her to rise. It felt as if his fingers singed her skin.

"Don't get up at your usual crack of dawn, Cal,"

Gretchen chided. "For once, sleep in. I don't want you overdoing things. Today was a busy day for you."

"Yes, ma'am." She turned to Pam and Tom, who had also risen. "It was great to see you both. Thanks for having me. I'll stop by tomorrow for a few minutes and pick up Essie's bowl."

"Thank Essie for everyone," Tom said. "There are days I pine for anything Essie's made." He smiled. "It's good to have you back home, Cal."

"Thanks."

They all murmured their good nights. Nick escorted her to his car. He still had his hand on her elbow, guiding her along.

As they got out of earshot, she testily said, "I'm not an old woman. I can walk to the car on my own."

Nick let go instantly. "Sorry," he said sharply. Still, his good manners prevailed as he opened her door and closed it once she swung her legs inside the car. She regretted her peevish tone.

As he slipped in the driver's seat, she apologized. "I'm sorry. I've always been someone who did for herself. It's been hard these last few months, being helpless and having to be waited upon. I didn't mean to be petty or rude. You were being a gentleman. I wasn't reciprocating as a lady should."

He didn't look at her. "Okay. I understand."

He started the car and the air conditioning came on full blast. She shivered.

"Too cold?"

"A little."

He glanced over at her. "Would you like the top down instead?"

She smiled. "I'd love that."

Nick rolled down the windows and then hit a button. The convertible's top rose and folded back into the rear as he turned off the air conditioning.

'I like it down myself but a lot of women don't want the wind to mess up their hair."

She stroked her ponytail. 'Mine's pulled back. I actually enjoy the breeze running through my hair when the top is down."

He backed out of the driveway and pulled onto the tree-lined street. They'd only traveled two blocks when they spotted the barricades.

'Looks like a summer block party. We can go around. I know a back way."

He turned right and they went the long way, around the city park. Callie noted the lights were on. 'Looks like softball's being played tonight."

'Yeah. Friday night church league."

She caught a note of wistfulness in his voice. 'Do you miss playing?"

Nick didn't answer. At first, she thought he hadn't heard her. Finally, he cleared his throat.

'I miss it every day," he admitted. 'I didn't when I quit. I'd gotten tired of team politics. Guys complaining about injuries. Guys doping up so they could play hurt. Not to mention the clubhouse politics."

He turned left, driving away from the park and more toward the heart of town.

'In broadcasting, part of me would be second-guessing what pitch would be thrown next—what pitch should be thrown next—while at the same time I was trying to be Matthew McConaughey-smooth and analytical. That grew tiresome."

He sighed. 'I didn't really miss pitching until I came back to Aurora. That's when it finally hit me that I'd never play baseball again." He grew quiet for a moment. 'Don't get me wrong. I don't pine away, thinking I'm not a man anymore because I'm not throw fastballs and changeups on a regular basis. But every now and then, I drift over to watch the summer leagues or even the high school games. It's there I feel it again—the excitement, the camaraderie, the ballet-like beauty. That's when I miss it most."

He made the turn around the town square and gradually increased his speed as they headed back toward Noble Oaks.

"So, do you miss acting yet? Being Jessica?"

Callie eyed him speculatively. "You know my character's name? I thought you didn't watch my show."

Nick shrugged. "Just something I picked up. Cultural icon and all that you are. You're pretty famous."

"You didn't seem to know anything about my career before. Did you look up *Sumner Falls* on Wikipedia?" she teased. "Or Google me?"

"Maybe I heard it from Miz C. She brags on you all the time to anyone who'll listen."

She thought about his words. "I'll bet you didn't listen much before. Why?"

He eased into the long drive at Noble Oaks and pulled past the house until they reached his cottage. He shut off the engine and unbuckled his seat belt, turning to face her.

"I thought you were a selfish bitch who pretty much ignored a remarkable old lady," he said bluntly. "She's so proud of you. I'd been here a couple of years and you'd never come down once for a visit. I grew close to her and I knew she was hurting."

Callie winced. It had been too long since she'd come home. But she talked to Aunt C all the time, practically every day by phone. Plus, taping the show drained her. Between it and her volunteer work, she didn't have a moment to call her own. However, in her heart, she knew she could've made the time to come back to Aurora.

She stared at Nick and admitted, "You're right. I don't have any excuse. I never realized it, but I was being selfish."

"I don't think you are. Now that I've met you. You have a lot on your plate. You're like your team's MVP. Your show and its ratings revolve around you. It's like you're the starting pitcher every day. And you've got just enough Southern in you that you probably feel responsible for the welfare of everyone on the show, from the actors to stagehands to the janitor."

Tears sprang to her eyes. "You don't know the half of it," she whispered. "Primetime television dramas are in big trouble across the board. Ratings are down. Networks are canceling shows left and right because they can't compete with premium cable or streaming services. They're being replaced by reality TV and game shows. I've wanted to quit for a while now, even before the... the accident. I was afraid to, though. So many people depend upon me. Renewing my contract could make the difference for *Sumner* Falls remaining on the air or it being canceled. How can I even think of taking a chance and jeopardizing the show's future with so many people's futures at stake?"

She turned away and brushed at the tears that spilled down her cheeks. "I feel selfish for wanting to quit, but I got my wish. I'm not doing the show now. I'm on a year's leave of absence. The show's tanking in the ratings. I feel guilty every morning I wake up, and yet I still don't want to go back to playing Jessica again. The thought turns my stomach."

She turned back and faced him. "I want to do other things. I'm bored. I'm tired of being Jessica. I wish I'd

never heard of her, even if she has been my bread and
butter for ten years. I want to try new projects. Theater
again. Maybe films someday. I want more than the life I
have, Nick."

She shook her head. "I'm unhappy every single day I
wake up but I don't know how to change things."

Nick wrapped a hand around her nape and pulled
her to him.

Chapter Eighteen

NICK'S LIPS met Callie's. As they touched, he inhaled the honeysuckle scent clinging to her skin that had nearly driven him crazy as he shared her dessert. He hadn't remembered one bite that went into his mouth —only the constant shoveling motion he'd made in an effort not to lick the honeysuckle from her neck.

He sensed her stiffen for a moment, her neck and mouth rigid beneath his fingers and lips. Then a quick hitch of her breath occurred and suddenly she relaxed.

It was invitation enough.

He pulled her closer, his left arm closing around her waist and drawing her nearer to him. The bucket seats made it a little awkward but Nick refused to let a little thing like car dynamics stop him as he unbuckled her seat belt and slid his seat back without missing a beat.

He gently rubbed his lips across hers, thrilled when a little moan escaped from her. Her lips parted slightly and he urged her to open more to him.

A shiver went through him. She tasted sweeter than she smelled. As good as he'd imagined last night, as thoughts of doing this very thing kept him awake until just before dawn. No, reality was better. Way better.

Nick stroked her neck, urging her even closer as he explored her sweetness. A hunger rose in him unlike any before. He wanted more of her, now, to be inside her, stroking the entire length of her, crushing her beneath him, drawing close together until they were one.

His hands dropped to her waist. He lifted her into his lap, setting her back against the driver's door. He buried his lips against her throat. The scent of honeysuckle surrounded him, swirling around him. He tugged the elastic band from her hair and tossed it out the window, pushing his hands into her honeyed waves.

Nick found her lips again, hungrily taking from her warmth. His heart beat fast, joining hers in a rapid tango. He slipped her top button through its slit as he trailed kisses down her throat.

* * *

She wasn't afraid.

That was Callie's first thought, blindsiding her. She had lived with fear for months now, practically afraid of her own skinny shadow, not to mention jumping like a startled rabbit when she turned on the TV or radio and heard a male voice come into the room.

But this was different. Nick was different. His mouth on hers, his body pressed close to her, only made her feel safe. Secure.

And turned on. Big time.

She shivered as his lips nibbled down the long column of her throat. A good shiver. Actually, a *great* shiver, in her opinion. She'd felt little sexual pings with men she'd dated in the past. Little tingles and vibes that made things pleasant for her.

But this...

She sighed again, a heated throb taking possession of

her. Another moan escaped her lips—and she was not the moaning type. She never had been.

Until now.

"Oh..." She couldn't help it. Another whimper popped out. She sounded like some ingénue being ravished by a wealthy tycoon, cameras rolling, getting it all down on tape. And yet she went with the emotion, the roller coaster dizziness that invaded her as much as Nick's masculine scent filled her.

His mouth found hers again, demanding, controlling, pushing her for more. Callie clung to him like a drowning victim did her rescuer, afraid to let go. Afraid he would let her go. She pushed her fingers into his coal black hair, snuggling as close as she could get to him.

His hand found her breast and palmed it. She could feel it swelling to fit his hand. Slowly, Nick dragged a thumb across her nipple, back and forth, the teasing motion stealing her breath as much as his drugging kiss. She could no longer think coherently.

He slid another two buttons open and slipped his hand inside her shirt. He pulled his mouth from hers and looked down. He eased open the front clasp of her bra. She needed him to touch her warmth.

But as he peeled back the material, she came to her senses.

"No!" exploded from her lips.

He couldn't see those hideous scars. She wouldn't let him see her greatest shame. All the warm, rich feelings fled as she frantically pushed against him.

She began twisting, scrambling to get away. She shoved at him, kneeing him viciously in the process as she climbed back into her seat and threw the passenger door open.

A loud expletive shook the night as he fired it in her direction. She glanced back and witnessed him doubled over in pain, not able to jump out of the car and grab onto her. She hurried unsteadily back up the drive, re-hooking her bra and struggling to button her blouse as she went.

As she turned the corner, she heard him yell, "What the hell just happened?"

Her nervous fingers tried three times before the last button slid into place. She rounded another corner and slowed, realizing that Nick was in no shape to follow her.

She drew a cleansing breath and ran her fingers through her mussed hair, catching his scent on her skin as she did so. She smoothed her hair back into place as best she could and started up the porch steps, hoping it was late enough for Aunt C and Essie to have retired for the night. As always, one of them had left the porch light on for her, much as they had back in her high school dating days.

As she tried to turn the unyielding knob of the front door in her hands, it hit her.

"Dammit, you idiot ballplayer. The stupid door's locked." She remembered how he'd gone back to secure it after she'd come out onto the porch hours earlier.

Her purse was still in his car. And she'd sooner be a pig on a roasting spit than go back now and get it. Not that he could stop her. Callie realized just how aroused Nick had been and how her sudden departure probably left him incapacitated for more than a few minutes. Not that she'd done it on purpose. She'd freaked out without warning.

But she had to get out. Before things went too far.

Before he saw her scars. Before he saw how ugly she'd become.

Tears welled in her eyes as she leaned against the door. She had never really wanted a man before. Not like that. Oh, sure, she'd felt the sexual pull when things heated up between her and a guy. When it had led to sex, it had felt fine. Nothing like the rocket's red glare and bombs bursting in the air, but it was pretty darn okay.

Yet what had happened in that fiery red convertible was like nothing she'd ever been a party to. Just one kiss and she'd been a goner. It was as if she were a racecar engine and Nick the driver that knew just how to pamper her to get her motor revving at optimum levels. Every touch, every kiss, lit a fire within her that even now caused her blood to pulse like an Indy 500 car.

What had that been about?

They weren't even friends. They didn't really like each other. Well, that wasn't exactly true. They had revealed an awful lot to one another in a few encounters. She still didn't get that. The way they communicated, it was almost if they'd always known each other.

He definitely intrigued the hell out of her. He was talented and smart and doing something that most people talked about and never acted upon. She'd heard it said that everyone had one book in him, but few ever took the time to get it down on paper. Even fewer did and found it was good, much less publishable. Nick had worked hard at his craft for years and now had several bestsellers to his credit. He seemed to be heading to the pinnacle of his profession. His second profession. He'd already had enormous success in his first.

Callie had done exactly what she guessed Nick had done. She'd Googled him earlier that afternoon before she napped. She gleaned enough information from the articles she'd read to understand that he hadn't just been a paid professional, but he'd been the best on a consistently good team. Cream of the crop, MVP-good.

Even the stuff she'd located on his short career in broadcasting raved about his smooth analytical style, how he could get to the heart of what was going on and interpret the innuendoes of the game succinctly and easily for the viewing audience. It was a major disappointment when he'd vacated his seat in the booth at ESPN mid-season.

Only to vanish. At least to the world it seemed that way. Callie realized he'd slipped into the world of Nick Van Sandt and his myriad of characters.

They weren't friends yet—but they might be. He had the intellect she appreciated and a sly sense of humor, which she thoroughly enjoyed. Of course, the fact that she leaped out of his car, damaging both his ego and his groin without a word of explanation, might affect the becoming-friends part.

As well as the more. Becoming more.

She blew a deep breath out. Wow. If the man kissed like there was no tomorrow, what would it be like to be more intimate with him? It pained her to know that she'd probably never know now. It was for the best, though.

In fact, Nick had done something amazing for her. He'd freed her from her irrational fears. All the anxiety she'd experienced seemed to have melted into thin air. A surge of confidence permeated her. She even seemed to be standing a bit taller.

She'd been right to come home to Aurora.

Yet now she wanted to run back to New York, her tail tucked between her legs. She was too chicken to face Nick after what had happened. After all, she'd never planned on staying in Aurora permanently. And Aurora was where he'd planted roots.

As she pushed away from the door and walked down the porch steps, she knew she was lying to herself. She had wanted to stay in Aurora indefinitely. She still wanted to see Nick. Desperately. She just didn't trust what would happen when she did. It hurt to envision his reaction when he saw what had been done to her. No, she was right to put distance between them. She was damaged goods.

Callie leaned around the house cautiously. No Nick in sight. He'd probably stumbled into his cottage and had an ice pack—or at least a bag of frozen peas—strategically placed right about now. She walked down the long drive, hoping he'd been too absorbed to notice she'd left her purse on the floorboard of his car. She would retrieve it and her keys, sneak in through the kitchen door, and no one would be the wiser.

Callie went to the passenger side and leaned into the car, not wanting to open the door and then have to shut it.

Her purse wasn't there.

Shit.

"Looking for this?" a familiar voice said over her shoulder.

She whirled. "How did you sneak up on me?" she huffed. "I have excellent hearing."

He held up her purse. "I played army men and spies and all kinds of fun games growing up. I was the quietest kid on my block. I'd even slink into the kitchen and filch hot cookies while Mom's back was turned. She was certain I would make an excellent jewel thief or cat burglar one day."

She reached for her purse, but Nick held it just out of her grasp. "Thanks to you, Safety Boy, I'm locked out, so if you'd do me the courtesy of returning my purse?" She gave him her haughtiest Jessica glare, one that even caused the crew to give her a wide berth.

Nick looked over his shoulder at the main house. "Knowing Miz C, I'm sure you could've found a way to get in. I stay on her all the time about locking her doors and her windows."

Callie sniffed. "I still need my purse. Would you please hand it over?" Her impatience grew. She found she had to turn away. The questions in those midnight blue eyes were ones she didn't want to answer.

"Callie?" His voice was whisper soft. She faced him reluctantly.

"I can't," she said, a lump forming in her throat. She bit her lip hard, trying to stop the tremble that threatened to take over her entire body.

"Come here." He dropped the purse onto the ground and pulled her into his arms. She buried her face in his broad chest, her fingers bunching his shirtfront tightly.

"It's okay." He held her close, his arms encompassing her in a protective embrace. His gentle tone was more than she could bear. The sobs came in wild tremors. She clung to him and the solace his arms offered.

* * *

Callie babbled incoherently between sobs, but Nick didn't think what she said was important. Or if it were, she'd tell him when she needed him to know.

He'd figured it out before he made it to his doorstep. He felt like a moron. He'd watched her move, a little hesitantly at times. He'd poured over the news reports online. He knew how viciously she'd been attacked and how many stab wounds had been stitched up. Hell, she still had a nurse with her that put her through a rehab program on a daily basis.

"...Couldn't... couldn't let you... see..."

He finished it for her. "Couldn't let me see your scars?"

Her head popped up, a wild look in her watery eyes. "Yes," she hissed.

Callie pushed hard against his chest and stepped away from him, crossing her arms protectively over her middle. Nick watched the hard set of her mouth, her chin tilting slightly up, daring him to say more.

Which, of course, he did.

"What do you think happened between us, Callie?"

In response, she turned her back to him and scooped up her purse, slinging it over her shoulder. But she rose gingerly, and he knew she was hurting as she took a few steps away from him.

"Callie?"

She stopped in her tracks. He prayed she would turn around. That she wouldn't walk away and out of his life because she was the proud type who wouldn't budge an inch.

Just in case prayer didn't work, he thought he'd better sweeten the pot.

"It was never like that before for me. Not with anyone. Even..." He stopped a minute and decided to push on, his own pride be damned. "Even with my wife."

She turned slowly, her brow furrowed, worrying those sexy lips of hers to distraction.

Nick took a step forward, hoping she wouldn't bolt like a deer. She stayed. So did he.

"I... those... were the most intoxicating kisses I've ever tasted." He moved a few feet closer, his opened palms itching to take her in his arms again.

"I... me, too," she admitted.

Her gaze fell to the ground. He moved close enough until she could see his sneakers come into view. Quickly she looked up, and he became lost in her emerald eyes.

Gently he placed his hands on her shoulders, kneading her like a small kitten. "I was never good with girls back in high school. Later, women flung themselves at me when I hit the Big Show."

He closed the gap between them, his hands encompassing her waist. "It was always about sex. Quick, meaningless sex. Almost like I wasn't there. Not involved. Just watching from a distance."

Nick brought a hand to her cheek and stroked it. "Then I met Vanessa and thought it was love. We did it fast, slow, every way in-between. But I still seemed like an observer. I thought something was wrong with me."

He bent and brushed a kiss along her jaw. "Then I found out she didn't love me. Never had. Just used me to become famous. She never took the time to know me. Never even tried. I was just her meal ticket to the A-list."

He nibbled her earlobe. Shivers bolted through him at the contact and he knew Callie felt the same way as she gasped.

"In the end, she meant no more than a one-night stand with an unnamed groupie." His gaze met hers. "I only realized that just now. I didn't then. I thought the things I felt tonight came from made-up stuff in books and fairy tales."

"Me, too," she whispered.

Nick cupped her face in his hands. "Callie, there's something between us. I don't know what. I don't know what it may lead to. But you have to give it—give us—a chance. Please."

He watched her open her mouth to speak. Nothing came out. And then her words cut him like a knife.

"I'm damaged goods, Nick." Her voice was flat. Void of emotion. "You wouldn't really want to be with me." She turned to step away.

A physical pain darted through him. He couldn't let

this happen. He couldn't live with regret and what might have been.

"No." One word, full of anguish, escaped. He whipped her around so fast she lost her balance. She reached out to steady herself and he did what he'd always wanted one of his heroes to do—he literally swept her off her feet.

She squirmed as he carried her into the cottage and slammed the door with his foot. He eased her to her feet, pushing her back against the door, his body blocking her escape.

"No, Callie Chennault. You're not damaged goods. You're beautiful both inside and out—and I'm going to do whatever it takes to convince you of that."

Chapter Nineteen

HE COULDN'T BELIEVE *the scene that unfolded before his eyes. He watched Nick sweep up Jessica in his arms and march inside like a caveman dragging his woman back to his lair.*

He stood from the awkward crouch in the shrubbery, thankful that he finally could. His leg muscles screamed in protest as the blood began circulating again. He brought a hand to his mouth to stifle the fit of giggles lurking, waiting to escape. He couldn't afford to make his presence known.

Yet.

He'd left Jessica a little surprise and thought to do the same for Nick when they'd come home in the sleek convertible. Although he'd discovered that amazingly, they lived within a stone's throw of each other, he hadn't expected to find them together. Especially in that way.

Anger mixed with curiosity caused him to spy on their romantic interlude. They made out in the car like horny teenagers on a first date. Then, for some unknown reason, she'd fought and clawed her way out of the car, away from Lover Boy.

He'd actually thought for a moment to take Nick.

Bent over and obviously feeling major discomfort as he hobbled to his doorway, he would be an easy target. But easy didn't interest him. Fun did. He hadn't planned thoroughly. He could spend days—even weeks—amidst his plans. He knew he didn't want to rush this.

With Nick, he wanted to get it right. Wanted the Golden Boy to suffer as he had those years growing up. He needed more time to decide how he would end the superstar's life.

And he especially needed to be sure Nick understood why.

All this would require much thought. He refused to go for the quick way out. He'd begun to toy with the idea that it might add to the fun to take the two of them into Death's arms at the same time and place.

That would be a true masterpiece. And since it seemed as if these beautiful people were having, or about to embark upon an affair, it would be easier to catch them off-guard as they spent time together, exploring the newness of their relationship.

He felt the stiff erection spring to life with just the thought of this marvelous plan.

No, they had more time because he had much to think about.

But their days were numbered.

Chapter Twenty

NICK'S WORDS hung in the charged air. Callie swallowed hard, afraid to even breathe. His eyes were dark as night, pinning her against the door as much as his athlete's body.

He leaned down, his mouth hovering mere inches from hers. "We can do this the easy way or the hard way. I'm game for either."

He cupped her face in his hands, his thumbs stroking her cheeks, his eyes burning with what she recognized as desire.

"Nick—"

His mouth stopped her from saying more. Her head spun as wave after wave assaulted her mouth. No coherent thought came, and she certainly couldn't have voiced it if it did. Her body's fire flamed higher with his every touch. Her knees began to buckle. She thought she was falling but she never hit the ground.

Because she was in Nick's arms again. Somehow, he'd caught her, laying her gently on the bed, then sitting next to her. Concern etched his brow.

"You okay?" he asked softly, brushing the hair back from her face.

"I... guess. Why?"

He grinned. "You fainted on me."

"I did not!"

A smug look crossed his handsome face. "You did. I must say, Miss Chennault, that in all my experience in kissing, I have never caused a lady to pass out from sheer delight." He winked at her. "I must be very, very good. Despite the fact that I'm way out of practice."

She was dumbfounded. Yet, it would explain how she got from one room to another without remembering the short journey. And her body still felt heated from his drugging kisses.

Of which she wanted more.

Her eyes must have betrayed that thought. She noted a subtle change come over him. But he remained where he was, his large hands wrapped around her smaller ones.

"I think you should rest a little while." He stood but seemed reluctant to release her. Finally, he dropped her hands and backed away from the bed.

The thought of him leaving brought an ache to her heart. "Don't go." Her voice shook with who knows what emotion she felt. She didn't dare put a name to it.

"Okay." He took a step over to a club chair sitting in the corner. He sat on its edge, never taking his eyes from her.

An emptiness filled her. The distance between them was a gulf wider than the Grand Canyon. She sat up, unwilling to pretend the void didn't exist.

He sprang to his feet and crossed the space between them in two strides. He knelt beside her, a hand gently resting on her knee.

"I feel... a little shaky," she told him. "Would you... lie down with me?"

An unreadable look passed across his features. "Okay."

Nick moved to the foot of the bed as she lay back against the down-filled pillow. He leaned over and slipped off her sandals and placed them on the floor. He did the same with his shoes before he eased onto the bed.

"Hold me," she whispered, not believing what she'd asked.

She barely knew him and yet she needed him now. Him and only him. The why and the how? She'd think about those tomorrow. Hey, it worked for Scarlett O'Hara.

Nick pulled her into his arms. Her head rested against his heart. A sense of total relaxation came over her, mixed with a few stray butterflies still floating around inside her stomach.

He kissed the top of her head. "Go to sleep, Callie. You're safe."

She knew that. As she closed her eyes, she realized this was the only place in the world where she wanted to be.

In Nick's arms.

* * *

Callie stirred. Nick sensed his time in paradise was about to end. Never had he been as content as he had for the past two hours with Callie next to him.

At first, he'd reveled in her very nearness. The subtle scent of honeysuckle wafting up, teasing him. When she moaned softly in her sleep, his arms tightened around her, wanting to ward off the bad dreams.

But most of all, Nick had come home. He was in Aurora, which had become a state of mind as much as an actual spot on the map. He knew this small town would always be home to him, no matter where his travels took him. He ran here to heal the emotional wounds Vanessa inflicted. Aurora was the refuge that gave him new life and confidence to emerge in the literary world as Nick Van Sandt.

And now Aurora held Callie and she was here, in his arms. He spoke the truth when he told her that although he had sexual experience, he didn't have much experience knowing women—or knowing anything about love. But Callie was a woman he wanted to know.

And love.

That revelation didn't frighten him as he would have suspected. Instead, he longed to spend time with her. Talk to her. Make her laugh. Have her read what he wrote. Enjoy meals together. Make love.

He smiled to himself and brushed a kiss on her temple. Hell, he wanted the whole package–his writing *and* Callie. He wanted to learn everything about her. See her perform. Become one with her. He wanted happiness and kids and a dog and a cat and a big house so they'd all have plenty of room to grow. And love.

Thoughts of a lifetime commitment with someone he barely knew should have scared the hell out of him. He'd sworn never to get seriously involved with a woman again, much less marry one. Especially another self-absorbed actress.

Yet, it was happening just like Tom told him it did. Tom said the first time he spoke to Pam, he knew. *He just knew.* The feeling only grew stronger the more he got to know her. Nick remembered Tom shaking his head in wonder as he recalled the magic. Nick was now experiencing the same certainty regarding Callie Chennault.

Already he knew Callie was smart, accomplished,

sensitive, beautiful—and she had a sense of humor. Their sexual chemistry was the stuff men dreamed of. If plain old kissing could light the kind of heat they'd had going earlier, making love would ignite the covers in a four-alarm fire.

Or at least set off the smoke detectors.

But he knew this was different from anything else he'd ever experienced, because simply holding her close seemed enough. If that's all the gods of fortune gave him for the rest of his life, he could die a happy man.

Of course, Nick had to convince her of all this. That was a tall order. He'd figured out that she was skittish around men. He couldn't blame her. Plus, she had the hang-up about her appearance since her attack. He had to try and find a way not to scare her off and let her know that no matter what physical imperfections the assault caused, she would always be perfect in his eyes.

Callie sneezed. She started in his arms and then began scrambling wildly. He held on, not enough to hurt her but enough to guarantee she wasn't going anywhere.

"It's me, Callie. Nick."

* * *

Callie forced herself back to reality, which turned out to be almost as good as the dream she'd awakened from.

"We were in Cancun," she murmured, calming as she curled into Nick's rock-hard chest.

"We were?" She heard the surprise in his voice.

"Yep. Piña coladas. A big blanket unfolded on a pristine, secluded beach. Lots of hot sun beaming down on us, warming our skin."

She caught the amusement in his eyes and smiled. "You just know those kinds of things in dreams."

Nick stroked her arm. "So, we were vacationing together. Maybe our honeymoon?"

She laughed. "Aren't you taking things a little fast? We haven't even been on a date yet."

"Hmm." He pressed a kiss on her brow. "We could count tonight. I mean, we rode in the same car. We shared dessert."

"That is pretty personal," she agreed.

"We also had the obligatory first date goodnight kiss," he added.

She grinned. "Which one?"

He grinned right back. "It's not like we have to single out a particular one. Here we are in bed. I guess the night turned out better than either of us expected."

The thought should have appalled her. She didn't take relationships lightly, but she found herself enjoying the idea. Of being with Nick. Of being in bed with Nick. Really in bed.

"I can't tell you what a relief it is not to be afraid of you," she confessed. "Besides Detective Waggoner, I haven't been easy in a man's company in months. Well, until tonight. Being around Eric and Tom seemed like old times again. Pam's idea of a barbecue was a good start."

"What about being with me?"

She reached up and placed a finger against his lips. "You're talking too much. Shut up and kiss me."

She knew it was a cop-out, but she didn't want to keep analyzing herself when she had an unbelievable hunk of hotness next to her.

"Maybe tomorrow." Nick sat up, taking her with him. He released her, bent and slipped on his shoes, and then picked up her sandals.

She took them, a frown on her face. "I guess this is good night?"

He smiled. "Well, I suppose there's always the oblig-atory goodnight kiss..." His voice trailed off as he studied her mouth. Her stomach lurched in that funny way, so she cut her eyes to her sandals and concentrated on putting them on.

She stood slowly, not wanting a repeat performance from earlier.

"Walk you home?" he asked, a hint of mischief in his eyes.

"Okay."

She made her way back to his small den and picked up her purse from the floor, sliding it onto her shoulder. Nick opened the door. As they stepped onto the porch, he entwined his fingers through hers. Callie went giddy with the contact. It was like sixth grade all over, when a boy would hold your hand for the first time. Once upon a time, that had been the best feeling in the world.

She considered their linked fingers and smiled. It still was. They strolled slowly to the main house, no words necessary, as he guided her to the back porch.

As he gazed into her eyes, Callie knew things had changed between them. It was a good change but she didn't understand the depth of it. For now, they had formed a bond. She wouldn't question it. It was enough to know Nick was in her court.

He brushed a quick kiss against her mouth. It made her long for more contact, but he stepped back from her, dropping her hand.

"See me tomorrow? For dinner?"

"I can't think of anything I'd like better." Her reply surprised her. She usually censored her feelings, espe-cially at the beginning of a relationship. If you could call this a relationship. "Will we kiss?"

Nick's eyes met hers. "I think we could manage a little of that." He gazed at her longingly. "I'd like to make you dinner. I'm no Essie, but I can grill a steak better than Bobby Flay. Plus, I toss a mean salad. Seven?"

"Seven," she echoed.

They stood looking at each other, both reluctant for the night to end. Suddenly, he pulled her into his arms for a quick, searing kiss. Just as quickly, he released her.

"That was a preview. Like coming attractions at the movies."

She giggled. "I would give that preview a thumbs up."

"Where's your key?" he asked. "You need to go to bed."

She raised an eyebrow at him.

"I need you to go in and go to sleep. For your sake as much as mine."

She dug in her purse and pulled out her house key. He took it and inserted it into the lock.

"Damn," he said softly.

"It wasn't locked?"

"No. I'm going to have to have another come-to-Jesus meeting with Miz C and Essie."

He handed her the key. "Good night."

"Good night."

She stepped into the dark kitchen. She turned to close the door and impulsively blew Nick a kiss. He caught it and tucked it into his pocket.

Callie shut the door and turned the deadbolt before she placed her purse on the counter. She was emotionally wrung out. She opened the refrigerator and took out a bottled water, downing almost half of it before closing the door. She took the bottle with her as she went up the back staircase to her room.

A single light glowed on the nightstand. Essie must have left it on for her. She stepped into the room and shut the door, noticing that Wolf wasn't on her bed. Aunt C had probably spoiled him rotten all night and the dog had opted to sleep with her instead.

As she turned, her eyes went to the single, long-stemmed red rose lying across her pillow. Curiosity filled her. Why would Essie put a flower on her pillow?

She walked to the bed and picked it up. The flower had just begun to open. Its sweet, heavy aroma filled the air around her. She wondered if she still had a bud vase somewhere. If not, she knew where Essie collected them downstairs.

Then her eyes fell to an envelope on which the stem had rested. A creepy feeling edged up her spine. Her mouth went dry. Still, something compelled her to open it. Her hands shook as she did so.

She pulled out a single sheet of stationery, holding her breath as she unfolded it.

Thinking of you, dearest Jessica.
  Fondly, Lipstick Larry
  (No, not the fool you encountered. Your REAL and BIGGEST fan. Surprise!)

Chapter Twenty-One

NICK SLOWLY WALKED down the drive leading to his cottage. A satisfied, mellow feeling encompassed him. He couldn't remember the last time he'd been so content. Not even e-mailing a finished, edited manuscript to his editor in New York gave him quite the peace of mind he now possessed.

All because he was in love.

His friends would've thought he had lost his mind. It didn't matter. Nick had the exact feeling Tom spoke of. It ran deeper than any desire he'd ever experienced. He'd gone from instantly disliking Callie on principle, to being undeniably attracted to her against his will, to finding out what an incredibly interesting person she was.

All that—and the sexual heat they generated. He could still taste her. Still smell the honeysuckle. Even now, he wanted to turn and find her and pull her close for one more addictive kiss. Actually, he could go for more than a kiss, but he knew he would do this right. He would take it nice and slow. He had fallen—hard, fast, and as thorough as any man could.

But he couldn't expect Callie to do the same.

She would take some persuading, especially in her present state of mind. Then again, convincing her to fall for him would be a whole lot of fun. He grinned. He couldn't wait to wage his campaign.

A piercing scream shattered the stillness of the August night. Panic flooded him as he tore back up the gravel drive toward the main house. His gut told him Callie was in trouble.

He reached the back door, remembering that she had locked the dead bolt behind her. His keys to the main house sat on a table back at his place. He bunched his T-shirt around his hand and punched a pane of glass in the lattice works of the door. Glass shattered, spilling onto the ceramic tile of the kitchen floor. He thrust a hand through, careful not to drag his wrist against the jagged edge.

Unlocking the door, he threw it opened and raced up the stairs. Unsure of which was her room, he headed toward a sliver of light near the end of the hallway. Nick threw the door open. It crashed against the wall.

Callie was slumped on the floor, curled into a tight ball. He raced to her and pulled her to her feet.

"Are you hurt?" he asked, careful to temper his tone. Behind him he heard a noise. He turned. Miz C rolled up in her wheelchair and Essie stood in the doorway, frightened looks on both their faces.

He turned back to Callie. She was white as a sheet. Her teeth chattered as if she'd been stuck out in a blizzard without a coat. Her lips moved wordlessly.

But it was her eyes that scared Nick the most. They had a blank, dazed look, as if she were going into shock.

* * *

Callie tried to get out the words, but fear locked her voice box. Somehow, she realized Nick was there and she threw her arms around him, burying her face. The tears came, melting the numbness that had frozen her.

"He's here," she gasped. "Here. In Aurora."

"Who, Callie?" Nick asked her gently.

Oh, thank God he wasn't yelling at her. She didn't think she could take that. She lifted her face and met his troubled eyes. "The rose. The note," she whispered.

The effort caused her to release her death grip from him and she slid down into a puddle at his feet.

He followed her down, taking her hands in his, rubbing them, talking to her in soothing tones. She didn't listen to his words at first. All she could think about was the horrible note.

"It's from... him."

She reached and picked up the sheet that had fallen to the floor. Wordlessly, she handed it to Nick. She watched as his eyes went stormy.

He stared at her with a fierce protectiveness. Something stirred inside her. A calm washed over her. She wouldn't have to face this alone.

She had Nick.

She pulled in a cleansing yoga breath and expelled it slowly. She smiled weakly at her aunt and Essie, still hovering in the doorway, their faces full of anxiety.

"I'm fine—but we've really got to start locking our doors."

* * *

Nick observed that Callie's eyes were almost back to normal. Some color had returned. He stood and pulled her to her feet.

"Don't touch anything. Let's go to Miz C's sitting room and call the police."

He wrapped his arm around her waist and pulled her to him. He stroked her hair in a soothing motion, all the while fighting the bile that churned in fury inside him.

Who left the note?

He was well versed in the Lipstick Larry murders. He'd followed them as he did any unusual crime, always sifting for details that he might one day incorporate into one of his novels. He'd scoured the news stories even more closely when he'd Googled Callie. No other similar murders had occurred since the suspect was taken into custody.

This note said Larry was still out there. And he had his eye on Callie. Nick remembered reading one article that said the man charged with her attack and the brutal series of murders of the girls that favored Callie denied his involvement with anything other than his stalking and attack on her.

Could he be telling the truth?

Nick guided Callie down the hallway. He had sat many a time in this room over the last three years as Miz C talked about the old days. He loved listening to her stories about Aurora's past and all the changes she'd seen in her lifetime. The old lady had become a good friend to him. She had helped him begin to mend and create a new, more normal life.

He led Callie to a floral love seat. As she sat, Nick heard gravel crunching outside. It hit him that Eric must be bringing Gretchen home from the barbeque. He gave Callie's hand a squeeze.

"I'll be right back." He hurried from the room, wanting to catch Eric before he left.

As he hit the bottom of the stairs, he stumbled and

caught himself. He flicked on a nearby light switch, only to have his stomach turn inside out.

Callie's fluffy white dog lay on the marble entryway, his throat slashed. Nick remembered how friendly the dog had been. Despite his guard-like stature, the pooch probably never met a stranger.

He opened the front door and stepped onto the porch. He spied Eric and Gretchen and didn't hesitate to interrupt them.

"We could use a little help in here."

The kissing couple pulled apart quickly. Both heads turned at the same time. He motioned them up to the porch. As they hurried up the walk, Gretchen broke into a trot.

"Callie?" she called out worriedly.

He nodded. "Wait." He reached out to stop her from rushing inside.

Nick glanced from his cousin to Gretchen. "Callie's fine but she's had a fright. We were about to call the police when you arrived." He took a deep breath. "Lipstick Larry left her a note in her bedroom."

Gretchen gasped, her hand going to her throat. "How did he escape?"

He shook his head. "I don't think he had to. Come on up. Callie needs a good looking over. And then we need to talk about this." He stopped before he opened the door. "Prepare yourself. Wolf is right inside. It isn't pretty."

The trio met Essie sitting on the floor next to the still dog, stroking his fur, shaking her head.

"I'm puttin' on tea and coffee. I suspect we'll be wanting both." She bit her lip. "Mr. Eric, you call somebody to come get Wolf here so I can clean up the floor. I don't want Miss Callie seeing her baby this way."

Eric was already lifting his cell phone from his belt to call the station. Those gathered waited as he spat out instructions before they continued upstairs to the sitting room.

* * *

Gretchen flew to Callie's side, immediately grabbing her wrist to check her pulse.

"It's fast." She did a quick once-over and seemed satisfied. She sat next to Callie on the love seat. "Try to take some yoga breaths."

She did as Gretchen instructed. She leaned back into the sofa's cushions and closed her eyes, not wanting to think about everything but knowing she needed to confront things head on. She'd never wimped out before. She wasn't going to start now, especially with all the support around her. She braced herself and opened her eyes.

"Better?" Eric asked. When she nodded, he said, "Tell me everything. Don't leave out any detail. You never know what's important."

"I went up to my room. There was a light on. I assumed Essie left it on. Maybe. I'm not sure now."

"She did," her aunt confirmed. "She said she would as she left my room after she settled me for the night."

"Okay. Good to know. Anyway, I walked in and spied a rose lying on my pillow. I couldn't imagine why Essie would leave it there and not place it in a vase. It seemed so... odd. I went and picked it up.

"That's when I noticed the envelope."

She bit her lip to stop its trembling. Nick came and perched on the arm of the sofa. He gently massaged the back of her neck. Some of the tension eased.

She continued, ignoring the questioning glance

Gretchen threw her way. "No name was on the front. It was unsealed." She watched Eric and Nick exchange a look. "I removed the sheet of paper inside and unfolded it."

Nick's arm went around her shoulder. She drew strength from that. "I opened it. It was addressed to Jessica."

The room grew unnaturally quiet. She broke the silence.

"It was from Lipstick Larry. It said something like it was from the real Larry and not the fool I'd encountered."

She reached up to her shoulder. Nick covered her hand with his.

"We left the note on the floor," he told Eric. "Obviously, Callie touched it. She handed it to me so my prints are on it, as well. We left after that. I didn't want anything disturbed. There could even be something else he left behind in the room that we didn't see."

"I'm going to go do a preliminary once-over in Callie's bedroom," Eric said. "I'll have two men here in a few minutes. I want all y'all to stay put. I'm also going to check over the rest of the house before they get here."

"Essie!" Callie cried out. "She's downstairs. What if he's still—"

"I doubt it," Eric reassured her. "You would've known if he'd stayed around. I'm just looking for an open window. That kind of thing. How he got in."

Nick spoke up. "The back door to the kitchen was unlocked tonight. Callie went in that way when we came home. I don't know if anything else is unlocked."

Gretchen's eyebrows shot up as she looked from Callie to Nick and back again. Callie sensed a guilty blush creep up her neck.

"Stay here, everybody," Eric reiterated. "I'll be back in a few minutes."

Gretchen stood. "Miz C, would you mind if I took your blood pressure and pulse? You look a little peaked." She walked over to her hostess.

"Why, certainly, dear. I'm all right, though. Just a little worn out by all this excitement."

Nick slipped into the seat next to her. She grasped his hands tightly.

"Miz C, I think it's about time you not only started locking up, but you need to look into an alarm system."

"Oh, dear. That sounds complicated, Nick. Who in Aurora would install such a thing? I suppose we'll have to go into New Orleans for that."

"I'll take care of it in the morning. I'm sure Eric can help us put a rush on things."

"I'm sorry, Aunt C. I don't want you or Essie in any danger. Maybe I should go back to New York. They had me under—"

"No," Nick cut in. "You aren't going anywhere."

Gretchen shot Callie a satisfied smile. The redhead then looked over at Nick. "I agree. We need to find out what's going on here before she goes traipsing off."

"Traipsing?" Callie laughed. "I think a little Southern is creeping into you, Gretchen."

The nurse nodded. "I do like it here. Not the heat. And the humidity is wreaking havoc with my hair. Other than that, this is a good place. Good people. Good food." She paused a beat. "I could see staying here. Permanently."

"Especially for the good men?" Callandra threw in, a teasing light in her eyes.

Gretchen flushed bright crimson to her roots. "Oh, hell," she muttered. "Why not admit it?" She turned to

Nick. "I don't care what you or anyone else thinks. I am absolutely, one hundred and ten percent crazy in love with your silly cousin," she proclaimed. "Nothing like this has ever happened to me before. One look at him would've done it, but when that lazy drawl slides out of those sexy lips, I am a goner. That and all the opening my doors and helping me from the car—it's amazing. Don't any of you tell him. I don't want to scare him off."

Callandra patted Gretchen's hand. "A Southern man is a true gentleman, Gretchen. He definitely knows how to treat a lady. Eric has always been such a good boy. Nice looking, full of fun, very respectful. You can't go wrong with our wonderful sheriff."

Essie walked in carrying a tray, Eric following behind her, trying to smother a grin behind his hand. Callie wondered just how long he'd been standing there. Essie poured out coffee and tea for everyone as Eric spoke.

"Everything else was secure so our perp must've come in that open back door."

"Miz C has agreed to let me arrange for an alarm system to be installed first thing tomorrow," Nick shared.

Eric nodded, pleased. "That's a terrific idea, Miz C. I have a buddy from college who has his own place over to New Orleans. He does good work and his rates are reasonable."

"Then give Nick the information, dear." She sighed. "I suppose it's something I should have done a long time ago."

Eric took a sip of his coffee as the doorbell sounded. "That'll be my boys. Nick, if you'll let them in? Cal, I'd like to do a formal interview with you now."

He stood as Nick left the room. "Ladies, if you'll

stay here and out of harm's way, we'll be about our business. In fact, if you'd like to go back to bed, Miz C, I won't be needing to talk to you anymore tonight. I'll pick your brain tomorrow after you've gotten some rest."

"I don't know what I could contribute, Eric. Both Essie and I went to bed quite early tonight."

He patted her shoulder. "You never know, Miz C. Sometimes, it's the little things that we tend to overlook that help us catch a break in a case. I'll swing by tomorrow morning and visit with you and Essie together."

"I'll take you to your room and get you settled, Miz C," Gretchen volunteered, wheeling the old woman through the door to her bedroom as Essie followed them.

Callie stood. "We could go downstairs, Eric."

"Sure thing, honey. Why don't we take the back stairs and go sit in the kitchen?" He let her lead the way.

She noticed the entire bottom floor was brightly lit as she entered the kitchen. She could hear the low murmur of voices coming from the front part of the house. She sat at the oval oak table in the breakfast nook, smoothing her hand across the crocheted place mat in front of her.

Eric joined her and pulled out a pad and pen. He studied her a moment. "Before we get started, Cal, there's something you need to know." He hesitated.

"No," she whispered. Without him voicing it, she instantly knew. Wolf hadn't been in her room. When they'd gone to her aunt's sitting room, the dog hadn't appeared. That meant something had happened to him.

"Is he... gone?" she choked out.

Eric nodded.

"Can I see him?"

"No," he said firmly. "That wouldn't be a good idea.

I've taken care of Wolf."

She swallowed hard, a lump filling her throat. "That sick bastard," she got out. "He hurt my baby. Oh, God. Wolf."

Tears spilled down her cheeks and she angrily brushed them away. She would mourn in private for her dog later. Right now, she needed to help her friend do everything he could to find this piece of shit.

She nodded at him, her resolve firm. "Let's start. Ask away."

"I'll need a timeline, Cal. Everything from the moment you left Pam's until you found the letter." He gave her a crooked smile. "Since there seems to be a bit of a gap, I'll need to know where you were and whom you were with."

She swept back her hair and then crossed her arms. "I was with Nick the entire time. We came the long way home. There was a block party going on so we went around by the park."

She leaned forward, her elbows on the table, her fingers folded together, under her chin.

"We sat in the car for a while. Then we... had words. I got out and came around to the front door. I'd stomped off without my purse and the door was locked so I went back to get it."

She sighed. "Nick... persuaded me to come into the cottage to talk." She noticed Eric fighting a smile. She shrugged. "All you're getting out of me, Eric La Rue, is that we spent some time making up."

He nodded sagely. "Making up is fun to do."

"Tell me about it. Anyway, we were probably together a couple of hours at the cottage before he walked me home. The back door was closer so I came in that way and went straight up the back staircase to my room. You know the rest."

He scribbled a few notes and rested the pen atop his notepad. "I'll need to contact NYPD, Cal. They may have someone fly down here and check things out. It could be some crackpot, for all we know. Nothing to do with this Lipstick Larry fellow. But I'm sure you're aware that the guy they have in custody has been making noises about how he didn't kill anyone."

"I know. The D.A.'s office told me they were going to try him first on the charges of my attack. Then they were going to move on to the murders, which would give them more time to prepare."

"That's still a good strategy. Especially if he's only involved in your case. That would put him away and keep him away so you wouldn't have to worry about him. We still have to give some credence to the nut who wrote this note to you." Eric ran a hand through his hair. "He could be a nobody who wants to believe he's Lipstick Larry."

"Or he could be the real deal," she said. "Either way, someone out there will probably pay me another visit."

"I'll put a man on the house immediately," Eric assured her. "I don't want you going anywhere alone."

"She won't," Nick said from the doorway. "As of this moment, Callie and I are Siamese twins."

Chapter Twenty-Two

NICK'S EYES sprang open at the creak in the hall. He slipped his hand underneath the pillow and rolled silently from the bed, gun in hand, and cracked open the door.

It was Essie coming down the hall. She carried a tray with coffee, toast, and a magnolia swimming in a small glass bowl. The morning newspaper was tucked under her arm. He slipped into the corridor and closed the door behind him, tucking the gun into the back of his waistband.

"Good morning, Mr. Nick," she whispered. "I'm just bringing Miz Callandra her breakfast. She wakes pretty early, you know. Even with all those goings-on last night, she'll be wanting her sports page and Dear Abby like usual."

He took the tray and paper from the cook. "I'll take it to her, Essie. I want to visit with her a spell."

Essie shot him a mischievous look. "You know she don't succumb to sweet talk, Mr. Nick. I'd give it to her straight up, like a good soldier."

He raised his brows. "Just what is it you think I'm going to talk to her about, Essie?"

She clucked her tongue. "Miss Callie's an early riser, too. I expect you got about ten minutes before she starts stirring."

He winked at her and continued down the hall. He tapped gently on the door before he entered. He found Callandra Chennault seated in her wheelchair already, staring out her window.

"Morning, Miz C," he drawled. "Got your breakfast here. I'm sure the Saints are gonna lose that pre-season game tonight so you can head straight to the comics."

"Set the tray here." She returned her troubled gaze to the front lawn. He spotted the squad car in the drive.

"He's here for Callie's protection, Miz C."

"Much good that'll do if I can't remember to lock a damn door and keep a madman out," she snapped.

Nick rested a hand on her shoulder. "It's not your fault. You've never had cause to be safety conscious before. No one could've predicted this would happen. Not with the arrest and Callie's ID of her attacker."

Callandra dabbed her eyes with a lace handkerchief. "I hate this. She was doing so much better. She was learning to relax again. Now all this." The old woman lifted saddened eyes. "I was able to help her heal once, long ago. But I can't protect her from... this monster."

He sat opposite her. "We'll do everything to keep her safe. Eric's contacted NYPD. One of his patrolmen will be right outside at all times. And she's got me."

Callandra sniffed. "Exactly what does that mean, young man?" She looked him up and down. "I know you must have stayed the night. Your clothes are rumpled and your hair hasn't been properly combed. I don't think you just happened to be coming for a visit this early in the morning. Tell me, what exactly are your intentions regarding my Callie?"

He took a moment and decided to take Essie's advice and march straight into battle. 'I intend to marry her, ma'am. She only knows I've started to like her a little." He shook his head. 'She has no idea I've fallen in love with her. It'll be as much a surprise to her as it was to me."

He stood. 'But I guaran-damn-tee you that I won't let her out of my sight. If Callie's resistant to the idea, I'll simply wear her down until she surrenders. Patience is one of my strong points."

Callandra rewarded him with a gracious smile. 'I always knew the two of you would hit if off once you met. You'll make beautiful babies for me to spoil."

Nick cracked a series of knuckles in reply before he found his voice. 'Let's don't frighten her off with baby talk, Miz C. I need to work up to that." He bent and kissed her cheek. 'I can promise you that I'll take the best care of her. From now on. Scout's honor—and I was an Eagle Scout."

'I assume you'll be staying with us indefinitely?"

'I did sleep on top of the covers on my side of the bed last night," he revealed. 'What sleep I got. I was wound pretty tightly after the cops left."

'Well, I can't tell you how relieved I am that you were here. I think we'll all feel a little more secure with a man in the house."

She paused. 'I told you before, Nick. I need to replace you with a full-time gardener. Your writing and time with Callie will leave my flowers sadly neglected if I don't. I will speak to Eric today about it. As long as you'll be staying in the main house, why don't we offer the cottage along with the position? I'm sure you'll want to get something larger for the two of you. Eventually."

'When this is over. Until then, I'm stuck like glue to her." He grinned. 'I think it's going to be a lot of fun."

He turned to go then glanced over his shoulder, "Wish me luck."

Nick returned to Callie's room and entered quietly. She was starting to stir. A frown crossed her face as if the idea of facing a new day disturbed her. He leaned down and kissed her brow.

A slight smile turned up the corners of her mouth. She stretched and then snuggled back into her pillow. He stood and watched her at rest. Her simple beauty shone against the starched white pillowcase. Her flawless skin needed no trace of make-up.

For him, the essence of Callie was her unadorned hair in soft waves about her face. He knelt beside her and brushed a lock from her cheek before he kissed her.

* * *

Callie woke to Nick's kiss. For a moment, she would have believed she was Sleeping Beauty being awakened from the wicked spell placed upon her. Nick's hands were soft on her shoulders, his mouth slowly becoming more insistent.

"No," she said, pushing him away. She covered her mouth with her hand. "I have never kissed anyone first thing in the morning. Morning breath. Dead man's mouth. Yuck. It's embarrassing."

He laughed. "Don't tell me you've never had a lover roll you over and kiss you awake."

She pushed up to a sitting position. "Honestly? I'm always up early. If I did have an overnight guest in my bed, I sure as hell made it to my toothbrush before any romance commenced."

He stroked her cheek. "Well, this overnight guest spent last night above the covers and let you sleep.

Surely, that deserves a tiny reward for showing such restraint?"

She scooted to the other side of the bed and slipped out. "You're out of luck, La Chappelle. I'm in the zone in the morning and I've got my routine. Making out with you is not a part of it."

He grinned wryly at her. "So much for genteel Southern manners. I'll keep that in mind. For next time."

She opened a drawer and pulled out yoga pants, a T-shirt, and a sports bra. "Why don't you go downstairs? Essie will get you some coffee. You look like the type that needs a morning jumpstart of caffeine."

He plopped into the room's only chair. "Nope. I'm going Biblical on you. *'Where you go, I will go, and where you lodge, I will lodge.'* Impressed? Got that from Sunday school in East Texas. Ruth hooking up for the long ride."

"Well, Ruth honey, I'll be right on the other side of that door, so lodge there." She entered the bathroom and gave Nick a little wave before she closed the door.

Callie reached for her toothbrush but gripped the counter as a wave of nerves hit. She waited for it to pass. They came off and on since the attack. She knew despite her bantering with Nick that she was just this side of being scared out of her mind by whoever out there wrote that vile note.

That—and the fact that Nick was just a few feet on the other side of the door. Thinking about him caused her hands to shake as she squirted more toothpaste into the sink than onto her toothbrush.

The fact that he stayed with her last night touched her to the core. He'd been the perfect gentleman, perched on his side of the bed, on top of the sheets and comforter. Callie didn't think she would be able to sleep with what had happened, but Nick's presence brought a sense of security that had been sorely lacking. She'd dropped off into a satisfying sleep, uninterrupted until morning. That hadn't happened since the stalker's attack.

She wondered if Nick truly meant they would be joined at the hip. She rinsed her mouth and changed into her yoga clothes. When she came out, her mat was rolled out. Nick sat next to it atop Gretchen's mat, his legs crossed Indian-style, his hands turned palms up, resting on his knees.

"Let's get going," he said. "I've only heard of Downward Dog. That sounds like a good place to start."

* * *

Callie sensed the door opening from the subtle breeze in the air. She fought to keep her face placid, her eyes relaxed, her breathing steady. Gretchen must be getting an eyeful, what with Nick next to her, both in Corpse pose, the final meditative pose of the series.

"That's it," she said, slowly opening her eyes to see Gretchen's obvious interest as she gazed down at them.

Nick sat up. "That was way cool," he proclaimed. "Oh, hey, Gretchen. Callie's been putting me through some yoga poses. I wish I would've known about this when I was pitching. I feel absolutely amazing."

They both stood and rolled up their mats. Nick took both and set them in the corner of the room.

"Now what?"

Gretchen's lips twitched. "You can leave us, Sir Galahad. Callie has a massage session. Go shave and shower and give us some girl time."

Nick stood his ground. "Afraid I can't do that, Gretchen."

"Well, you cranky bastard. How on earth am I supposed to pump Callie about you with you still here in the room?" Gretchen opened the portable table and busied herself adjusting it.

Nick smiled like the Cheshire Cat. "If she's not talking, I am." He threw a triumphant look at Callie.

Callie protested. "No one is talking because there's nothing to talk about. Period." She rolled her neck, trying to work out a kink that had settled into it. "Just go. I'm fine. Besides, you know how private a massage is."

He gave her a mock leer. "Yeah, I know."

"Seriously, Nick," Gretchen chimed in. "We're fine. There's a cop on duty outside. Go get ready. I promise that we won't leave this room."

He looked from one to the other. "Only because I need some fresh clothes. I'll run home and clean up and meet you both downstairs at breakfast. By then, I'll have brought my stuff over." His gaze went to the closet. "I hope you didn't bring a ton of clothes, sweetheart. You're going to have to make some room for me."

She gasped. She didn't have time to register if it were from shock or excitement. "You are not moving into my room, Nick La Chappelle. No way."

"Way. Get used to it." He crossed to her and planted a hard kiss on her mouth that shook her down to her toes. "See you both downstairs." He sauntered out of the room.

Gretchen's jaw dropped in amazement. "I guess I don't even have to ask. That kiss smacked of possession. I guess you and Nick are a couple. Like it or not."

Chapter Twenty-Three

CALLIE WATCHED the passing scenery as they headed into New Orleans. They were going into town to talk with Bill O'Grady, the alarm system specialist that Eric recommended.

"I don't see why I had to come into town with you," she complained. "I was perfectly safe at Noble Oaks."

"No," Nick said. "You will be safer once this system is installed. Don't forget, we're peas in a pod, remember?"

"Nick," she said firmly, "I think you are taking this white-knight-in-shining-armor thing a touch too seriously. Eric has a man on the house. He said NYPD would be sending Detective Waggoner down to follow up. The alarm system will be put in today, more than likely. You don't owe me anything."

Nick whipped off onto the shoulder of the road and slammed the gearshift into park. He took her chin firmly in hand.

"Look at me, Callie Chennault. I'm dead serious. I'm going to be your shadow until this thing is through." His voice gentled. "Closer than your shadow if you'll let me."

She understood his underlying meaning. "Nick, I know you're attracted to me."

His smoldering gaze gave her pause.

"Okay. We're attracted to each other," she amended. "Still, we live very different lives. I'll eventually leave Aurora and head back to New York. I'm not interested in some fling while I'm here."

His hand slid to her nape, drawing her closer to him. "Neither am I, Callie."

She could feel her pulse leap in her throat. "What are you saying?"

He kissed her gently, slowly, yet the sizzle was still there. His mouth moved on hers with delicious ease. Her heart told her this man was the best thing that had ever happened to her.

Even so, she pulled away.

"If the kiss doesn't tell you what you need to know, Callie, then the words will." He paused and she found herself mesmerized by his midnight blue eyes.

When he spoke, his sincerity shone like a beacon from a lighthouse. "As a writer, I should be better at this. Just remember that I usually do several re-writes before my dialogue sees print."

Nick took her hand in his, slowly running his thumb across her knuckles. Frissons of excitement rippled down her spine. Never had a man's simple touch driven her this crazy.

"I love you." He sighed. "It hit me fast as lightning strikes. It's not just our chemistry, although there's plenty of that. It's you. And us. We have a lot in common, Callie. We come from small towns and we still have small town values. We're both successful artists but the money doesn't mean jack shit. It's what we do and the challenge we seek. You're the most interesting woman I've ever met, and you don't give me an inch.

Even though we've only known each other for a week, it's as if I've known you my whole life.

"Callie Chennault—I want to spend the rest of my life with you."

His declaration stunned her. *Love?* She actually agreed with what he'd said. They were cut from the same cloth. She enjoyed spending time with him. She felt at ease around him and was also exhilarated by him. Was that enough to build a lifetime together?

"But... we haven't even had sex," she blurted out. "Oh, God, where did that come from?"

Nick smiled at her, that Redford smile again, making her insides go liquid.

"I could be happy kissing you for hours every single day as it is. Making love to you will just be the bonus."

He took both her hands in his. "Don't I get extra credit points for admitting I love you and want to be with you from now until we're old and gray, even before we've had sex? I'm thinking that's pretty darn chivalrous."

"Oh, Nick." She threw her arms around his neck. Her voice quivered with emotion. She kissed *him* this time, long and thorough.

Callie pulled away suddenly, crossing her arms in front of her. "But... you haven't really... seen me, Nick. Not... not what he did to me. It's not pretty. I'll never look the way I used to."

He placed his palm against her cheek. "Honey, a few scars won't change how I feel about you." He put his hand over his heart. "My heart is telling me to go for the brass ring. I want you and our careers and babies and the whole nine yards."

"Babies?" she croaked. "We're already talking babies?"

'Shit! I told Miz C not to bring it up and here I am spilling those beans."

Callie cocked her head. "You've already talked to Aunt C about this?"

"A Southern gentleman always makes his good intentions known to the bride's family." He gave her a swift kiss. "Seriously, if you want to go back and live in New York, we will. I can write anywhere. My editor and publisher would be thrilled to have me close by. My agent would do a happy dance. I'd like, though, to keep a place here for us always to have a home to come to in the South."

'I just threw out I was going back to New York because I was scared at what you'd said," she admitted. "You know what we've talked about. I really don't know what I want to do yet, acting-wise."

"Then just tell me you know you want one thing for sure. Me."

Tears cascaded down her cheeks. "Oh, I do, Nick. I really do." He embraced her and she whispered, 'I'm afraid this has all been some dream and I'll wake up. That we'll still be two people who like to antagonize the hell out of each other."

He chuckled. "Oh, I don't think that'll change at all, hon. But we'll be stuck with each other, for better or worse. I like the sound of that. A lot."

"Me, too."

* * *

"That pretty much covers things," Bill O'Grady said. "We can have everything taken care of by suppertime. Eric giving me a heads up sure helped. Don't worry about your aunt learning how to work things. I'll take extra care explaining it to her."

Callie picked up one of the business cards that sat in a holder at the table's center. She scribbled a few lines on the back of it and handed it to the large Irishman.

"That's my business manager's address. Send the final bill to him and whatever monthly fees there are. I don't want Aunt C to pay a dime on this."

O'Grady tore apart the copies, stapling the card she'd given him to the one he kept. He pushed the other over to her. "Will do, Miss Chennault. I do have one more thing to ask."

He grinned sheepishly. "My wife and I, well, we're huge fans and the DVR is set to record every episode of *Sumner Falls*. Even the repeats. If she finds out that you were in here and I didn't ask for your autograph, I'd best be looking for another place to sleep. Permanently."

She smiled graciously. "Not a problem. If you'd like, I can have an 8x10 glossy sent to you."

"Whoa!" O'Grady shouted. "I would be the hero of the month at my house. If it's not too much trouble."

"I'll see that you get one. What's your wife's name?"

"Betty Lou." He smiled. "She looks a little like Betty Rubble from the Flintstones. At least I always tell her so. All guys know Betty was the better-looking one."

"How about a selfie?" Callie added.

"You don't mind?" O'Grady asked.

"Not a bit."

The alarm expert whipped out his phone and posed with Callie, thanking her profusely.

Nick stood and offered his hand. "Thanks for your time, Bill." He told her, "I'll call Miz C and tell her to expect the alarm company truck within the hour."

"I've got a couple of calls to make, too," she replied, as they both pulled out their cells.

She left a message on Beth's voice mail. "Sorry I didn't reach you in person." She found the address on her receipt and repeated it aloud. "By the way, you aren't going to believe what's happened down here. Let's just say there's nothing like homegrown boys."

Callie smiled as she ended the call, knowing Beth would return her call the minute she listened to the message. She dialed her business manager and told him about the upcoming bills for the alarm system.

"Ready?" Nick asked.

"Sure. I'm getting a little hungry, though. Maybe we can snag a po'boy before we go back?"

"Let's head over to the square."

They were parked about half a dozen blocks from Jackson Square, the heart of the French Quarter. Nick took her hand in his, his fingers warm and strong. The rightness of it surprised her. She'd gone from a man-avoider to a woman in love in less than a week. All because of Nick.

They turned off Canal onto Decatur, walking leisurely in the hot morning sun until they reached Jackson Square. St. Louis Cathedral loomed large.

"I remember the first time Aunt C brought me down here." She pointed toward the church. "We went in. Candles glowed everywhere. It smelled a little musty but I was sure God lived there. I thought it was the most beautiful church in the entire world. I still do."

He gave her fingers a squeeze. "I like the place on the corner there. Want to try it?"

"Sure."

They crossed the street and entered the oyster bar. Its black-and-white tiles gleamed as much as the long mahogany bar. The small place was busy, with white-aproned servers cutting between chairs with their laden trays, as whirring ceiling fans kept the flow of air conditioning constant.

"There's a table." He led her to it as a waitress appeared.

"Two shrimp po'boys and a side order of hush puppies. And two mint iced teas."

"You got it." The server flashed a smile and left them.

"How did you know exactly what I wanted?"

He laid a hand over hers. "You just look like a shrimp-and-hush-puppy kinda gal. I guess great minds think—and eat—alike."

They talked over their sandwiches, which came with slender, salted fries and creamy coleslaw. She found out a little about Nick's playing days and even shared a few stories of the backstage gossip behind *Sumner Falls*. Before she realized it, the restaurant had almost emptied, the lunch rush over. She'd lost all track of time as they spoke.

Nick paid the bill and they stepped from the cool air conditioning back into the steamy heat of New Orleans. Callie took in all the street vendors lining Jackson Square, hawking their wares or performing for loose change.

Nick pointed to one of them. "Hey, see that lady with the pink fedora? She's really good. She did a drawing of Elvis, Eric, and me once, years ago."

He guided her to one of the sidewalk artists lining the square. Example caricatures of her work were displayed under the shade of a tree.

"Afternoon, ma'am. We'd like to get our portrait done. In color," he added.

The woman, dressed in a bohemian style and wearing Birkenstock sandals, nodded.

"Sit there," she indicated. "No talking for fifteen minutes."

Callie sat and Nick moved next to her. His arm went

around her waist, pulling her close. She stared across the square at the statue of Jackson perched upon his war steed.

Could life get any better than this?

Despite her present troubles, contentment poured through her. Serenity blanketed her, as real as Nick's arm about her.

"It's finished. It's good," the artist proclaimed.

Callie came out of her reverie. How long had she been daydreaming? She peered at the sketch and smiled. The artist portrayed her as dreamy and delicate. Nick was strong and grinning from ear to ear. Tiny hearts had been drawn about them in the air. The cartooned couple looked totally in love.

"Thank you," Nick told the woman, pressing a bill into her hand. She tucked it down her blouse and rolled up the paper, handing it to him.

"We'll come back," he promised.

They strolled toward the market when he spotted a carriage.

"Come on. It'll be fun. I've never done anything touristy like this before." He spoke to the driver briefly and handed Callie up before he climbed in after her.

Throwing an arm around her shoulders, he told her, "We're off to see the Garden District."

"Oh, I love it there. Every house has its own distinct beauty."

"And its own story," he added. "Maybe I'll be inspired to start something new."

She rested her hand on his thigh. "Well, it worked for Anne Rice. She didn't do too shabbily."

He shuddered. "Her stuff creeps me out. Vampires always scared the hell out of me. I used to sleep with the covers tucked behind my neck when I was a kid because Elvis swore vampires would come visit me in the night.

Every morning, I'd run to the mirror and check my throat to make sure no bloodsucker had stopped by for a midnight snack of Nick."

She snorted. "I think Lestat is romantic and charming. Even if he is a little egotistical sometimes. Besides, Rice's descriptions are wonderful. I'd love to have the chance to play a character that complex."

She put her head on his shoulder as the driver guided the horses to St. Charles. They spent a good two hours in the Garden District, pointing out the houses they liked and making up stories about the various owners. It pleased her to see they had similar tastes, from their love of wraparound porches to grand old cypress trees.

"Would you like to live along here?" Nick asked.

Callie considered it. "It would be nice but I prefer a smaller place. After living in New York all these years, I think I'd enjoy a less hectic pace. NOLA has too many people, including too many tourists. I really cherish my privacy."

"Me, too." Nick brushed his lips against hers and Callie surrendered to the moment.

They disembarked where they'd started from and he insisted they stop at Café du Monde.

"How can you be a block from the best beignets in the world and not succumb?" he asked teasingly.

She agreed, despite the fact that she was still full from lunch, and they joined the line waiting to grab a table. Nick maneuvered her around several people and they snagged a spot just as a couple was leaving. They ordered café au laits and two plates of beignets, which appeared nearly as soon as they spoke.

"I used to love coming here every summer," he revealed. "It was one of the places Aunt Olivia would bring Mom and me. I thought these were the best donuts in the world. Plus the best hot chocolate. No matter what the temperature, I had to have my hot chocolate."

"How long did you stay?"

He shrugged. "Usually a month. Mom would come the entire time, too. We always had a blast."

"Are you an only child?"

"Yep." He bit into his last bite of beignet and moaned. Callie leaned over with a napkin and wiped away his powdered sugar mustache.

"Mom missed living here. She and Aunt Olivia were thick as thieves. Still are."

"Where does your mom live?"

He sipped his coffee. "With Olivia now. About five years ago, she retired and left East Texas for good. She always wanted to come back to Aurora. Aunt O was already a widow and they've been living together ever since, causing trouble."

"Do you miss your dad?" she asked quietly. She thought of the angry shouts and slaps she'd grown up with and how grateful she was when her father was no longer around.

"Sometimes. He was a traveling salesman. Gone from home a lot. Mostly, it was Mom and me. She actually taught me how to pitch. She'd been an ace pitcher in softball growing up. She's the one that got me interested in the game."

He laughed. "She never would let me play football. One of those mamas that didn't want to see her boy tackled to shreds. I sure took shit from the guys for not being allowed to play football. In Texas, it's sacrosanct."

Nick eyed her remaining beignet. "Are you going to finish that?"

"No. I'm full. Especially after all those buttered hush puppies."

He switched plates with her and tore off a bite. 'Still, I played basketball in the winter. Baseball both spring and summer, and then the fall ball when I got older. I didn't miss out on too much. My dad didn't see many games, though. He spent most of his time gone on the road. It was always business with him. Not much left over for Mom or me."

She rested her hand atop his. 'I guess we both fell a little short in the dad department. I supposed our other relatives made up for it, though." She paused, wanting to tell him a little more of her story.

'My mom died when I was twelve. Breast cancer. She was sick for a long time before that. After she passed, Aunt C and Essie were all the family I had."

Nick washed down his last bite. 'I'm lucky. I still have Mom and all my cousins. That's why I came back to Aurora. I... needed to be around family. I finally figured out that's what's most important." He gave her a heated glance.

'Oh, Mom's gonna cut off my nuts and deep fry them," he suddenly proclaimed.

'What?" She laughed. 'That sure came from left field."

He ran his fingers through his thick, dark hair. 'Way out from left field. Mom and Aunt O got back from their trip to Branson last night. They go every year around this time. I forgot to call and check on her."

'I'm sure you can explain a lot was going on last night."

He nodded. 'Yeah. Eric's probably brought them up to speed." He stood. 'Come on. We need to head home. We'll drop in on Mom and let you two ladies get acquainted."

Nick flashed a wicked smile. 'I might be able to stay out of the doghouse by presenting her with my fiancée."

She swallowed. "That sounds... serious."

He gave her a quick kiss. "I am serious, honey. I'm just sorry I don't have a ring on that finger yet to let the male population know you're taken."

"Things have happened pretty fast."

He lifted her hand to his lips and pressed a kiss into her palm. "You look tired, else I'd say let's go ring shopping right now."

Her emotions threatened to overwhelm her so she told him, "I am a little tired. This has been a pretty full day. I haven't even taken my afternoon nap!"

"Then let's go home. I'll call Mom and tell her we're coming over tomorrow instead. Do you think you can walk back to the car?"

"I'm fine. If I get tired, you can carry me."

Nick swept her off her feet in a single move. "Good thing you're light."

"Nick La Chappelle, put me down," she ordered.

He kept walking.

Her face flamed. "Oh, this is embarrassing. Please, please, put me down."

He stopped. "Are you sure?"

"Yes." She ducked her head, hating the attention they were drawing.

Nick set her on the sidewalk and got down on one knee, taking both of her hands in his.

"What are you doing? Nick, are you crazy?"

He grinned shamelessly. "Crazy for you. Be quiet. I want to make this official. I know I told you I loved you and wanted to spend the rest of my life with you—but I never really asked you to marry me."

She sensed the crowd gathering around them. Her cheeks burned bright red. "Nick!"

"Callie, I love you more than sleeping late on a rainy Saturday. I love you more than jambalaya or pecan pralines. I love you more than pitching a no-hitter in the seventh game of the World Series.

'I love you and want us to spend every minute of every day together until we're too old to remember each other's names. Will you do me the honor of becoming my wife?"

She couldn't help but laugh at his outrageously romantic proposal. 'Yes, yes, yes. I will marry you and sleep late with you and feed you pecan pralines and even watch the Series with you. Now, will you get up?"

Nick rose and pulled her into his arms for a searing kiss. Vaguely, she heard applause surrounding them. When he finally pulled his mouth from hers, Callie realized not only had the crowd's numbers swelled, but several people were shooting videos and taking pictures with their smart phones. Everyone around them wore a smile.

Nick took her hand in his and waved to the crowd. 'Gotta go, folks. We need to talk about rings and babies and all kinds of important things." He took her hand and pulled her through those gathered, hurrying her down the street.

'Stop," she ordered after they'd passed two blocks. 'I'm totally out of breath."

'Sorry. I couldn't resist." He ran a finger down her cheek. 'You're just so cute when you blush."

She shook her head. 'What have I gotten myself into?"

He whispered in her ear. 'I can't wait to get myself into you."

Nick laced his fingers through hers and escorted her a few more blocks and around the corner to the car. Her face burned at his racy comment. She would pull on her sunglasses the minute they got into the convertible. She wished she hadn't left them on the dashboard in the first place.

When they reached the car, he groaned. "Not a ticket. Come on, I'm parked fine. There's no meter." He lifted the windshield wiper and froze.

"What's wrong?" She noticed a blank envelope resting on the glass. The pit of her stomach grew icy.

"Get in," he ordered, unlocking the car and practically shoving her inside. He locked her door and slammed it before walking around to retrieve the envelope. He opened his own door and got in, locking it the minute it shut.

Silence weighed heavily inside the car. Callie bit her lip. The wonderful, beautiful, romantic day faded as she stared at the envelope in his hands.

"It could be anything," he said, trying to convince them both. "An advertisement. A coupon."

"It's not. Just open it."

As before, the envelope wasn't sealed. Nick and Eric had discussed that no trace of DNA would be left that way. Since the previous note hadn't had any fingerprints on it, Callie assumed this one wouldn't, either. She watched him pull out the folded slip of paper and open it, turning it around since it was upside down.

She watched as he read it, his eyes going dark as the color drained from his face. He refolded it and started to put it back in the envelope.

"I want to read it."

"No. It's just more crap. I'll give it to Eric."

Callie wrapped her fingers around his wrist. "We're in this together. Please. I need to see it."

Reluctantly, he handed it over. With shaking hands, she unfolded it.

. . .

Nick—

Hope you are having fun today. Because it could be your last.

Lipstick Larry

P.S. Believe it or not, I actually want you dead more than her.

Chapter Twenty-Four

CARS PACKED the drive at Noble Oaks as Nick and Callie returned. He'd called Eric as he'd raced out of the city, relating what they'd found. Eric told him Detective Waggoner had arrived from New York and would be among those waiting when they reached Aurora.

He took in Callie as he swung into the driveway. She appeared so fragile in the leather bucket seat, her arms wrapped around her protectively. Her eyes stared dully, straight ahead.

"It's not your fault," he told her for the third time.

She quickly turned and shot daggers at him. "Of course, it is. He wants *me*! He's mad because he's seen you with me. When I think how stupid we were to parade our feelings in front of the entire French Quarter. He was *watching* us, Nick. He probably had his camera out, snapping pictures of our proposal. We've inflamed him. The entire situation has gotten out of hand. I'm not going to risk your life. This is between him and me."

He cut the engine and glared at her. "What exactly does that mean, Callie? You're just cutting me loose?"

"Yes." Her harsh tone belied the frightened look in her eyes.

"What happened to love? Seeing each other through thick and thin?"

"I believe you're talking about the wedding vows and that's through sickness and in health, for better or worse, till death us do part." She unfastened her seat belt and stared hard at him. "We aren't married and we haven't proclaimed any public vows or made any promises. I declare this relationship officially over before it's even begun. That way this raving lunatic won't see the need to let death part us."

She threw open her door and eased out. Nick jumped out and went around to her side of the car. One look told him how physically and emotionally depleted Callie was.

But she would hear him out.

He gently took her arm. "Listen. You are not going to fight this guy alone. I love you. I don't care if the world knows—let alone this douchebag. We're in this together, Callie, united we stand. I'm not going to run out on you at the first sign of trouble."

She tugged, trying to get away from him but he held on firmly. Finally, she stopped struggling. She raised tear-filled eyes to his.

"Don't you see it's because I love you that I'm not willing to sacrifice you? I don't want to see you killed. If you're not involved with me, he won't see you as a threat. He'll leave you alone. I won't let him hurt you, Nick. I couldn't save Wolf—but I can try to save you."

Nick pulled her to him, enfolding her in his arms. He felt the tremors run through her as she sobbed.

"Baby, I won't walk away from you," he whispered in her ear. "If I can't be with you, I might as well be dead."

Callie looked up at him, biting her lips to try and get back under control.

"Other than getting this stupid note, I just had the best damn day of my entire thirty-five years," he told her. "I'm not going to let some psycho come between us. I don't have to say the public vows or have the piece of paper to know there isn't anything I wouldn't do for you. I will stand by you and I'll tell you, sweetheart— when this is all over—it'll be the two of us left. Together. Stalker, be damned."

She collapsed against him, her fingers bunching his shirt tightly. Nick stroked her hair. He looked up and saw Eric, Gretchen, and a man he assumed was the New York cop.

"Come inside," Eric ordered quietly.

Callie pulled away from him. She spotted the cop and ran to him, throwing her arms around him. A pang of jealousy pulled at Nick, despite the fact that the man was old enough to be her father.

"I'm so glad you're here, Waggoner," Callie said. "This has turned into a nightmare." She gestured for Nick to come. He moved up to where they stood.

"This is Nick." She took a deep breath. "My... fiancé."

Nothing else Callie could've said would have made him prouder. He realized in that moment that she had committed to him. He thrust out a hand.

"Sorry to meet you under such circumstances, Detective."

The cop grunted as he shook hands. "You're deep in the midst of things now, Nick. Makes sense, though, that he'd want to go after you. You're a roadblock between him and Callie. The idiot we arrested back in New York hollered day and night that he wasn't a murderer. That he didn't have anything to do with the other dead girls that resembled Callie." He glanced around. "Let's continue this conversation inside."

They went up the porch steps, Eric and Gretchen in front of them. He spotted Miz C the minute they entered the foyer. Both and he and Callie went to her.

"I'm so sorry," Callie apologized over and over. "I would never have come here if I would have dreamed this wasn't over."

Callandra's stubborn chin went up a notch. "And I would thrash you soundly if you hadn't come home. You're where you are loved, my dear. Even Dorothy Gale knew there's no place like home."

The old woman pointed a finger at Nick. "You need to watch yourself, too, young man. You and Callie must follow whatever instructions Detective Waggoner gives you until this madman is in custody. I wouldn't want anything to interfere with..." Her voice trailed off as she looked mortified.

He grinned. "You haven't let any cats from their bags, Miz C. Callie knows I'm nuts about her. We're engaged. We've even talked about where we'll live. But we haven't done any negotiating on how many babies. Satisfied?"

Callandra beamed at them. "Immensely." Her eyes sparkled as she took in her niece. "Despite Nick's occasional bursts of sarcasm, he is quite a fine man." She took Callie's hands in hers. "When this situation has been resolved, I know you two will be very happy together."

"I don't mean to intrude, ma'am," Waggoner said, "but Sheriff La Rue and I need to speak to these two in private."

"Of course, Detective. Take as much time as you need. We must catch this lunatic. When you're done, we would be honored to have you stay to supper this evening."

"That would be nice. Thank you." Waggoner looked to Eric. "Where would you like to do this?"

Eric indicated the parlor and the four of them adjourned there. Eric shut the doors behind them. Nick led Callie to a large, brocaded sofa and sat beside her.

Waggoner took a seat in the oyster-colored wing chair opposite them. "Tell me everything. From the minute you found the first note last night until you found the second one today. Don't leave out any detail."

Callie began the story and Nick interjected his take on things every now and then. Waggoner scrawled a few notes as they spoke, but mostly he listened. When they finished, he placed his notepad on the coffee table.

"May I see the note from today?"

Nick fished the envelope from his pocket. "I figured there wouldn't be prints on it."

"True, but you never know. Sometimes, they get sloppy when they get bold."

The detective removed a plastic bag from his pocket, as well as a glove. He slipped on the glove before taking the note and reading it several times. Eric stood over his shoulder, reading the text, too. Finally, Waggoner put the envelope and letter into the evidence bag and handed it to Eric, who stepped from the room.

"I won't give you the soft sell, Nick. In plain English, this monster has a fixation on Callie. Quite frankly, the longer we've had Simon Bills in custody, the more I've doubted his link to the serial murders of young blonds."

Waggoner turned to Callie. "We've discovered no solid proof to tie him to a single girl. Everything that we thought was evidence in the murders proved to be nothing more than news clippings of Lipstick Larry's exploits. You and I know that Bills is the guy who attacked you. You ID'd him. We found the knife with your blood on it in his medicine cabinet. The whole shrine he'd set up in your honor in his apartment. The log where he kept a record of your movements and all the times he followed you. We can get an easy conviction on his stalking and attack on you. That's why I pushed for that case to be brought to trial first. We could get one lunatic off the streets while we bought time for the murder investigation."

The detective stood and began pacing the room. "But the guy's not that smart. Our serial killer had to be smooth enough to get these girls to come with him willingly, to wherever he plays his private games with them. He's left virtually no evidence. That takes a clever man. Simon Bills doesn't fit the killer's pattern or IQ. He confronted you on a public street. He was hostile, not self-contained. You were even able to manipulate him for a while. I doubt you could've done that with our real perp.

"Moreover, Bills panicked. He got messy with you. The murderer is a calm, rational guy. He takes his time. He leaves no trace." He frowned. "I think he's the one behind these two notes. He's followed you to Louisiana and wants to play the game out to its finish."

Nick put a protective arm around Callie. He felt the tremors running through her body.

"How do we catch him?" he asked.

Waggoner returned to his seat. "Obviously, he's in the area. A stranger will stand out among locals in a town this size. I know Aurora is bigger than you remembered it, Callie, with a lot of tourists coming through. Still, he's got to be staying somewhere nearby. And someone's got to remember him. The Aurora PD has begun canvassing the area already."

The cop blew out a long breath. "In the meantime,

you both get round-the-clock protection. Eric has brought in the FBI since the case has crossed state lines. They'll create a profile. We'll tap the phones. Then, we wait."

"All that could take a long time," Callie pointed out. "I don't know how long I can live like a bird in a gilded cage."

Waggoner gave her a hard look. "It's either that or let him succeed, Callie."

"We could flush him out," Nick suggested. "He wants me out of the way. You could use me to set a trap."

"No!"

He recognized the panic in Callie's voice and knew she was close to the breaking point. She gripped his hand tightly. "No way, Nick. I just found you and decided you're worth keeping. I'm not going to lose you in some failed, heroic attempt to catch a killer. This isn't one of your books."

"Nick does have a point," interjected Waggoner. "We could get someone in with his general build and coloring. I'll have to work on that with Eric and the FBI." He nodded at Nick. "Callie's right. No foolish attempts at bravery required. You got the girl and she's a real peach. Don't blow it now. Let law enforcement do their job."

He stood. "I've got a few things to check on. I'm sure you'd like a little time alone to unwind. I know this must've been a rough day." Waggoner leaned over and kissed Callie's cheek. "Good to see you again, kid. Sorry it's under such rotten circumstances." He shook hands with Nick and gave him a curt nod before leaving the parlor.

Nick didn't care what the cop said. Callie might go

stir-crazy before this killer was caught. They needed time to explore their budding relationship and get on with their lives without this hanging over them.

Plotting was his forte. Given time, he knew he could come up with a way to catch the killer.

Chapter Twenty-Five

HE DROVE PAST NOBLE OAKS, *taking care not to slow his car. He didn't want to seem suspicious in the least. He threw a quick glance to his right and realized the drive was filled with vehicles. He smiled. As they say, the plot now thickened.*

He'd been coming by to see if he could catch a glimpse of her. She walked a lot in the mornings. The property was large and totally unprotected. He could have taken her numerous times.

Instead, he spied the expensive convertible, top up today, speed past him. He'd made a U-turn and decided to follow them at a discreet distance. They'd gone into New Orleans, to a security company. It didn't surprise him. She would be upset after finding his presents.

It was what happened after that which really surprised him. The little slut had been down here no more than a week and she was all over the ball player. He had stars in his eyes, obviously fooled by what she really was. Still, it made for fun to follow them for a while. He'd gotten bored, though, and gone back to the car and left a note, knowing it would crank up things a notch.

He knew the police had contacted not only the morons

at NYPD, but also those at the FBI since the action had now crossed state lines. Wouldn't it be delicious to read what their profilers said about him?

Of course, things would be more dangerous now. The chance of getting caught had multiplied. They were on their guard. Despite that, he wanted to toy with them a little longer. He needed the excitement that brought. And it would only complete his work to take them out together. Maybe in their little love nest in back of the main house.

He wanted to lull them into a false sense of security. Only then could the fun and games begin. He would kill Jessica first—slowly, with great skill, showing off the talents he had polished to perfection. He wanted her to suffer as his dear mama had. He would force Nick to watch.

And then he would kill him. Swiftly, with as much pain and force as he could muster. Nick might've ruined his life, but he wouldn't let the superstar have the satisfaction of knowing that.

Oh, to think sweet freedom came at such a heavy price.

But what fun it would be to finally earn that freedom.

Chapter Twenty-Six

"THE WIFE and I have always thought about retiring to Florida, but if the food's always this good and there's no snow to speak of? I might need to change her mind."

Those gathered around the table laughed at Detective Waggoner's comment.

"Callie was hell-bent on coming back here, Uncle Paul," Gretchen said. "Now, I understand why." She smiled to herself, and Callie knew it wasn't simply the appetizing food her nurse spoke of.

"Weren't you supposed to make dessert tonight?" she asked.

Gretchen beamed. "I did. I only watched Essie making the beans and cornbread. I did help fry up the catfish, though."

"What is it about this cornbread?" Waggoner asked. "It's so rich. My wife would kill for a bite of this."

"It's the broccoli in it," Essie announced as she swung through the door with a glass casserole dish. "That and lots of butter." She smiled at the detective. "You think fettuccini's a heart attack on a plate? It ain't got nothin' on my cornbread."

The cook set the dessert in front of Gretchen. "I'll

be back with bowls, honey, but I thought you might want to be the one to dish up your mud." Essie sashayed back out the door, whistling all the way.

Callie noticed Eric sitting up straighter, leaning over to look at the dessert. He broke out in a huge grin.

"Gretchen, you made Mississippi Mud!" He reached a finger out to take a sample but quickly stopped and withdrew his hand, reddening slightly. Callie observed Aunt C frowning at him.

"We tried one batch but it wasn't up to Essie's standards. The second try did the trick, though," Gretchen said. Her eyes shot to Eric. "I have had a taste, and it is one luscious mess of goodness."

Essie brought in deep ceramic bowls, and soon everyone had the heavenly chocolate dessert before them, Eric once again piling his with a mountain of Cool Whip on top. Callie had only picked at her dinner, despite the fact that Essie prepared some of her favorite foods. The note on the car and Wolf being gone dampened not only her spirits but her appetite.

Still, Gretchen was watching her—and it was chocolate, a sacred food group. She spooned a bite into her mouth and sighed upon contact.

"Oh, Gretch, you did it," she told her friend. "Pam will be so jealous. Her mud's never turned out this well."

"Maybe when this is all over, we can host our own barbecue, Callie. Especially since Nick's quite the grill expert."

"Speaking of being over, Gretchen," Waggoner interrupted, looking at Callandra. Callie figured she knew what was coming. "It wouldn't be a bad idea, Mrs. Chennault, for you, Essie, and Gretchen to relocate into town for a while."

Aunt C glared at the policeman, her chin tilted high

as anger sparked in her eyes. "I will not be run from my own home, sir, and I would certainly never abandon my niece. We have the new security system in place. Nick is now sleeping in the main house. There are men on duty outside. I don't see why I should leave the comfort of my own home."

"If you insist. It was merely a suggestion." The detective looked back at Gretchen. "You might need to give me seconds," he added, passing his bowl to his niece.

Callie sighed. "I think I'm going to call it a day," she announced. "But don't let me break up the dinner party."

She stood. Immediately, Nick was on his feet, too.

"Goodnight everyone," he said for both of them, taking her elbow and leading her from the room.

They walked up the stairs at a leisurely pace, Nick matching her slow tread.

"I think you need a long soak in a hot tub, ma'am."

"You read my mind," she told him.

He opened the door to her room. "Wait here." He entered the room and checked it and the bathroom before he motioned her in.

"I've locked the other door leading from the bathroom to the adjoining bedroom. I'll go start your water."

He headed into the bathroom and Callie heard the sound of running water begin. She slipped off her sandals and nudged them under the bed with her toes as she pulled the elastic-coated rubber band from her ponytail.

She checked the mirror above the antique dresser and fluffed her hair before removing the diamond studs she wore every day and sliding her watch off her wrist.

"I'll wait out here for you," Nick said, watching her in the mirror.

She turned. "Really, I'll—"

"I'll be waiting. Gather up what you need." He plopped into the club chair by the bed and stretched his long legs in front of him.

She decided arguing wouldn't change anything so she did as he said and went into the bathroom.

"Lock the door," he hollered.

"Yes, sir," she muttered under her breath, turning the lock into place.

The bathroom was steamy and smelled of honeysuckle. He must've seen her bath crystals and dumped a handful into the water. She stripped and wound her hair high up on her head and secured it with a few pins. She avoided looking into the mirror and climbed into the claw-foot tub. The temperature was absolutely perfect. She shut off the faucet and sank, grabbing her bath pillow to slip behind her neck.

A loud pounding on the door gave her a start. "What?" she yelled.

"How pruney do you need to be?"

Callie realized the water had cooled considerably. She must have fallen asleep.

"I'll be out in a minute."

Quickly, she scrubbed and rinsed herself and released the stopper. Nick had thoughtfully placed a towel along the edge of the tub. She stood and wrapped it around her, gently patting along where her scars lay. Fortunately, the mirror was steamed up, preventing her from seeing them.

She rubbed moisturizer into her face and dusted on her honeysuckle-scented powder before she slipped into her lace thong and sleeveless nightgown. She'd always slept in old T-shirts before, usually men's, but they weren't long enough to cover her flaws. Gretchen found several silk gowns that went just to her knee. They were comfortable and made Callie feel less self-conscious about her Frankenstein-looking patchwork of scars.

She grabbed her kimono from the hook on the door and slipped into it before emerging from the bathroom. Nick sat in the chair, the scrapbook from the nightstand across his lap, his bare feet propped on the bed. His chest was bare. He wore blue pajama pants the color of his eyes.

Callie walked into the room, her heart beating wildly. She tried to calm herself before she spoke. "Having fun?"

He closed the book and set it on the table. "I didn't know you edited your middle school newspaper."

"That was in my *I want to be a journalist and light world on fire* days."

"And the plays. You had the lead in every production in high school from freshman year on."

She shrugged. "I found my niche. Whatever role I wanted, I could slip it on. Like a second skin."

He stood. "You were also homecoming queen. Quite a résumé, Ms. Chennault."

She laughed. "That last one was a fluke. The most popular girl in my class turned up with a nasty case of shingles the week before the homecoming game and dance. She always won everything. I think between the backlash of her grabbing every honor since grade school and her not being able to attend the game to be crowned caused a voters' revolt. I lucked out."

"And you were Most Likely to Succeed?" He took a few steps toward her.

The quick quip died in her throat at the hungry look in his eyes. She took a step back.

"Nick, I can't." She defensively crossed her arms in front of her.

"I haven't asked you to do anything, hon."

Callie gave him a tremulous smile. "Your mouth might not be saying any words but your eyes are speaking volumes. Like you're the Big Bad Wolf and I'm Little Red Riding Hood."

"What are they saying?"

"Things I don't want to talk about," Callie admitted. "Look, Nick, I come out to this bare-chested, broad-shouldered, gladiator hunk action. We've had this whirlwind romance and part of me is wondering just what I've gotten myself into. I don't think I can physically or emotionally handle taking us to the next level right now."

She waved a hand in exasperation. "Where are you sleeping tonight? You can't sleep on top of the covers in here again."

He frowned, a look that would match Aunt C's most lethal glare any day. "Where else do you think I would be?"

"Nick," she whispered. "I'm scared. Of you. You're a lot of man."

He closed the distance between them and put strong hands on her shoulders. He ran his hands up and down her arms, trying to reassure her.

"Don't be," he whispered back, his gaze intense. Those midnight blue eyes turned dark with desire.

Callie shivered. "But I am. I know you want to protect me, but who's going to protect me from you?"

"I don't get it."

She shook her head. "I've always taken care of myself, from the time I was really young. The few relationships I've had with men have always been on my terms. I called the shots. I kept my emotional distance. If they tried to close that distance, I cut them loose. I'm not any good at letting someone else look out for me."

"Oh, babe." Nick pulled her into his arms. She

could feel his heart racing. "Don't you know I feel the same way?"

She remained silent, her throat thick with unshed tears.

Nick kissed her hair. "I haven't been too great in the relationship department either. I told you I was too shy and then too famous. I never really let anyone get close until my marriage. Even then, I was merely skating along the surface. I never really knew how broken it was until the day it ended."

Tenderly, he kissed her brow. "This is really a first for me, too. Getting to really know someone. Share things. Thoughts. Feelings. Small talk."

He tilted her chin up. "We'll go as slowly as we need to. I know it's tough with what's hanging over you, but I don't ever want you to be afraid of me. Okay?"

She nodded. "Okay."

He brushed a quick kiss across her lips and released her. He looked around the room. "It's either sleep on the bed, the chair, or the floor in front of the locked door. I'll do whichever you want, but I'm here. For good."

"You'd sleep on the floor for me?" Callie grinned mischievously at him.

"Yeah. If I had to."

"Or all scrunched up in the chair?"

He bit back a smile. "Yeah. If I need to."

She grew serious. "I don't know how much I'm ready to give yet, Nick. But my own personal bodyguard in bed might be nice."

She walked to the near side of the bed and began to turn down the comforter. He went to the other side and matched her moves. She slipped under the sheet while he switched off the overhead light before he climbed into bed.

"Oh, wait. Do you want me to leave the light on in the bathroom?"

"No. I'll be fine. You know, having my bodyguard nearby is like having the teddy bear I slept with when I was a kid."

He leaned over and turned off the light on the nightstand. She rolled onto her side. Nick scooted up behind her and threw an arm around her, drawing her close. Callie finally dropped off to sleep, knowing Nick would be there all through the night.

Chapter Twenty-Seven

NICK ENJOYED Callie nestled against him, her face burrowed against his heart. He gently stroked her hair, not wanting to disturb her sleep. She'd lain awake a long time in his arms last night. He knew she missed Wolf and was still worried about the threat against both of them.

He eased from the bed and brought the covers back over her. Miz C liked her air conditioning strong and the vent blew directly across the bed. His throat was dry because of it and he wanted a drink of water. He moved quietly across the hardwood floor and slipped into the bathroom, closing the door before flicking on the light.

Just then, a song began chirping loudly from Callie's cell phone sitting on the counter. He quickly answered it, hoping the ringing hadn't awakened her.

"Hello?" he said softly.

Silence greeted him. Then a throaty female laughed.

"Well, I know I don't have a wrong number because I've got Callie on speed dial. I'm just surprised that she's not the one answering. Or maybe I'm not, after that cryptic message she left me yesterday."

"Uh... Callie's sleeping right now. Can I have her call you back?"

Again, the amused laugh. "Just tell me one thing. Are you a homegrown boy?"

Nick didn't know what to say to that—or whom he would be saying it to. "I guess you might say that," he said warily.

A sudden tapping on the door startled him. He opened the door to see Callie standing there. With his cell phone in her hand.

"It's your mom," she said dryly. "I gather that's for me?"

"Shit." He spoke into the phone. "Here's Callie." He passed over her phone and took his cell from her.

"Hey, Mom."

"The bright and sunny routine doesn't cut it. You're usually grumpy before your first cup of coffee. And I have a feeling if we were in the same room, I wouldn't be smelling any coffee on your breath."

Nick crossed to the chair and sat. He noticed Callie had closed the bathroom door behind her. He ran a hand through his hair.

"Okay. It's like this. I'm sorry I didn't call to see how Branson was. There's just a lot happening. A lot, Mom. I really need to see you today to talk about it." He took a deep breath. "And there's someone I want you to meet."

His mother chuckled. Nick relaxed a little bit.

"Eric told Olivia and me some of what's going on. However, it did surprise me that I'd leave town and return after only a week to find my baby involved with someone who would be answering his phone at seven in the morning."

Heat rose up his neck. He felt like a sixteen-year-old caught making out in the driveway after he thought his mom had gone to bed.

"It's not like that. Well, it sort of is. I mean, we haven't even slept together yet. Well, we actually did the last two nights, but that's only because this psycho is after Callie, and there's no way I would ever leave her alone. I even make her lock the door when she goes to the bathroom."

Nick took a deep breath. "Mom. I know I sound crazy and confused—but I love her. She doesn't take shit off me and she's smart and funny and sweet and talented. You're going to love her."

Without any hesitation, he heard, "So, do you two want to come over for breakfast?"

He laughed. "Mom, you are the greatest. Your French toast would be terrific. Callie needs a little fattening up. How about an hour?"

"I'll see you both then. Bye, sweetie."

He ended the call and shook his head. A moment later, Callie came out doing the same thing.

"My best friend from New York is dying to meet you. Beth said you sounded sexy as hell. She actually knows who you are. Her husband is Mr. Sports Central. She's picked up quite a bit since they've been married. She can spout ERAs and MVPs like there's no tomorrow."

He laughed. "We're having breakfast with my mom in an hour. Think you can handle that?"

Callie frowned. "Can we make it an hour and a half? I need to do some stretching with Gretchen before I hit the shower. We did a lot of moving around NOLA yesterday. I'm pretty stiff and don't want to skimp on my exercises."

He went and nuzzled her neck. "I know, no morning breath kisses."

She laughed and nipped him on the neck, too. "Go

shower. I'll get Gretchen to help me run through my exercises."

Nick watched her open the bedroom door and cross the hall. She knocked and then stepped into Gretchen's room, closing the door behind her. He called his mom back and told her they'd be a little later than planned.

And turned crimson when she laughed.

* * *

Callie fiddled with the slender gold chain around her neck as Nick drove into town.

What if his mom didn't like her? She'd sure sounded surprised to hear a woman answer his phone. Her face flamed again with embarrassment, thinking that Aunt C would have been mortified if put in the same position.

Nick reached across and pulled her hand toward him, grazing his lips against her knuckles. "Relax. Mom's very cool. Sweet, but up front. She will love you. I know it."

She swallowed. Her throat was desert dry. She started to lick her lips, but she didn't want to mess up her lip gloss. She wanted to make a good impression on Nick's mom after such a dismal start.

He turned onto a cul-de-sac and into a driveway. She noted the patrol car following them parked directly across the street. She couldn't think about that now. The stalker. The cops shadowing her. She had enough to be nervous about with meeting her future mother-in-law.

Callie examined the charming ranch house. An oasis of colorful flowers flooded the front beds and surrounded two oak trees on both sides of the yard. White wicker chairs graced the wraparound porch.

Nick opened her door. "You look great. You are great." He leaned down to kiss her.

"Don't," she warned. "The last thing I need is a messy mouth when I meet your mom."

He grinned, his lips grazing her cheek instead. "Then promise me I can mess with you later." He took her hand, interlaced his fingers with hers, and walked her to the front porch. The door opened immediately.

The petite woman standing there appeared nothing like Nick. She was blond with hazel eyes and an outdoor tan. Her eyes sparkled, full of energy and mischief. That part she definitely passed along to her son.

"Hey, Mom." Nick leaned down and pecked her cheek. He pulled Callie up a step. "This is Callie Chennault."

Callie smiled, drawing on Jessica's confidence in any social situation. "Hello, Mrs. La Chappelle. It's so nice to meet you."

"Please. Call me Maggie." She took Callie's hands in hers. "Go on in, Nick. Olivia's waiting in the kitchen. She's cooked enough to feed an army."

He raised an eyebrow. "And you'll be...?"

"Doing the girl talk thing over OJ or hot tea. Callie's choice. Now, scoot."

Nick shrugged. "Don't be mad if nothing's left." He walked into the house and closed the door behind him.

Maggie indicated they sit. Callie eased into a chair, her butterfly production in full swing.

"What would you like to drink?"

"Tea would be nice. Thank you." She watched as Mrs. La Chappelle poured hot water from a carafe into an elegant china cup. Callie opened a packet of Earl Grey and dipped the teabag into the cup. The motion soothed her somewhat.

"I would tell you I'm a fan but I've never seen your

show," Nick's mother said matter-of-factly as she poured herself a glass of juice. "However, my sister, Olivia, is mad for *Sumner Falls* and thinks you're the most talented actress on TV. She also said you were Pam's best friend during your teen years and that the two of you have remained close ever since. You definitely have Olivia's stamp of approval."

Maggie paused and sized her up. Callie found herself swallowing nervously, dunking her teabag like a maniac. She was afraid to speak. Afraid she'd say the wrong thing. She didn't realize how much she wanted this woman's approval until now.

"Nick is my only child." Maggie's voice softened as she began to speak. "There isn't anything I wouldn't do for him. We've always been close. My husband traveled quite a bit for work, and my boy and I found we enjoyed each other's company."

His mother took a sip of her orange juice then continued. "Nick has had a lot of professional success, both in sports and now his writing career. He's experienced very little of that personally, though. He thinks he's a rock and that he doesn't need anyone." Her level gaze caused Callie to pause dunking her teabag, in mid-air.

"It's hurt me to see how lonely he's been for so many years. You can imagine how surprised I was to come home after barely a week away, and he has a spring in his step and the humor back in his voice. His smile is reaching his eyes for the first time in a long time. I can see how happy he is."

Maggie leaned over and took Callie's hand. "If you've done all that for him in less than a week, then you have my blessing to hang around as long as you want." She frowned. "Just don't hurt him, Callie. If you aren't serious about having a relationship with him, tell him and move on. Let him go now before it hurts too much."

She squeezed Maggie's hand. "I'm not perfect but I will tell you this. I never knew I could admire a man as much as I do Nick. In a few short days, he's become my world. If anything, I'd be the one to fall apart if he left. I plan to be rocking next to him in the old folks' home seventy years from now, ma'am." She paused. "Looking for love was the last thing on my mind when I arrived in Aurora. It hit me clear out of the blue, like a shock of lightning. I know in my heart that Nick is the best thing that will ever happen to me. I'd be a fool to let him go."

Maggie's eyes filled with tears. She let out a long sigh and stood, her arms opening wide. "Then welcome to the family, Callie."

Chapter Twenty-Eight

TWO DAYS HAD PASSED since the note appeared on Nick's windshield. Except for meeting Nick's mom, Callie hadn't left Noble Oaks, even staying inside the house instead of taking her usual walks. She was beginning to feel boxed in. She closed the Eleanor Roosevelt biography in her lap. She'd been on the same page for twenty minutes now, but she couldn't concentrate on the words.

She glanced at Nick, sprawled on the floor, his back resting against the living room sofa. A frown creased his brow. His mouth was set in stone. Obviously, writing wasn't going very well.

"Dammit," he proclaimed, sliding the laptop onto the floor. He stood, stretching his arms, and then dropping them to his sides. "Absolutely nothing is coming to me. I have hit the proverbial brick wall."

He sat on the arm of the chair she sat in. His fingers began to massage her neck absently.

"Do you think I can help?" she asked. "I've actually brainstormed with our writers several times when they were doing long-range plotting for the show." She smiled as a few memories of those late night bull sessions emerged. "It was actually pretty fun."

"Fun?" He gave her a wry smile. "To me, writing is like having teeth extracted with no anesthesia. Or it's the most exhilarating roller coaster ride in the world. No in-between. Famine or feast."

She faced him. "No, seriously. Maybe I could help. You said you're beginning a new book. What happens first to get things rolling along?"

He shrugged. "I have no idea. I always start with my characters first. I have to see them in my mind's eye. I have to know their names. Then I start fiddling with their backstory. Why they're like they are. Then I create character profiles. What they like and dislike. How they would react in certain situations."

Nick stood and began to pace as he spoke. "Half the background stuff I do never sees the page, but it helps me know who they are and how they became that way."

"And then?"

He stopped pacing. "Once I have them nailed down, then I go for the story. I have a file of interesting crimes I clip from newspapers. I also scan several newspapers online and cut and paste story ideas into Word docs. Anything to jumpstart me."

"Why don't we look at some of those first?"

He looked horrified. "Before I have my characters? I haven't even settled on their names yet."

She smiled at him. "Indulge me. Pull up something for us to go over."

"I have never done it this way before," he grumbled. "This just doesn't seem right."

He sat on the sofa and reached for his laptop, his fingers flying over the keys as he called up the information she'd asked for. She took a seat next to him.

He sighed. "You know, I'm sorry if I sound anal. I've

actually read quite a few books on the writing process. Gone to conferences. There are lots of writers who come up with their storyline first. It's just never been the way I operate. I guess you're pulling me from my comfort zone."

Callie squeezed his bicep. "It's okay, Big Boy. We artists all have our little idiosyncrasies."

Nick clicked on a file. "Here are some I've squirreled away that seem pretty workable."

Callie began to read, using the scroll key to zip through the stories he had saved.

"Hmmm. This is interesting. A bar owner who killed off his obnoxious patrons one by one. I also like this one, the second-string quarterback who knocked off his competition so he could land the starting job."

"Let me think." She closed her eyes, trying to enter Nick's dark world of crime and death. She wondered if this were a wise move on her part, as she sensed her body tensing. No, she wouldn't let her real life problems consume her. She would simply process things as he did. Distance herself from the material. Think of it as a script.

Then she had the germ of an idea.

"Wait. What about this." She opened her eyes to find his midnight blue ones staring into hers. Callie got that tingle that only Nick could give her. She shrugged it off, trying to get down to business.

"What about a sociopath who's a cop?"

He nodded slowly. She could see his wheels beginning to turn as he spoke. "Maybe when he can't get the evidence he wants, he simply eliminates the suspect. A little like Dexter Morgan. Except not as adorable. That could work."

"He could have this really sympathetic D.A. as a love interest," she suggested.

269

Nick's eyes lit up. "Maybe his best friend—say it was his partner—was killed in the line of duty right in front of him. The guy winds up getting off on a technicality. That sticks in our man's craw. That could be his first murder. Bring his partner's killer to justice."

Excitement spread across his face. She thought a moment. "Was he born a sociopath? Or did he develop into one? Did society's rules and this killer getting off create something in him that made him fall off the legal path? Was it always in him? Or as a cop, does he think he's above the law?"

Nick's excitement was now visible. "My mind is racing. I've got to start getting this down." His fingers flew over the keyboard.

Callie smiled to herself. She had some ideas of her own. She went to the desk and pulled out pen and paper since she was too lazy to go upstairs for her iPad. She returned to sit next to Nick. She began plotting, her thoughts almost coming too fast to get everything down on paper.

A knock at the door interrupted their work. Essie stepped in, rolling a cart of sandwiches and soft drinks. A bouquet of fresh flowers accompanied the meal. Essie traded out the vase with one on the coffee table.

"Those flowers are beautifully arranged," Callie told her.

"Mr. Eric came through and helped Miz Callandra find a new gardener. He cut these and even arranged them himself." The cook smiled. "Miss Gretchen's gonna have her nose out of joint. She's been having fun doing up the flowers."

Nick hit save and slid his laptop under the sofa. He placed the plates and drinks on the table as they spoke. "I guess I need to move the rest of my stuff out of the caretaker's cottage."

Essie nodded. "Miz C knew you didn't have much since the place came furnished. She asked me to see if you could move your things over to the red room this afternoon so the new young man can get settled in. He said he don't have much either."

"My clothes are all pretty much here. I just have my books. Two filing cabinets of research and odds and ends. It won't take me long, Essie. I'll get to it right after lunch."

"You do that. I'm heading back to town now to the salon. You need anything else?"

"No. We're good. Thanks for lunch."

She left and Callie bit into her sandwich. "Yum. Essie makes the best chicken salad on the planet. I think I've tried every deli in New York, but none comes close to hers."

Nick smiled. "Are you still thinking about us living in New York part of the year?"

"I don't really know. I have decided I'm not returning to *Sumner Falls*."

"Really?" He took her free hand. "I know that had to be a hard decision."

"I need to call my agent and the show's producers. My heart isn't in it anymore. I think that would show on screen. I've always given my best and I couldn't let down the fans with a lukewarm performance."

"Have you thought about doing theater? If so, we definitely need to be in New York. Or films?" He frowned. "I guess we can always go to California."

Callie squeezed his hand. "That wasn't a good place for you. I don't want to bring up any unhappy memories."

Nick brought her hand to his lips and kissed each knuckle tenderly. "Baby, wherever we go, I'll make new memories with you."

Her heart melted at his romantic words. "I love you," she whispered.

His smile quickened her pulse. His eyes spoke of the unspoken promises between them. "I love you more."

Nick pulled her to him. His mouth came down on hers possessively, thoroughly ravaging every inch of her lips, her teeth, her tongue. She trembled at his every touch even as she drew closer still, never wanting it to end.

Finally, he pulled away, his eyes gleaming. They both panted as if they'd just sprinted hundreds of yards and were physically spent. Nick stroked her cheek, his fingers like a flickering flame, branding her as his.

"We might need to invest in some flame-retardant sheets," he quipped. "Else the house might burn down around us."

She realized she was shivering—with both emotion and desire. Nick wrapped an arm around her to steady her, drawing her next to him. He reached over and put her plate in their shared lap.

"How about a little lunch?"

He brought a quartered sandwich to her lips, which still trembled from his touch. Callie nibbled at it, trying to calm her racing heart. She chewed thoughtfully. It amazed her, the depth of her emotions for this man.

"I still like your first idea best," she told him. "An apartment in New York and a larger place here. Lots of films are shot in New York as it is. If some director really wants me—and who's to say an ex-TV star will even be marketable—I'll only take a project if it's shot in the city."

He took a huge chunk of the remainder of her sandwich. "No. Don't turn down anything you really want to do. We can always rent a place in California for the short term if need be. I can write anywhere. Have laptop, will travel."

Nick took another bite and her sandwich became history. "Just don't drag me to any fashion shows or Spago or—"

Callie silenced him with a kiss. "I'm not much into that." She reached to the other plate and they started in on his sandwich. "Besides, we'll have to actually find a place here. I'd love for Aurora to be our permanent base. If you like my apartment in New York, we can keep it. It's paid for and has plenty of space. I'm sure you'll have to put your own spin on a few rooms, though. I can't see you liking my girly comforter and throw pillows much."

Lacking a sandwich, he playfully nibbled on her fingers. "Something tells me that if it's your bedroom, I won't be focusing on the furnishings." He growled low. She lost it, laughing aloud.

Nick pulled her to her feet. "I love to hear you laugh." He cupped her face and kissed her softly. "I better go move a few things."

"I'll help you."

"No. Stay here. There's not much. Besides, it would probably drive the cops crazy, you going back and forth like that. Why don't you check out this red room and clear some space for me? I won't be long."

He kissed her again, more deeply this time. She clung to him, her blood singing, wanting more than just a kiss.

"Hey, Sparky. Don't make me go up in flames," he teased. "Once I move in? Maybe we need to test out the bed in the red room."

Her pulse zoomed up her personal Richter scale. "I'd... I'd like that."

"Are you sure?" His eyes searched hers. "I don't

want to push you if you aren't ready." He smiled, then teased, "Hey, I'm already a sure thing. You may not have the ring on your finger yet, but I'm yours for life."

She put her arms around his neck. "I'm very sure."

Callie couldn't believe she felt so loved that she was able to move past the assault, past the scars. Loving Nick —and him loving her in return—made her brave and strong.

She brushed a light kiss on his mouth and pulled away. "Go get moving. Then we can move on to better things. Like that novel we're collaborating on. I got down some wicked smart ideas before Essie brought lunch."

Nick cupped her buttocks and pulled her closer to him. "So, writing is what you have in mind for your future?"

She bit her lip. "That. And some other stuff. Hop to it, La Chappelle."

He released her and left the room. She went upstairs to the red guest room. It connected to her bedroom with the adjoining Jack and Jill bathroom in the middle. The walnut furniture fit well with the burgundy drapes and comforter. She supposed at one point the furnishings might have actually been red. Tradition died hard in the South, though. She checked and found all the drawers were empty. She moved a few knickknacks around on the dresser, clearing space for his laptop and personal accessories.

As she worked, the thought of starting on a writing project with Nick excited her. She'd never written professionally before, but she'd always had a flair for it back in school. She loved writing short stories and poetry. Or maybe Nick could write something with her in mind. He'd never done a screenplay before but with his talent and the Nick Van Sandt name recognition, it would be easier than he thought. She wondered who his agent was and if he or she focused strictly on publishing or had Hollywood connections.

Callie slid a chair and table over some to make room for his two filing cabinets. This room would be perfect to work in. It had a small sitting area with a desk nearby, and the light was good. Suddenly, a great plot thread hit her. She rushed back downstairs to get her thoughts onto paper.

She curled up on the sofa and began scribbling. She'd barely begun when her cell phone rang. She almost let it go to voice mail but then decided she better answer it. Beth had promised to call back when she had more time for them to talk about Nick. Glancing at her watch, she bet Beth had put down her son for his afternoon nap.

She pulled the cell from her pocket and answered it.

"Hello?"

Silence greeted her.

"Hello?" she repeated.

Nothing. The quiet spooked her. She realized she should've noticed the Caller ID before she answered but she had assumed it was Beth. She pulled the phone away from her ear. It was Waggoner calling. Maybe he was driving and had hit a dead zone.

"Hey, Waggoner. I can't hear you. I'm going to hang up. Try again. Call me back."

Callie started to end the call when an eerie moan rose in her ear. It was low. Gut wrenching. Fear gripped her, paralyzing her.

"Waggoner? Is that you?" she whispered.

Again, a noise. This time a gasp of pain. Adrenaline surged through her.

"Who is this?" she asked, her voice stronger.

"Callie?" a voice croaked. "Hang up."

"Detective Waggoner?" Her heart twisted at the anguish in his voice.

A muffled chuckle. "Too late to say goodbye, Jessica. He didn't crack until the end, though. I'll bet Nick will be the same way."

A dial tone buzzed in her ear. Callie dropped her cell, a scream building in her throat.

Instead, what came out was a soft wheeze. "Nick. Nick!"

Chapter Twenty-Nine

NICK NODDED to the cop in his squad car as he crossed the drive and came back in through the kitchen door. He tapped in the security code, as the system was armed at all times. Balancing two boxes he'd hurriedly crammed with several research books, he set them on the kitchen table.

He wondered if he should take the boxes upstairs and unload them. That way he could use them to make another trip. Then he froze. The hairs on the back of his neck stood at attention.

Something was wrong.

Instinctively, he knew Callie was in trouble. He raced up the back stairs, opening doors, calling to her, trying to figure out which one was the red room. She wasn't in any of them. He would have asked Miz C, but she was at her weekly hair appointment and Gretchen had gone with her. Essie had mentioned she was going back into town, so Nick assumed she would be picking up the pair soon.

He raced back down the stairs and heard a noise. He stopped, trying to track where it came from. It was faint, a soft keening, coming from where he and Callie spent the morning. He ran to the living room doors and threw them open.

He froze, not ready for the sight in front of him.

She lay curled in a fetal position, her face deathly white, drained of all color. She held a throw pillow close, her arms wrapped tightly about it, as her head bobbed back and forth in denial. Her lips moved as the odd sound came from them. It would haunt him forever.

"Callie?"

He approached her slowly, not wanting his movement to startle her. She stared straight ahead, unseeing, as he took a series of steps in her direction. He reached the sofa and knelt beside her. She looked worse up close. The phrase *'death warmed over'* flitted across his mind.

"Callie?" he asked again, not sure he would get a response.

But something connected deep inside her. Her eyes met his. The keening stopped. Her lips formed words but nothing came out. Nick gripped her icy hands in his. The contact seemed to break the logjam.

"Nick?"

"I'm here, baby."

"He's... gone."

He rubbed her hands, trying to restore some warmth. "Who's gone?" he asked gently.

Her head bobbed furiously as a torrent of words poured out. "We have to call Eric. We have to call Eric. Now. He has to know. I need Eric to know. Now." She jerked her hands away and clutched his shirt in desperation. "Now," she repeated, burying her face against his chest, her arms encircling him, holding on as if her life depended on him being her anchor.

"Okay, baby. Okay." He pulled his phone from his pocket and hit Eric's name.

"Hey, buddy." Nick tried to keep his tone light and casual, but Callie pulled the phone from him.

"Eric?" Her voice was barely above a whisper. "Come to Noble Oaks. Right away."

He watched her nod as he sat beside her. "Yes. It is." She drew a deep breath and expelled it. In a flat voice, she said, "Detective Waggoner is... dead."

She dropped the phone next to her and put her head in his lap. Nick was stunned by her revelation. Still, he didn't ask anything. He stroked her hair, hoping his gesture reassured her.

Less than five minutes later, he heard a police siren approaching, followed by car doors slamming outside. Callie sat up, wrapping her arms about her.

"Go let him in."

He reluctantly left her, knowing they were the only ones home. He hurried to the front door and opened it, punching in the code as Eric rushed in.

His cousin had a million questions in his eyes but Nick shrugged helplessly. "I don't know," he said softly. "I just don't know." He paused. "She's in the living room. She's in a bad way."

Eric laid a hand on his shoulder. "Give me a few minutes alone with her." He crossed the foyer and entered the living room, shutting the doors behind him.

Nick paced impatiently for over ten minutes before the doors opened again. Eric stepped into the foyer and closed them behind him.

"She seems okay but I'm sending Doc over to see her." Eric shook his head. "Lipstick Larry called her. She heard Waggoner dying over the phone, calling out to her. The fucker somehow got to him. Or at least he did a good enough job convincing Callie that Waggoner's dead."

Nick felt as if he were a balloon suddenly deflated.

All the life whooshed out of him. What must Callie feel like?

He started toward the door. Eric stopped him. "I'll start a search for Waggoner. He's not answering his phone. I checked on the way over. No one's seen him all day. If his cell's on, we'll be able to locate him. Wherever he is."

Eric's eyes betrayed his thoughts. "Keep her here, Nick. Keep her safe."

His cousin brought in two deputies that had been stationed outside. He situated one inside the front door and the other just outside the kitchen door with strict orders.

"Don't leave your post for any reason. I don't care if Jesus Himself appears for the Second Coming and invites you to Paradise for an eternal feast. You are not to move. Understand?"

Both men nodded and took their positions. Eric left to attend to business. Nick escorted him out and rearmed the alarm. He knew he had to see Callie.

As he made his way to the living room, he wondered how to comfort her.

She sat on the sofa, her knees drawn to her chest, her arms wrapped around them. Her forehead, which rested on her knees, but her head sprang up as he entered the room. He was surprised to see no tears. In fact, he witnessed no emotion at all. As he crossed the room, though, he did see a deadly calm on her face.

Nick sat next to her, unsure what to do or say. He draped an arm along the back of the sofa, not knowing if he should even touch her.

Callie's gaze met his. Determination began to set in. Her eyes focused. Her jaw locked.

"I will kill him myself," she said coldly, her voice void of any emotion. "I will kill this motherfucker."

Nick didn't doubt her for a moment. "Can you talk about it?"

She drew in a few long, deep breaths and he knew she'd reverted to her yoga training. "He tortured him, Nick. Waggoner was a tough, tough cop. I can't imagine what it took to break him—or what he might've told this creep." She shuddered. "I don't want to. But it's beyond personal now."

His hand found her neck and began massaging the tension from it. "What do you want us to do?"

She met his gaze. "Remember when you said you wanted to be the bait?" She paused. "I'm ready to draw him out now. Me. *I'm* the one he wants. *I'm* who he'll get."

His heart slammed against his ribcage in violent protest. "No way, Callie. Absolutely not."

She jerked away from him. "I have to do this. If not..." Her voice faded. She stared out the large bay window that overlooked the front lawn.

"If not, what?" he demanded.

She turned back to him. "You'll be next. And he'll make it even worse. Because somehow he knows how much I love you."

His stomach clenched in fear. For Callie. For himself. He'd just found this amazing woman. He couldn't risk losing her. He would do whatever it took to protect her. Though he'd racked his brain for the past two days, trying to figure out a plan himself, nothing had materialized.

Nick took Callie's hands in his, his own determination to end this nightmare equal to hers.

"What do you have in mind?"

Chapter Thirty

HE WAS SO *proud of himself. He believed this was his best work yet. He'd filmed the entire incident on his cell.*

It had been so easy. Just like every time before, no one ever suspected him. He appeared so average. So trustworthy. Detective Waggoner hadn't seen what hit him.

He hated to brag, but to do what he had done, especially to a seasoned NYPD detective? It made him float as if on air. Of course, the Rohypnol helped accomplish part of the plan. He had to give credit where it was due. Roofies ruled his blueprint of pain.

Naturally, he'd shared with Paul—he guessed they were close enough that he could use the man's first name—who he was once he came to his full senses. Too bad Paul had hollered himself hoarse, screaming obscenities in that lovely Brooklyn (or was it a Bronx?) accent. He didn't have much of a voice when the fun really began.

Fortunately, he'd captured every lovely moment. He just loved the ease of using his iPhone. And after downloading the video to his laptop, with a few minor shifts through the magic of editing, he'd had a nice little condensed snippet to play for Jessica. Oh, she'd sounded be-

yond frightened. He'd gotten under her skin. Figuratively. Not literally, of course.

That fun was yet to come.

He was ready now. Ready to take on his most important work. It would be his crowning achievement. He'd learned a lot about a person's threshold of pain while he'd diligently practiced.

All that practice would now make for the perfect kill.

No—kills. He couldn't forget about Nick.

BOTH CALLIE and Nick met her aunt, Essie, and Gretchen as they arrived home from their visit to Aurora's only beauty salon.

"What do you think of my new cut?" Gretchen twirled in front of them, her hand primping her hair. "It cost a third of what I would pay in New York. And look at this shade of pink." She held out a hand for Callie's inspection as she peered over her shoulder. "Did she call this shell pink, Miz C?"

Essie wheeled Callandra Chennault in. Her aunt immediately asked, "What's wrong?"

Gretchen stopped admiring her new manicure. She glanced around, spying the patrolman standing inside the front door.

"Something's happened." Callie tried to keep the tightness from her voice. "He's... Eric will be here soon."

Gretchen took her hand. "Are you okay, Callie? Is it Lipstick Larry? Has he sent another note?"

Nick spoke up. "We're not sure yet. Eric will be getting back to us really soon. Why don't we go sit in the kitchen and see if Essie can rustle us up something sweet?"

She fought the urge to blurt out what she'd heard to Gretchen. After all, it was her friend's uncle. Maybe Eric would prove her wrong. Maybe this maniac had only toyed with her. Made her believe that Detective Waggoner was dead.

In her heart, Callie knew that wasn't the case. She tried to keep the guilt at bay. She had gotten Paul Waggoner involved in this case—and now he was dead. How on earth would Gretchen handle this horrible truth?

The shrill ring of the phone interrupted her thoughts.

"I'll get it." She walked to the table by the front stairs and lifted the receiver, trying not to show any hesitancy in case it was him again.

"Noble Oaks."

"Cal? It's Eric. I'm on my way over."

"Is it... what we thought?"

"Yeah. We pinged Waggoner's cell and found him inside that abandoned gas station out on Route Thirty."

She knew the answer but asked anyway. "Was it bad, Eric? Did he suffer?"

Her friend's silence spoke volumes. Finally, he said, "Try not to think about it, Cal. You don't want those images in your head. That's exactly what this bastard wants." He paused. "Is Gretchen there? If she is, don't say anything about Paul until I get there. I'd like to break it to her in person. She seemed to really think highly of him and his wife. They really stood by her after her divorce from that jerk, Phil."

"All right. Why don't you come around to the back? We'll be in the kitchen."

Callie turned. Everyone had already left the foyer. She counted on all her acting skills now. She didn't want to cry. She certainly didn't want to reveal anything to Gretchen.

Instead, she let the Jessica part of her take over. The part that could keep a cool head in a hot situation. The part that could let anger burn inside while she appeared composed and collected to anyone observing her.

She entered the kitchen. Essie had opened Tupperware containers of oatmeal raisin and chocolate macadamia nut cookies. Nick was pouring iced tea into tall glasses. She shared a knowing look with Aunt C, who probably knew something bad was afoot but was smart enough to wait for Eric and not press the matter further.

They didn't wait long. Aurora's sheriff arrived within ten minutes of his call. Callie spotted him park his car and stride across the yard to the back door.

Gretchen jumped up. "I'll let him in." She punched in the code and opened the door and spoke to Eric a moment before murmuring, "All right." She stepped outside and closed the door behind her.

Callandra motioned for Essie to sit and join them. "What is this about, Callie?"

She maintained her air of calm, though her insides churned. "Lipstick Larry phoned my cell while you were out. He had Detective Waggoner with him." She paused. "Paul is dead, Aunt C. Eric is telling Gretchen now."

Callandra took her hand. "Are you all right, dear?"

She nodded grimly. "I'm holding it together."

They all turned to look out the window. Gretchen sobbed, holding onto Eric with whitened knuckles.

Callandra glanced at Nick. "Have you thought about eloping? And staying away for a very long time?"

Nick sighed heavily. "Don't think I haven't considered it, Miz C. No 'around the world in eighty days', either. More like five thousand and eighty. Moving to Paris or Rome or Timbuktu permanently. At this point, I'd be willing to enter the witness protection program."

He shrugged. "But Callie didn't like any of the names the marshals picked out for her. Myrtle. Eloise. Maybelle. Can't say I blame her." He shook his head. "No, seriously. We will definitely hang around to see this S.O.B.'s hide nailed to the wall."

He took Callie's hand in his. "We will see this creep brought down. Else we'll be looking over our shoulders the rest of our lives."

The door opened. Eric and a shaken Gretchen, her face stained with tears, entered. Callie immediately went to her friend and enveloped her in a hug.

"I'm so sorry, Gretch. I feel it's my fault since he came down here to help me."

Gretchen pulled away, shaking her head. "Don't ever say that, Callie. Uncle Paul loved you like his own kid. He would've done anything to see you safe." Her voice broke. "If you'll excuse me. I need to go call my aunt and see about making the arrangements to take Uncle Paul back to New York."

"Of course, dear." After Gretchen left the room, Callandra turned to Eric. "Please. Sit," she commanded. "Tell us what you can."

He took a chair at the table and absently reached for a cookie. "You don't need to hear details." He looked at Callie. "It was similar to what was done to the girls in New York, the ones who resembled you. Although the coroner believes Paul died early this morning. He's doing the autopsy now. We'll know more after that."

Eric frowned as he chewed. "Could it have been a recording you heard, Cal? A killer of this caliber would think nothing of recording his crimes and playing them back multiple times for his pleasure."

She thought a moment. "It's possible. I heard

Paul in pain. He called my name and told me to hang up. Then... *he*... came back on the phone. It very well could have been recorded previously. Or somehow edited and spliced together." She shuddered. "I cannot comprehend the diabolical cruelty, though."

Eric stood. "I have a lot to do. I've already alerted NYPD. The FBI is totally in charge at this point. They had one field agent on the case, but we're about to be overrun by them. Things will pretty much be out of my hands at that point."

"Thanks for everything you've done, Eric."

He hesitated. "I don't want you to think I'm bailing on you, Cal." He swallowed. "However, the FBI does things its way. I may be cut out of the loop as far as details of the investigation go. I didn't want you to think I was letting you down in any way."

She stood and gave him a hug. "I would never think that. Besides, I don't know how much I really want to be apprised of. At any rate, I have Nick to watch over me."

Eric laughed. "That's like letting the wolf in to guard the sheep, Cal." He kissed her cheek. "Thanks for understanding my position—or lack of it now. Tell Gretchen I'll call later, as soon as I can. I've got to get over to the autopsy."

"Will do." She let him out and reset the alarm.

"I am feeling drained," she declared. "I think I'll go lie down for a while." She looked at Essie. "I'm not really hungry for dinner. If I want something later, I'll just make a sandwich."

"I'll walk you upstairs." Nick pushed his chair from the table and let her lead them up the back staircase to her room without a word.

He opened the door and did his usual once-over before allowing her inside. She sat on the bed, her hands absently twisting.

Nick joined her. "Are you going to be okay? I know you're made of strong stuff to withstand everything you've been through up till now, but Waggoner's death is a pretty severe blow."

Callie knew in that moment what she needed. She was ready. She wanted to lose herself and find salvation the only way she knew how.

She looked at him with clear eyes, knowing her face held a determined expression.

"Make love to me, Nick. Take me away from all this —if only for a little while."

Chapter Thirty-Two

CALLIE'S WORDS took Nick aback.

"Are you sure?" Even as he asked, he knew the answer. Resolve reflected in the depths of her darkened green eyes, burning into his.

He framed her face with his hands. Her fingers wrapped tightly around his wrists.

"I want to live, Nick. I don't want to be afraid anymore. I don't want him to force me to hide from my own shadow."

Her hold tightened. "I can be weak and give in to terror and fear. Or I can be strong and meet him head on." She smiled. "But I need you by my side, no matter what happens."

She gazed into his eyes, hers shining with love and a heat that scalded him. "You are my other half, Nick. You are my soulmate. I can do anything... if you're with me. I want to show you how much I love you. I need to cement that connection between us. I need to draw from your strength. Now."

He didn't miss a beat. The bond he already felt with her was stronger than anything he'd experienced. He was ready to move their relationship to the next level.

Despite the yearning inside him for that physical consummation, he knew he needed to take it slowly. Callie's words might say one thing but he suspected a little fear of men still lingered inside her.

Nick drew her close to him. He softly brushed his lips against hers. Her hands slid up his arms and locked around the back of his neck. He continued his kisses, his thumbs gliding back and forth across her cheekbones. The heady scent of honeysuckle on her skin heightened every breath he took as he drank her in. He inhaled the richness, his hands sliding to her throat. One hand slipped around the nape of her neck, while the other moved lower.

He sensed the rightness of the moment. He slipped his tongue inside her mouth. Her moan assured him he wasn't rushing her. He had explored her mouth thoroughly before, but this time it sent his pulse racing out of control.

And not just his pulse.

He sensed her confidence growing with each kiss. She began to answer the stroke of his tongue with her own. A low whimper in the back of her throat made him smile. As her body relaxed, Nick understood without words that she'd told him she knew she would always be safe in his hands.

Their kisses became deeper, brandishing a fire unbeknownst to him. With each one, they became longer, more possessive, more demanding than anything that came before it. He lost all track of time. Only now, with Callie, did this moment exist. No past. No tomorrow. Only the constant assault of his mouth on hers, taking, giving, sharing, loving.

Nick tore his lips from hers, burying them against the slender column of her throat. If someone lit a match in the room, he'd go up in an instant and take her with him. He'd never known such heat, such need, such passion. He leaned her back onto the bed, nibbling his way along her jaw as one hand worked at the buttons on her blouse.

He opened it and pushed it aside. He sensed the slight tension now running through her, a slender thread that he was determined to unravel. His mouth moved back to hers, demanding her attention as his hands kneaded her shoulders. He would make her forget her attacker. Forget the scars left behind from the assault. He wanted her here with him, in this moment, this magic moment of fire and heat and desire.

His hands slowly dropped to her breasts, where he continued his touch. His heady invasion of her mouth never let up. He wanted her breathless, totally focused on their lovemaking. Her nails dug into his clothed back. He realized he needed her flesh touching his. He leaned up and raised the polo shirt over his head, tossing it aside.

* * *

Callie's eyes were closed, enjoying every ripple of emotion running through her. Nick's mouth left her suddenly. Before she could protest, he was next to her, his bare chest hot against her, causing her to throb out of control.

He murmured against her mouth, "This has got to go," as he pulled down her bra straps. His lips trailed over her bare shoulder, sending thrills of pleasure shooting through her. He unhooked the bra and slipped it from under her. It went sailing across the room.

Skin met skin, sending her heartbeat racing wildly. She knew even with the curtains drawn in the late afternoon light, he would be able to see the start of the scars.

Suddenly... it didn't matter. It never would again.

Nick entwined his fingers with hers, pushing them up onto the pillow by her face. His eyes held a look of love and passion that warmed her to her core.

"I love you," he whispered. Then he grinned. "And I'm just getting warmed up."

He moved to her breast and began teasing her nipple with his tongue. She gasped in pleasure. Her hips rose inadvertently against him.

He lifted his head and smiled that heartbreaking smile. "Oh, I'll get there, honey. It's just going to take some time. I want us to enjoy every second of this."

Nick lingered over first one breast and then the other as she writhed urgently under him. Everything about this man revved her engine—every look, every scent, every hard plane of muscle that danced under her fingertips.

And the best was yet to come.

He released her hands and slid his mouth down to her belly as he unzipped her khaki capris. She felt him slide the espadrilles from her feet and then gently tug the capris and her thong off. He quickly shed his jeans and boxers. His hands then moved back up her calves.

Callie watched as Nick's eyes fell over her naked body. They paused a moment along her right side, trailing along where the scars descended from under her breastbone down to her upper thigh. Her breathing stopped a moment as he studied her.

She didn't see pity. Or revulsion. That's what she'd most feared. Instead, she witnessed an overwhelming love shining in his eyes. And she felt it in every feather-soft kiss he planted along the row of blemished skin. His gentleness, his concern, moved her to tears.

His kisses continued up her body until they reached

her chin. He frowned at her, his eyes going wide.

"Why the tears? Did I hurt you?"

She framed his tanned face in her hands. "No. I'm just so happy. Don't you know women cry when we're deliriously happy?"

He visibly relaxed. His hand stroked her cheek. "I thought they screamed at the top of their lungs. Or laughed themselves silly."

"Sometimes." She couldn't help but smile at him.

"Did I tell you I love you, Callie Chennault? That I love every golden hair on your head. Every sarcastic remark that comes out of that lush mouth. Every inch of this heavenly body which, by the way, I can't wait to fit closer to mine."

"Even my scars?"

He kissed her softly. "Especially your scars. Because they're a part of you, sweetheart. I love your body and your sense of humor and how smart you are, not just with a snappy comeback at my expense, you know. I'm sorry you suffered the way you have but in a round-about way, these scars brought you home. To me. And a lifetime of tomorrows."

He kissed her again, hard and swift, causing her to pulse with need. "I'm head over heels for you, babe." He pulled her close. "And I'm never letting you go."

Callie's blood sang as it rushed through her veins. This meant everything to her. "You couldn't chase me away, La Chappelle. Even if you tried. I'm like that insufferable piece of gum that sticks to your shoe and refuses to come off."

Nick slid a finger into her. She gasped at the intimate touch.

"I think I've got a lock on my target," he whispered. He stroked her slowly, then quickly, then slowly again, as their passion heated. She whimpered and twisted beneath his hand, climaxing with a violent shudder that left her weak as a kitten. Then he held her tightly and rolled so that she was atop him.

He smiled up lazily at her as he lightly rested his hands on her hips. "You're in charge, Beautiful. Do with me as you wish."

Callie's throat tightened. She realized Nick had purposefully put her in the position to control their pace. He wanted her to have confidence in what they were doing. Together. She would be the one at the helm. An overwhelming sense of love and possessiveness flooded her.

She returned his smile. "Then you better hold on. You're in for the ride of your life, Baseball Boy."

Callie made love to him with an abandon she'd never experienced. She'd never been freer, more open, more a partner to a man than in this single time of making love. And when she came again, with him inside her, she finally understood the beauty of what that meant. She'd experienced little tingles in the past. Having sex made her feel really good at times, like a hard workout brought a great physical rush.

But she'd never had the explosions of wow-ness that she'd heard other women talk about.

With Nick, everything changed. When the waves of pleasure hit, she went with them, clinging to him, treasuring this precious connection they'd made. After, spent beyond words, she lay curled in the shelter of his protective arms, almost too tired to think.

No one would come between her and this man. She would fight to the death to guard Nick from the killer's touch of evil. She would be ready for him.

Callie knew when their inevitable confrontation ended, only one of them would remain standing.

And alive.

Chapter Thirty-Three

CALLIE AWOKE FEELING... satisfied. Yes, that was the right word. Immensely content. Almost smug, in fact, as she watched the man sleeping next to her.

Any woman in America would recognize that Nick La Chappelle was a twenty on a one-to-ten scale. He oozed sex appeal—even asleep. The thick, dark hair that curled slightly at his nape, the high cheekbones and sensual mouth, and the muscular chest her hand now rested on were only the start. Nick was the whole package. Physical perfection, as well as intelligence, and he possessed the most attractive feature a man could—a sense of humor.

She snuggled closer to him, her head resting on his shoulder. Even asleep, he pulled her closer, a small smile appearing at the corner of his mouth.

They'd made love three times since yesterday afternoon, each more fulfilling than the last. Callie should be bone tired but she could've run the New York Marathon in record time, she suspected—and this from a girl who hated running with a passion. This athlete-turned-author had turned her life upside down in little more than a week.

She wouldn't trade anything for him.

An intense possessiveness crept over her. She had never been the jealous type in the past, yet she knew from her own experience how someone in the public eye attracted massive attention from the opposite sex. She could handle fans flirting with Nick—as long as none of them took it beyond flirtation. If they did, she realized she would be ready to sweep in like an avenging angel.

Why such an enormous change?

She supposed love did that to people. She—who had never been in love and never gone looking for it—never suspected it would find her here in Aurora. Now she had given her heart to another. With joy.

It felt good. It felt right. It felt amazing.

She inhaled deeply, getting immense pleasure from Nick's musky scent. She couldn't get over the fact that this drop-dead, gorgeous, hot-bodied hunk had proclaimed an old-fashioned commitment to her. Despite all the trouble she was in and all the baggage that came with being associated with someone famous, he'd signed up for the long haul.

Callie sighed in utter contentment.

His hand suddenly brushed a lock of hair from her cheek. She looked up to find him smiling at her.

"Sleep well?"

"Yes." Her insides quivered. Just being near him had her feeling as if she were a bowl of Jell-O, all boneless and wobbly.

Nick kissed her leisurely, thoroughly, bringing her pulse close to heart attack status. Every touch brought new thrills. The best thing was they would have a lifetime together to explore them.

"Hmm," he said. "You didn't even leap out of bed to dive for your toothbrush."

She jerked, realizing that he was exactly right. In

every previous relationship, she was always conscious about every small detail. Now, only thoughts of Nick filled her mind.

She played with the hairs on his chest, smoothing them as she spoke. "I guess you've turned my head enough so that I didn't have time to think about it."

His soulful eyes gaze pinned hers. "It just took a good Southern boy knowing how to treat you. That's all."

But his eyes spoke the unspoken—that they had a connection deeper than anything either had encountered before.

"Hey, you need to get up and do your exercises," he reminded her. His eyes swept over her playfully. "I can't have you getting lazy and out of shape on me."

He kissed her again and she luxuriated in his taste and touch. "I don't know if I'll ever want to get out of bed again," she admitted.

Nick groaned. "Don't tempt me." He slipped from the bed. "I'll go check on Gretchen. I doubt she'll have time to put you through your paces this morning. She's probably leaving soon for New York." He pulled on his jeans as he spoke.

The thought saddened her, the whole mess of worms opened again in her mind. "Okay. I'll run through what Gretchen calls my basic routine and then shower. I'll see you in a little while."

Callie walked into the bathroom and closed the door behind her. Her eyes fell on her image in the mirror. She studied herself intently.

Nothing physically had changed. The ugly scars were still there, evident in their shock of red running along her side. It was her attitude toward them had magically changed. She no longer thought of herself as ruined. Embarrassed to be seen by a man. Nick had made it apparent last night that she turned him on, scars or no scars. Confidence shot through her, like an adrenaline high. She finally liked herself again—and she really liked that Nick found her attractive.

She did her abbreviated morning yoga routine and quick stretches that Gretchen swore by before she showered and dressed. She figured after her extracurricular workout with Nick last night that she'd gotten plenty of exercise.

As she approached the kitchen, she heard voices. She pushed open the door to find a full house—Essie bustling around the stove, flipping pancakes and turning bacon, while Aunt C praised a top draft pick that had just signed with the Saints. Eric and Gretchen sat next to each other at one end of the table. Nick must have showered, too, since his hair still appeared damp. He was dressed in neatly pressed slacks and a dark blue polo shirt that matched his eyes.

"Callie, love. Come in," her aunt said when she noticed her hovering in the doorway. "Essie, more pancakes, please, and a cup of hot tea for Callie."

She sat and her eyes immediately went to Gretchen.

Her friend said, "Eric's arranged everything. I'm on the 10:10 flight direct to New York. He... well, he... Uncle Paul... will be on the same flight. Everything's taken care of at home. Eric's been simply amazing."

Callie placed a hand over Gretchen's. "When is the funeral?"

Gretchen took a deep breath. "Day after tomorrow. My aunt and I still have a lot of people to contact. The department wants to honor him properly since he died in the line of duty."

"I'm so sorry I can't be there with you."

Gretchen shook her head. "Don't worry about that.

Besides, I'll be back within the next two weeks." She glanced at Eric.

Callie watched something pass between them. She looked from Eric to Gretchen, a question on her lips but Eric answered it before she could put her thoughts into words.

"We might as well tell you now. Gretchen's bringing all her things back down here when she returns." He glanced around the table. "It's a permanent move. And I'm hoping something more permanent will come out of it." He took Gretchen's hand and smiled.

Callie glanced at her aunt and had to hide a smile. Aunt C sat in her wheelchair beaming as if she'd orchestrated the entire match.

They talked amiably while breakfasting, Callandra insisting that Gretchen return to stay at Noble Oaks for as long as she wished. Then Eric checked his watch.

"We need to shove off. It's getting late what with traffic and all." He stood. "Now Miz C, Callie, the FBI will be here at ten to meet with you and explain how they'll be running the investigation. Until they arrive, I still have my men on duty out front and behind the house. I'll be back as soon as Gretchen gets off."

Eric gave her a pointed look. "Cal, it goes without saying, but you don't go anywhere. Period."

"How about as far as the garden? Please? I need a little fresh air. I'm tired of being cooped up indoors."

Eric glanced at Nick, who promised his cousin, "I'll be no more than a stone's throw away. Guaranteed."

"Okay. I'll get the car. Gretchen?"

"I left my purse upstairs. I'll run get it. Callie?" Gretchen motioned for Callie to accompany her.

They left the kitchen. She took Gretchen's hand.

"I know this is a rough time for you, but I'm thrilled that you've decided to stay in Aurora. I couldn't be happier how things are working out between you and Eric. He's a doll. I know given time, he'll make you happy."

"Eric has been wonderful to me, both before and after Uncle Paul's death." Her friend smiled. "I believe we truly have a future together. I have to note, though, that you have a rather rosy glow about you today."

Callie couldn't fight the blush that sprang to her cheeks. "Let's just say that Nick and I are well suited. In every way."

"Will you guys stay here, too?"

"Things are so new for us. We haven't made any long-range plans. I feel certain, though, that we'll split time between here and New York."

"I hate leaving in the middle of your therapy. I've never abandoned a patient before."

"Come on, Gretchen. I'm doing so well physically. I can keep up my usual routines while you're gone but I feel stronger every day I'm here. I don't think I'll need you to play nursemaid anymore."

Gretchen's eyes gleamed. "I'm sure Nick will help in providing you a challenging workout if you need it."

Callie laughed. "Oh, that man will definitely keep me in shape."

Gretchen grabbed her purse and soon they were saying their goodbyes. A little prickle of sadness hit her as the car drove off. She waved, a smile on her face despite the awful circumstances of their parting.

"Need a little quiet time?" Nick draped an arm about her shoulders.

"Yeah. A little sunshine and a bench would be nice."

"I know just the place. It's one of my favorite spots in Miz C's garden."

They walked around to the back of the house and down a cobbled path into the lush greenery of the back-yard garden. She froze on the path when she spied a stranger bent over, pulling some weeds from the base of a rosebush.

"It's okay. He belongs here. He's the new gardener Essie told us about."

Nick tugged on her. Her legs went rubbery as they moved toward the man. He stood and took a handkerchief out to wipe his forehead. He turned as they approached.

A big smile broke out on his face. "Hi, Nick! Hi, Jessica! I'm Petey." He thrust out a gloved hand, grinning from ear to ear.

Callie recognized the signs of Down's syndrome in the gentle giant. She relaxed and returned his smile as she reached for his hand.

"Silly, silly," Petey said. He pulled off the gardening glove. "Don't wanna get you dirty. I'm Petey. Pleased to meet ya. I'm helping Miz C. She's really nice, you know."

"I sure do," she said. "She's my aunt. Are you going to work in her gardens, Petey?"

"Yep. Yep." He nodded several times. "I know how to mow and edge and water. I take care of things. Mama says I'm good at taking care of things. Especially flowers. I'm good with flowers. I love flowers, especially yellow. Yellow is my favorite, favorite color."

"Petey has a green thumb," Nick added. "He learns really fast. He's helped me a few times before with planting and fertilizing."

"What do you like to do besides work in the garden, Petey?" she asked.

"I like to eat ice cream and feed the ducks and I like to watch Jessica. Jessica's my favorite and favorite of all." He smiled shyly at her. "You're pretty. But you look different than on TV. Jessica has really red lips and fluffy hair. That's a ponytail. Jessica doesn't wear ponytails."

"Remember how I told you that this is really Callie? She just make believes she's Jessica on TV."

"Uh-huh," Petey agreed. "I make believe sometimes, don't I, Nick?"

"You sure do. Hey, we're going to sit here while you do the things on your list. Can you think of what you're supposed to do today?"

"I already made my new bed. And I cleaned my bowl. I eat Frosted Flakes every morning. Mama says I have to do that every day before I can go help Miz C. But now I gotta weed these beds and then I get to mow the front yard. Then I can go home and eat lunch with Mama and watch Jessica."

He beamed at Callie. "Mama said you can't be on the show because you came to visit Miz C. She saves shows of you on the DVR so I can watch them all the time. I don't like it when you're not on. I like watching when you come on the TV." He thought a minute. "Then Mama rides me back here. I get to come back and make the flowers pretty and sleep in my new bed cuz I'm a big boy. I'm learning to be 'sponsible."

"Well, you're doing a great job, Petey," she told him. "The flowers you arranged for inside the house are so pretty."

Nick chimed in. "We'd like to sit here and soak up some sun, Petey. Why don't you go ahead and mow the front yard now so that we can have a little peace and quiet? You can finish the weeding after you mow."

"Okay, Nick." He loped off.

After he'd gone, Nick said, "I met him in town once at The Sweet Shoppe. He's Joe Bob Borgan's boy. He is passionate about butter pecan ice cream and Jessica. The thing is, Petey really understands flowers. He's been living at home with his parents until now. They're getting on in age, though. I guess maybe they're trying to help him become a little more independent. The situation working here and having the cottage to go to is perfect."

"I'm glad he's here."

"I'm glad we've got the garden to ourselves." Nick led her to a bench for two and they sat. Immediately, the sweet smell of roses enveloped them.

Callie lost track of time as they basked in the sun in silence, happy in each other's company. She guessed Nick was plotting out happenings in his new book.

She, on the other hand, focused on ways to draw out Lipstick Larry.

Chapter Thirty-Four

SHE DIDN'T like Special Agent in Charge Phillips. Not even a little.

Callie's eyes roamed the room, taking in how Aunt C's gracious living room furniture had been pushed aside for all kinds of electronic equipment—listening devices, computers with screens, hard drives and printers, and card tables set up with area maps that beeped when touched.

The half-dozen field agents populating the room seemed to have as little personality as Agent Phillips. No, *Special Agent in Charge* Phillips. He kept saying it that way so she assumed it was a big deal for a federal agent to carry around that particular title.

Still, he put her on edge. She thought his incessant monologue might cause her to snap any minute now.

Callie stood. Agent Phillips droned on. She coughed gently. Agent Phillips droned on. She finally had enough. She cleared her throat. Loudly.

Agent Phillips stopped, peeved at the interruption.

'Have you ever thought to ask Nick or me about any of this, Special Agent in Charge Phillips?" Her foot tapped impatiently as she spoke. 'It seems to me we might be able to clue you in on a few firsthand details about this creep."

Phillips frowned at her. "I've read all your previous statements and those of Mr. La Chappelle, Ms. Chennault. As a civilian, I'd think you'd want to leave things to the experts. I have seventeen years at the bureau, nine of those as a SAC. I wasn't aware that in trying to keep you and Mr. La Chappelle alive, I would need to ask your permission regarding anything. If that's how NYPD ran things, no wonder—"

"Don't even say it," she warned, her voice low and threatening. "Paul Waggoner ran an impeccable investigation and you will not dishonor his memory in any way."

He shrugged. "As I was saying," and his eyes cut away from hers, though his words implied that she had rudely interrupted him. "Our UNSUB—Unknown Subject—Lipstick Larry—has to be in the immediate area. We've set twenty-four hour patrols at seven points along this sizeable property, including three sides of the lake. Your aunt and housekeeper are currently being escorted off the estate for their protection—"

"Wait a minute." This time Nick interrupted. "You can't tell me Miz C agreed to this."

"Whether she did or not is not up for discussion. She is vacating the premises for her safety." Phillips focused his glare on her. "And no, we did not ask. The federal government reserves the right to tell its citizens what is in their best interests in times of duress, such as this."

The French doors crashed open at that moment. In rolled Callandra Chennault. Her color was high. She seemed like one of God's avenging angels, minus a sword in hand. The old woman wheeled right up to Special Agent in Charge Phillips.

"I *will* say goodbye to my great-niece. Whether you

like it or not, young man." Her eyes narrowed as she studied him. "You may have torn me from my home, but you will *not* prevent me from having a word with Callie before I go."

Phillips opened his mouth and then thought better of it. He closed his jaw tightly, holding his thoughts to himself. Still, Callie read the disapproval on his face.

She went and knelt by the wheelchair. "I hope this won't be for long, Aunt C. I'm sorry they're forcing you and Essie from Noble Oaks."

Callandra frowned at everyone in the room in general. Conversation ceased. The lone sound came from the printer spitting out some document.

"It won't be for long, dear," her aunt said quietly. "I'll do anything in my power to see you safe. If it means spending a few nights somewhere else, so be it."

Callandra took in the surrounding audience of agents. This time her voice carried for all to hear. "I expect I won't find one stick of furniture out of place when this is done. Not one iota lost, gone, or misused, else I'll sue the pants off Uncle Sam." She glared especially hard at Agent Phillips. "You better get this son of a bitch, Mr. Special Agent in Charge. This is my Callie we're talking about. I hold *you* responsible for protecting every hair on her head."

Essie crossed the room to retrieve control of the wheelchair and its rider. Callandra took Callie's hands in hers. "You have Nick. That's what counts. I trust him much more than these G-men."

Callie kissed her aunt's cheek. "I'll call you tonight. Where are you staying?"

Callandra snorted. "I don't know. *He* refused to tell me much of anything." With a raised chin and a final look of disapproval thrown Agent Phillips' way, she motioned Essie to leave the room.

After she left, Phillips explained, "They're being taken to a safe house. I'm afraid you can't be in contact with one another." He raised a hand to cut off her protest. "It's really for the best. Mrs. Chennault will have a doctor on hand since she seems to be a bit delicate at the moment. You wouldn't want her endangered in any way, I'm sure."

The FBI agent had played the only card that Callie couldn't trump. Her aunt's fragile health and the knowledge that the stalker might get to Aunt C or Essie, as he had Paul Waggoner, kept her from further protests.

"Waggoner's superiors mentioned using a decoy that resembled Mr. La Chappelle to draw out the UNSUB. We have someone flying in from the Atlanta office that is a good physical match to him. I also have a field agent in Dallas that bears a resemblance to you, Ms. Chennault. Both agents will be here by mid-afternoon, though they won't come directly to this location at first. We don't want to tip our hand.

"I would like to ask that the two of you work with them on your mannerisms. We can dress them in your similar fashion—and from a distance they may be mistaken for you—but our boy will be familiar enough with your body language to know they're imposters. Would you both be willing to help us?"

Callie glanced at Nick. He shrugged. She knew they really didn't have any choice in the matter.

"Bring them on. I've been through enough acting classes to put them through their paces. By the time I'm finished, the stalker won't be able to tell a difference," she promised.

* * *

He grinned at her confident words. Being a tech geek finally paid off. Cell-Finity Bug to the rescue! He'd been able to hack both of their cell phones more easily than their computers. Once he called the infected phones, they didn't ring—but it secretly turned on the phone's microphone. The beauty of the process meant that the phone's screen didn't display his call to it. It didn't even turn up in the call log. He'd even broken into their text messaging systems and had access to everything there. If the public only knew how many eavesdroppers had discovered this cell phone spy technology readily available on the Internet, there'd be mass riots.

Fortunately, the two lovebirds were typical smart phone owners and kept their phones near them at all times. He could hear any conversation from fifteen feet away—and they'd given him an earful.

It did surprise him that Jessica waited to have sex with the ballplayer until yesterday. He had assumed they were banging away somewhere else in the house or in the cottage out back since when he'd seen them together, they'd been as entangled as a stripper around a pole. But it was obvious what he'd listened to was a first-time encounter. With others that followed.

He wasn't sure how that made him feel. Thoughts of sex usually combined in his mind with violence.

Memories from his childhood flashed quickly in his mind. The parade of men. The tangled sheets. The scent of sex that lingered in the air. His mother's cries, which he thought were part of real distress in the beginning. Later, he learned that was not always the case.

He spied on her, too. When he was little, he'd slip into the room and hide behind an old swivel chair, turning it just so for a better glimpse of the action. What unfolded fascinated—yet repulsed him—at the same time. Once when he got caught by a john and she'd learned to lock the *door, he'd swiped the super's tools and drilled a small hole in the wall between her bedroom and the front room where he slept on a foldout couch. He hid it behind a cheap, framed print of Clark Gable and Vivien Leigh that she'd found at some garage sale.*

He'd watched. And he'd learned.

The images never left him.

He realized women used sex as leverage, just as they used their looks. As his mother's beauty faded over the years, so had the level of her clientele. Not to mention the money that came in. The way they lived continued to spiral downward until they hit rock bottom. Little to no food. The clothes on their backs. A pocketful of beatings— either courtesy of Mama or one of the string of men that marched through at all hours of the day and night.

It was that man's fault. He'd ruined Mama and her chance at a career on television when she was pretty and full of life. He'd seen pictures of her and every now and then, he'd spot a glimpse of the girl she'd once been, the one who longed to come into people's homes and make her mark.

Unfortunately, that one wasn't around anymore. But Nick was and he was close enough.

Nick could pay the toll. First, by watching Jessica die. And then when he didn't think he could suffer anymore, Nick would see that his suffering had just begun.

Chapter Thirty-Five

THE DARK SEDAN sped toward New Orleans, its air conditioning blasting away, trying to alleviate the intense heat and humidity lurking outside the tinted windows.

"We'll be situated in one of the airport hotels," Agent Phillips explained. "A large suite, which my people have already gone over with a fine-toothed comb."

Callie stared out the window at the passing scenery, her frustration mounting. She and Nick had brainstormed together, away from the prying eyes of the FBI, off and on for hours. They hadn't thought of a single situation where they could expose themselves to the killer and draw his attention while still coming out of the encounter alive.

Her mind drifted, playing out possible scenarios. The sudden roar of an airplane taking off made her realize they were close to their destination.

The car pulled up to the main entrance. In front and behind them, agents poured out of two separate cars, looking around like they were in a bad spy movie. It would almost have seemed comical if not for her bleak outlook.

They escorted Nick and her through the lobby and up to a suite where Ted and Brenda, the decoys, had already arrived. Greetings were exchanged and for the first time in a long time, she found herself outside the loop of fame.

"I am such a longtime fan, Mr. La Chappelle," Agent Brenda gushed. "I was at the Series where you pitched the no-hitter."

"Same here, Mr. La Chappelle." Agent Ted pumped Nick's hand enthusiastically. "My brother will spit shit when he hears I met you. You've been a huge idol of ours for years."

"I like how you brought such intelligence to the broadcast booth," Agent Brenda purred. "It's a shame you left when you did. Your replacements have all been so dull. And not nearly as easy on the eye."

"Please. Call me Nick." He slipped the baseball trading card from Agent Ted's hand and pulled a pen from Agent Phillips's pocket. "I'll bet you'd like that autographed." He scrawled his name and playing number across the bottom of the card.

She hid a smile. It was nice for once not being the one fawned over. It also brought home to her again that Nick was famous in his own right.

Nick returned the card and pen and gestured to her. "This is my fiancée, Callie Chennault."

Perfunctory greetings occurred this time, with no hint of enthusiasm. She thought she was going to like these two agents way more than SAC Phillips.

"Yes, I read the file on you, Ms. Chennault. So, you're an actress that's attracted a stalker," commented Agent Brenda, her bored voice indicating that this was a frequent nuisance. "I'm afraid I'm not familiar with you or your show."

"The file says that you're apparently a big deal," Agent Ted threw in. "We'll do our best to—"

Nick interrupted. "You guys are looking at a multiple Emmy-award winning actress," he stated, the vein in his temple throbbing. "Callie has also won all kinds of fan awards. She works with the SPCA and a battered women's shelter in New York, and is the person this douchebag is after. I'm just a secondary target. Get your priorities straight and focus on her—or this whole deal is off."

Nick's passionate defense of her surprised Callie—especially his loss of control. That let her know how really upset he was. She touched his arm and pulled him aside.

With a teasing smile and in a voice that only he could hear, she said, "Superman, I need you to calm down. Thanks for coming to my rescue when my legion of fans didn't materialize and recognize all my outstanding achievements but remember—I'm the diva here. I'll pull the prima donna act if need be."

Her teasing tone had the right effect on Nick. He visibly relaxed.

"I'm wound tighter than heading to the mound for the seventh game of the Series."

"Hey, even I know what that means. No need to explain. Come on. Let's get over there and put Ken and Barbie through their paces."

He glanced at the two FBI agents. "Do they really look like us? I don't quite picture myself as that pretty boy over there." He took her hand and glanced back in the agents' direction. "Besides, Agent Brenda is way too plain to be you."

Callie shrugged. "It would be a close enough resemblance from a distance. Height, coloring, weight. Those are all pretty much the same. Come on, big guy." She squeezed his hand and led him back to the huddled agents.

"I see no need to focus on speech patterns or inflections," Callie told them. "He shouldn't be up close and personal for that long. We need to work on your gait, the head tilts, your posture, hand gestures. Things like that."

They spent about fifteen minutes talking about their habits and demonstrating to the pair.

After a moment, Callie said, "Nick, why don't you go work with Agent Brenda here? You've observed me closely. You probably know more than I do about my gestures and how they look to others. I'll take Agent Ted here under my wing."

They both went to different rooms and worked for another hour, both checking on each other from time to time at the progress being made. Finally, Callie suggested putting the two agents together.

"We need you to interact as a couple. If this plays out as Agent Phillips believes, he may try to take us at the same time. You both need to be convincing enough not only as individuals, but as we are together."

"Do we need to demonstrate anything for them?" Nick asked, a mischievous gleam in his eye. He slipped an arm around her waist and moved in for a quick, hard kiss.

"Is this really necessary?" Agent Brenda whined.

The SAC barked out, "Yes. The UNSUB wants both of them. Ms. Chennault is right. He'll probably look for a situation to grab them together at the same time and place."

Phillips frowned. "We need to think about where to

turn your decoys loose. In public. But not too public. Definitely leaving Noble Oaks, since he seems to have tracked you from there before. We need for them to be on guard, even guarded, but somehow the guard must come down."

"How smart is this UNSUB?" Agent Ted asked. "I haven't read the profile on him."

"I'll get to that, but he's smart. Very smart. He kidnapped and killed several women in New York City and hasn't left any visible trace of evidence behind. Plus, an NYPD detective with decades of experience. Obviously, he's detailed-oriented. A planner."

Phillips put the decoys through their paces again, allowing her and Nick to make any adjustments they thought necessary. She sat as they watched the pair.

Nick parked next to her on the sofa. "Tired?" he whispered in her ear. "You look it."

"I'm beginning to feel it."

He rose and went to the other side of the room. He spoke a moment to Agent Phillips, who glanced at her.

"All right. Let's return you to Noble Oaks. I'm going to stay here, but Agent Crocker will see you home safely."

They had the same escort cars guide them out of the airport maze and to Aurora.

Nick's stomach growled as they pulled into the drive of the old mansion. "Hey, what're we going to do about dinner? There's no Essie to pamper us. Would you like to order a pizza? Aurora actually has a pizzeria now. It's pretty darn good, especially if you're interested in sausage and pepperoni. And hopefully, some mushrooms. Essie'll have the number posted on the fridge. Ham and pineapple pizza has become a favorite of Miz C's."

They got out of the car and let Agent Crocker show them inside the foyer.

"There are two men stationed in the living room. They're the only agents in the house. Several agents are still scattered about the property, monitoring the perimeter, so rest assured that no one can get inside. Please arm the alarm as I leave," Crocker instructed. "If you need anything, call Phillips."

Callie closed the door behind him and set the alarm. "We almost have the house to ourselves," she said quietly. "Finally."

They headed straight to the kitchen and she searched the refrigerator door for the take-out number.

"Hey, on second thought, I remember I've got a Di-Giorno's Pizza in the freezer at the cottage," Nick said. "It's almost as good as the real thing and a whole lot faster. Should I get it?"

She nodded. "Sounds good to me. I'll pre-heat the oven and toss us a salad."

"Be right back." Nick keyed in the code to allow him to open the rear door. She followed him, locking the door behind him, smiling through the glass as he signaled his thumbs-up approval. She re-armed the system and then turned on the oven to preheat before heading to the refrigerator.

Callie removed lettuce, tomatoes, black olives, mushrooms, cucumbers, and grated cheese. She took out a cutting board and chopped the ingredients, tossing everything in a large glass bowl and drizzling Essie's famous raspberry vinaigrette over it. She thought the salad dressing good enough to sell, but Essie was too humble about her talents. She simply bottled and gave it away to friends and family at Christmas and birthdays.

She glanced at the clock and wondered what was

taking Nick so long. Maybe he was having a hard time getting away from Petey. Callie had witnessed how much Petey loved to talk. He might be lonely as he spent nights away from his parents for the first time. Still, her own stomach rumbled even more loudly than Nick's had.

She decided to go get both of them and invite Petey to dinner if he hadn't already eaten with his folks. Aunt C had a tremendous sweet tooth and usually had no less than four different kinds of ice creams in the freezer. If no butter pecan were to be found, Callie believed she could find some flavor that would tempt Petey.

Placing the salad in the refrigerator to keep it cold, she entered the code. She unlocked and opened the back door and re-armed the alarm before she set out for the short walk to the cottage. This time her stomach nearly sang out in displeasure. Well, it was past eight-thirty. At this rate, they should probably gobble down the salad and settle for ham and cheese sandwiches. They could save the pizza for tomorrow.

Lights glowed in the bungalow's windows as dusk began to settle over Noble Oaks. Heat still rose from the ground in waves. The smell of cut grass mingled with the scent of magnolias and the sound of cicadas calling out to one another. She'd always thought of their song as the music of the night in the South.

It hit her that she hadn't missed New York at all since she'd returned to Aurora. Maybe they would make their permanent home here after all. She'd enjoyed toying around with writing ideas. Could that be the new direction of her career? If she changed to behind the camera, she wouldn't have to fight the stereotyping that would occur in front of it when she auditioned for future roles. She needed to consider it.

Writing intrigued her. Maybe she could collaborate

with Nick, though she sensed as a writer he was pretty much a loner. She could try something on her own. A novel might be too difficult to start with but she could write what she knew. What if she created a new television drama? Something set in a small town, with two rival families and all their extended family and friends. Maybe going in a new direction, such as writing, was the change of pace she needed. Plus, it would help distance her from Jessica.

A satisfied smile crossed her lips. Ideas started to fill her head as she continued down the drive to the cottage. She wondered if Nick would like to brainstorm some around as they ate dinner. Callie pictured a Southern matriarch like Aunt C trading barbs with the town's diabolical mayor. Political intrigue, romance, and a new business venture started to come to life in her head.

She stepped onto the tiny postage stamp of a porch. No doorbell meant she rapped loudly. She could hear the sound of the TV. She waited a moment and knocked again. Maybe Nick and Petey were back in the kitchen and couldn't hear her. When she knocked again and got no response, she decided to go inside.

She tried the handle and found the door was unlocked and pushed it open. "Nick? Petey?" she called. "Are you here?"

As she stepped into the room, the hairs on the back of her neck stood at attention. A quick scan of the room showed her that nothing seemed out of place. Some reality show blared from the TV. Maybe Petey was hard of hearing.

Yet as she crossed the room and headed toward the kitchen, a rush of fierce panic swept through her. She had to get out of here. Now.

Callie turned as the front door was pushed closed and locked.

Her eyes connected with a man in his mid-twenties. He was a couple of inches under six feet. Dark hair. Muddy brown eyes. Pleasant in a non-descript way. A sweet but bland smile. T-shirt and jeans. And blood spattered from the knees of his jeans to his sneakers.

No one had to tell her who he was.

Chapter Thirty-Six

"WHERE'S NICK?"

Callie surprised herself and tried not to let it show. She sounded so ordinary. As if she'd asked what time it was or what the weather was like.

The killer looked her up and down slowly. He nodded to himself, as if he were pleased about something.

Her insides revved up like a horse about to burst from the blocks at the Kentucky Derby. Adrenaline exploded in waves, bringing on an almost manic state. She thought she might take this guy on.

She fought that feeling, trying to force her mind to put on the brakes. No matter how physically charged she was, she couldn't act on impulse. He outweighed her by fifty pounds or more. And especially in her depleted condition, he would snap her like a twig. No, she would have to win the mind games with this psycho first.

And she had to know about Nick.

"I'm afraid Nick is no more," the stranger said sadly.

Callie met his eyes. "You're lying." She kept her voice low and calm. "It's not your style. You like to toy with your victims. Nick hasn't been here but ten minutes, tops."

He crossed his arms and leaned against the door, a slow smile spreading across his ordinary features. "You're familiar with my work. I'm flattered."

"Don't be."

He chuckled. "Well, I do love playing with my girls. Men don't interest me at all." He gazed at her with wistful fondness. "You were always the prize, Jessica. Nick just turned out to be an incidental loose end that I planned on tidying up somewhere down the road. Having the two of you in a single spot simply let me know fate had stepped in to guide me to my greatest work."

He'd called her Jessica. Callie didn't know if he was nuts enough not to be able to distinguish between her and her character, or if he played a game with her.

What should she do? The last time she'd found herself in a dangerous position, she'd tried to let Jessica do all the talking. That had almost worked until mouthy Callie Chennault stepped in for a moment and blew things.

Who was this man? What did he have against Nick? It seemed to her that he had some vendetta against Nick that was totally unrelated to his fixation on her. Or Jessica. What did he want with Jessica? She'd try to find out.

"Jessica isn't here right now. I'm Callie, her friend. I just want to know where Nick is."

He eyed her with a speculative gleam in those muddy brown eyes. "You can't fool me, Jessica. You may dress down like a little country girl in this bump on the map, trying to fool everyone—but I know the real you." He laughed. "Pretending to be this Callie is smart, though. It works some of the time. I know people still bother you, but it's really not a very good disguise. I recognized you. Other people do, too. I've seen them wait for you outside the studio in New York just to get your autograph. It can be twelve degrees with a harsh wind blowing, and there'll always be a few of Jessica's loyal legion waiting for her to appear."

"If you've seen me in New York, why didn't you ever come up and ask me for an autograph? I give them to fans all the time."

He frowned. "Because I'm not your fan. Because you're too perfect. Because you and all those like you kept her from a job."

"Who? Do you have a friend who is an actress? I can help get her an audition with our casting director."

"It's too late. She's dead."

Shit. Callie had hit a wall with this line. Where could she go now? She sensed she needed to keep him talking. She had to find a way to play for more time and hope Nick was alive somewhere in the cottage. Though every instinct told her to run, she refused to budge until she could find him. Without Nick, she didn't have a life.

She took a deep breath. She decided to go the sympathy angle. "I'm sorry."

"Are you?" he snapped. "You didn't know her. You wouldn't have given her a second glance on the street. It was people like you who broke her."

His face crumpled. He slid down the wall at his back, coming to rest on the ground with his hands braced on his knees. He seemed like a lost little boy all of a sudden, not an adult in his twenties.

She decided to press him while he seemed vulnerable. She had to learn why he did what he did to all those women—and learn why he was after Nick.

"Did you love her?" she asked softly.

"Yes." His voice was but a whisper. "I did. Years ago. The beatings pretty much killed the love."

His eyes glazed over, as if he were no longer in the present. His voice came from across a distance, almost childlike. She tamped down the revulsion building inside her.

"She was beautiful. Like an angel. I saw the pictures in books on a shelf in the closet. She wanted to be on TV. She used to rock me when I was little and tell me about going on auditions. How she was going to be famous. How she wanted to come into people's homes and be their friends. She'd been lonely and TV had always been her friend."

It was his mother he spoke of. But what were the connections?

Callie dared to take a few steps toward him. She knelt, still out of his reach, but she wanted to be on his level.

"Did she ever get to be on TV?"

"No. She had me instead. A one-night stand with a traveling salesman. She was working a convention as a floor model and hit it off with him. He lied about where he worked. Where he lived. What his real name was."

The bitterness flowed with each word that rapidly tumbled out. "She couldn't find him when she found out about me. Then her face got fat and her feet swollen and nobody wanted her. She had no money, no family, no friends that stuck around. Just me. Her little punching bag."

"She blamed you?"

"Sometimes. She would love on me one minute and punch out my lights the next. She couldn't afford a babysitter. She couldn't get an agent. Her looks faded. She did what she could to put food on the table. It always involved a line of men coming and going at all hours."

He sprang up and had her around the throat with one hand before she could move. He yanked her to her feet and slammed her into the wall. A rush of black clouded her vision, followed by a myriad of stars exploding in bright yellows and oranges.

He leaned close. "She always knew she was better than anyone on those crummy shows. I'll bet she could act rings around you, Jessica. You were the one that she hated the most. You had it all—the fame, the looks, the money. You and all those like you kept her from becoming a star."

His fingers tightened around her throat as his free hand stroked her breast. A shiver of revulsion ran through her as she fought the rising bile.

"Hot for me, Jessica?" he mused.

Callie brought her knee up hard into his groin, giving the thrust everything she had. Suddenly, the pressure on her throat ended as he fell back to the floor. She gulped in the sweet air. It made her lightheaded but she knew this was her one chance to escape.

Still dizzy, she took a shaky step over him with one leg in order to reach the door. As the other followed, his hand snaked around her ankle and sent her crashing to the floor. She tried to catch herself, falling on one wrist. She cried out in pain, knowing she'd broken it when she heard the snap.

The killer flipped her over and straddled her, his weight pinning her to the floor. Desperate to stay alive, she clawed at his face with her good hand. Bright red streaks appeared a moment later. He slapped her hard, twice, and she tasted blood in her mouth. He forced her arms above her head and yanked a ball of twine from his pocket, wrapping the string tightly around her joined wrists again and again. The pain from her injury caused her to go lightheaded and she was afraid she would pass out.

Callie could barely breathe with his weight on her, much less scream for help. Suddenly, she caught sight of a pair of handcuffs. He looped one cuff around her immobilized wrists, attaching the other to a chair leg. Now her arms were useless. She tried bucking him off but that proved futile. He was too heavy and her legs began to go numb from the pressure.

He stretched out on top of her, cooing in soft tones meant to calm her as he stroked her cheek. But she knew what lay ahead. She was aware of what had been done to the girls who resembled her. How long he'd tortured them.

His hands slipped to knead her breasts roughly, pinching the nipples, moving lower, between her legs. He cupped her and began to rub his palm against her slowly, smiling as he did.

Callie refused to cry. She refused to whimper. She would not give him a minute of pleasure, seeing her beg for her life. She would endure this. She would keep thinking. She would figure out how to get out of this mess. She had to.

She heard a noise and lifted her head, looking past him. His hands trailed down her thighs and calves to her feet. He slid off her sandals then slammed the heel of his hand down on her smallest toe. She gasped in pain, knowing he'd broken it.

"Payback," he muttered, as he slid down her body and began to lick her foot.

But she now knew where the noise came from. Beyond, in the arch of the kitchen, Nick dragged himself along the floor, an unfamiliar object in his hand. His face was a bloody mess. One eye swollen shut. But he moved with a single purpose. He was crawling to save her.

If this bastard saw Nick, he would kill him. She had to distract him. A calm descended upon her, bringing everything into a sharp focus.

She was ready for her close-up, Mr. De Mille.

"Oh," she moaned. She began writhing, twisting her torso, arching her back. "Oh, God, yes," she slurred out.

He stopped sucking her broken toe, a look of surprise on his face. Callie wet her lips and decided her Academy-winning performance was here and now.

"Please. Don't stop." Her chest heaved. "No one's done that before. I'm... I'm so fucking turned on by it."

He moved back up, sliding his body against hers. She swallowed hard, forcing her gag reflex to behave and gave him her best Jessica smile. The one that seduced every man. The one that made them putty in her capable hands.

"You want more?" His hardened penis pressed against her thigh.

"Yes," she whispered breathlessly, closing her eyes for fear they would betray her disgust. Seconds later, she was glad she'd done so.

The killer pushed his fingers into her hair, holding her head in place as he began to kiss her. His tongue forced her lips open and she met it with her own. She had done a love scene in acting class with a guy who'd had nasty garlic breath and the world's worst case of acne. The teacher let the bit go on for almost two minutes. It got more slobbery by the minute, like she was kissing a drooling Doberman. Callie drew on that memory and simply imagined this was Leonard. She'd made it through Leonard once. She would triumph again.

She wiggled seductively under him, pushing everything from her mind.

"I'm better than Nick, right?" he asked, his mouth coming off hers.

"Mmm, much better," she lied.

Then she heard an odd noise and felt a vibration. He gave a cry of anguish as he tensed, his entire body going stiff. He collapsed on top of her and didn't move.

Callie opened her eyes as Nick pulled the man off her. The killer lay on the floor, paralyzed, his eyes wide with fright. She bit her lip to steady herself as tears welled in her eyes.

Instead, she gazed at the man she loved. "Are you all right?" She eyed his bruised and battered face. "You look like one of your fastballs hit you in the face. Multiple times."

Nick crawled next to her, holding a hand against his ribcage. "I think he broke a few of these." He rubbed the area gently. "What about you?"

Callie's gaze cut to the killer. His eyes, filled with pain and anger, stared into hers. She knew he was conscious but he wasn't moving. She looked back at Nick.

"Stun gun," he got out. "Used it on me. Then kicked the shit out of me." His crooked grin caused her heart to flip over.

"Did research. For a book. Hero got tasered. Pain's unbelievable. Can attest to it now." He shook his head and studied the killer for a moment. "Right now he's paralyzed. Every single muscle's cramping tighter and tighter. Got no control over his body."

He brought a hand to her cheek and touched her reassuringly. "Need to get help." He pushed himself to an upright position, grimacing as he did. "Gotta get these off you."

He crawled to the stranger who had turned their

lives upside down and searched his pockets for the key. All the while the man's eyes never left her. Nick found the key and brought it back, releasing the handcuffs.

"Scissors," he gasped. He scooted over and opened a drawer in the coffee table and pulled out a pair. Returning to her, he cut through the twine that bound her wrists.

She sucked in a quick breath as pain shot through her. Nick's jaw tightened as he gently eased her arms down. "Your wrist. Swollen. Looks broken."

He glared at their attacker. "I want this bastard to go away for a long, long time." He reached out and smoothed her hair. "Come on, baby. Let's get you up and away from this fucker."

Somehow, Nick managed to get on his feet and help her rise. He escorted her to the sofa before he hobbled to the phone and punched in a number. She could hear the ringing in the silence of the cottage. Only Nick's labored breathing disturbed the quiet.

"It's La Chappelle." He paused. "We're out back. In the cottage. Bring your cuffs, Phillips. We got him."

Chapter Thirty-Seven

CALLIE SAT opposite Eric inside the Aurora Police Department. Nick sat next to her, his fingers linked through hers. She stole a glance at his bruised and swollen features, worrying anew at the pain he must have gone through while lying frozen, unable to defend himself, as the killer viciously attacked him. Nick insisted on leaving the hospital first thing this morning, though, after an overnight stay.

She also thought of poor Petey, who also suffered from the taser and had been found cowering in the locked bedroom closet of the cottage, babbling how his "friend" hurt him. The police got little out of the gardener, other than the fact that Lipstick Larry befriended Petey in town and bought him ice cream. Later, he offered to help Petey do his work, saying it would be fun for the two of them to work on the flowers together.

Petey kept talking about them playing hide and seek. The police surmised from his ramblings that the killer had hidden in the back floorboard of Mrs. Borgan's car when she brought Petey back from lunch, as they'd found hair and other fibers present in the car that matched his. He must have slipped out and remained hidden from her and the assigned agents' view while she and Petey carried in some groceries for him that were in the car's trunk.

Agent Phillips entered the room, nodding curtly at them before taking a seat at the table next to Eric.

"Good morning. Thank you for coming."

"Wouldn't have missed it, Special Agent Phillips," Nick told him. "I think Callie and I are ready for you to fill in the blanks for us."

He gave her fingers a light squeeze. The gesture provided her the bit of courage she needed to hear what would be revealed. They'd already learned from Eric that the two FBI agents inside Noble Oaks had been found dead, having died before she and Nick had arrived back from their session with their doubles.

"Perp's name is Raymond Morris. Birth certificate lists the mom as Genevieve Morris. Dad unknown. He was a bright kid. Off the charts in elementary school. Removed four times from his home due to suspected child abuse and the mother's alcoholism and arrests for prostitution."

Phillips shuffled the papers in front of him, pulling out one and studying it a moment.

"Mrs. Morris was found beaten to death when Ray was sixteen. Said he didn't kill her but no one else looked good for it, despite the long line of johns who regularly patronized her services. Spent six years in detention for the crime. Got out about eighteen months ago. Held a steady job but failed to meet with his parole officer last week. Turns out he'd gone AWOL from his job about a month earlier."

The agent turned a few more pages and cleared his throat. "Checked his last known address. Suspicious neighbor next door to the brownstone where he'd been renting a room told the cops that Morris told her that he was moving to Queens. Said his landlady decided to join her relatives down in Florida. No one saw her leave. Just took Morris' word."

"That was enough to get a warrant," Eric continued as Phillips took a sip of coffee. "They found a plethora of proof in the basement that will no doubt link Morris to the rapes and murders of the New York blonds. Plus the landlady's remains." He grimaced. "It wasn't pretty."

"But what about Nick?" she asked. "I thought I'd endangered his life by us becoming involved, but Morris told me he had already targeted Nick. He thought it was fate that we were both in Aurora and he could deal with us at the same time."

Phillips shrugged. "I haven't gotten that out of him yet. Nothing connects the two of them. We can get him on assault and battery on Mr. La Chappelle but I don't think the attempted murder charges would stick."

"But he told me he was going to kill Nick!" she exclaimed, wanting justice.

The SAC raised a hand. "He's waived all rights to an attorney—if we'll let him see Mr. La Chappelle. Alone."

Nick's eyebrows raised a notch. "Is that allowed?"

"Declining an attorney is his right. Stating he'd do so only unless he met with you?" Phillips shook his head. "I couldn't promise him you'd see him. He won't guarantee me anything unless I do."

"Then I'll see him," Nick stated, grim determination filling his face. "We have to have answers. If that's the way to get them, I'll be happy to cooperate."

Eric left the room and returned minutes later. "Everything's arranged. Morris is being brought to interrogation." He studied his cousin. "Sure you want to do this, buddy?"

"Positive. You'll all be watching, won't you? Don't you have one of those two-way glass set-ups?"

Eric nodded. "You bet. Let's head that way."

They all stood and filed down the hallway. Eric indicated a door and Callie entered a small room that overlooked Aurora's lone interrogation room. Eric and Agent Phillips followed her in. She watched as a deputy led Morris into the empty room and seated him at the table. She breathed a sigh of relief. His hands were cuffed. He wore leg shackles.

Nick entered the room, his battered face void of emotion. The deputy motioned for him to be seated across from Morris.

"I'll be right outside the door, Mr. La Chappelle. You just holler and I'll come a-running if you need me."

"Thanks, Officer."

The lawman left, closing the door behind him. Nick and Morris studied each other for a long moment. Callie explored one profile, then the other. A prickling crept through her. Her gut suddenly knew what this was about.

"I suppose I should ask you for your autograph?"

"No. Not that I'd give it to you anyway."

Morris stared at Nick. "You still don't get it, do you? Mr. Smooth. The poster boy for broadcasters. I'd always thought you were fairly smart."

"Smart enough not to butcher women."

"Way to go, bro. Nice comeback."

Callie watched as realization dawned on Nick's face. "You mean..."

Morris slammed his cuffed hands against the table's surface. "Exactly. Aren't you ready to welcome me to the family? Maybe I could be the best man when you marry that slut."

Nick's eyes flashed with anger, but he remained seated and silent.

"I grew up smart—and very, very poor, Nicky Boy. Mom caved and took the welfare. Moved every few months to beat the rent. Beating me up in her spare time was her only hobby, one she was really good at. Yeah, lots of love in the old Morris household."

Morris leaned back in his chair. "I was smart and small for my age. Basically, a geek without the glasses. Not an athletic bone in my body. Always got picked last in gym class. Wedgies in the locker room. The bullies shook me down for my lunch money over and over until they figured out I never had any. Then they'd be pissed and drag me to the toilet to swish my head around in for taking up their time. And those are the good memories, Nicky. Yeah, I had an awesome childhood."

He shifted in the chair. "My escape was to lose myself in TV. Just like Mom would. She wanted to be famous. The most popular actress on a long-running series. She came to New York with big dreams in her heart. Never made it because she got knocked up with me. She never mentioned my old man. I didn't dared ask.

"Then one day I was watching a Dodgers' game. Everyone from my neighborhood pulled for the Yankees, but I loved the Dodgers. Those clean, crisp uniforms. The beautiful ballpark in sunny California. I wished every night I could be on that team. Yeah, right —punky little Ray Morris who couldn't walk and chew gum at the same time, much less hit a ball. I dreamed about escaping and being a star athlete. Handsome. Rich. No one bullying me ever again."

Morris rested his arms on the table. "One spring night when the apartment was already baking in the heat, a new pitcher went out to the mound to pitch against the Mets. The announcers bragged on this rookie from Texas with a hundred-mile-an-hour fastball and a wicked change-up to match. They flashed your face on the screen.

"My mom had just seen a john out the door and turned around and got a glimpse of you. She fainted dead away." He laughed. "I freaked, man. Splashed cold water in her face. Thought the heat had done a number on her. But when she came to? She started cursing a blue streak.

Then she told me my dad looked exactly like you."

* * *

Nick remembered that night as if it were yesterday. He'd gone straight from high school into Triple A and only spent a season there before getting called to the big show the next spring. That night he'd pitched against the Mets had been his debut in front of the L.A. home crowd. He'd struck out fifteen batters despite all the butterflies in his stomach.

His parents had been there. He'd flown them out especially for that night.

"Did she see my... our dad in the crowd?"

Morris nodded. "You catch on real fast. She recognized him right away when the cameras cut to him, despite the fact that a few years had gone by. They even interviewed him between innings. He bragged on what a great kid you were. How talented and smart you were. How proud he was of his only son."

Morris stood up abruptly, his chair falling back against the wall. "You had everything. You got the looks and the talent and a great home. I lived in hell every day of my life. The old man fucked my mom once and never looked back."

Nick eyed his own flesh and blood, recognizing the killer now as a paler version of himself without all the advantages he'd been raised with. He couldn't imagine the horror of being brought up in such a hostile environment. It sickened him how his father had been in part responsible for the way this man turned out.

It had always been unspoken between him and his mom. They'd grown so close over the years as his dad traveled from coast to coast for his job over extended periods. Yet Nick had heard the times she'd cried, either from loneliness or when she found evidence of her husband's infidelity as she unpacked his bags. He tried his best to make it up to her. They both expressed silent relief when Dick La Chappelle passed away from a sudden heart attack after Nick's first season in the majors. He'd provided for his mom ever since.

He studied his half-brother, wishing he could change so many things and knowing he never could.

The deputy opened the door. "Agent Phillips would like to see you, sir."

Nick rose, a hurt in his heart pounding heavily. Pity —mixed with revulsion—warred within him as he thought of the atrocities committed at the hands of this man. Before he could speak, Raymond Morris did.

"Yeah, run away, golden boy. You wouldn't want to be seen with the likes of me." He snorted. "Don't worry, bro. I'll invite you to the execution. Should be another ten years down the road by the time all the appeals are exhausted."

A ghost of a smile crossed Morris's face. "Have fun with Jessica now. But be watching over your shoulder, though. If I ever get out, you two will be the first to know." His smile broadened. Nick knew pure evil danced across the killer's face.

His insides clenched tightly. He locked his jaw and left the room without another word.

Outside, the deputy led him to the room where Callie, Eric, and Phillips had viewed the interview.

"We have out of him what we needed and the motive," Phillips said. "No reason for you to stay in there with him any longer."

"Do you think they'll find him insane?" Nick asked. "With the circumstances of his childhood? His delusions of revenge on a dad he never knew? Callie symbolizing everything his poor mom wanted and never achieved?"

Phillips shrugged. "Not my call. My job was to find him. I've done that. He'll be tried in New York first on the serial murders before he would be returned to Louisiana to face the charges of Detective Waggoner's murder. He's proven canny enough that I don't think an insanity plea would be feasible. Not that a sly attorney won't try it."

A knot of fear twisted inside him as Nick watched his half-brother being led from the room. Would he and Callie be able to create a life together without always peering into the shadows, worried that Morris lurked there?

Epilogue

NICK OPENED the door to the living room and found Callie absently twisting the gold band on her finger as she chewed on her lip, her pen poised above the notebook in her lap. He grinned, knowing she must be hard at work on her new series. He'd thought it a terrific idea when she shared she was thinking of stepping behind the scenes and creating her own show. They tossed out ideas for characters and plots the entire time they honeymooned in Cancun.

"You busy?" he asked.

When Callie caught sight of him, a smile lit her face. It gave him chills every time he looked at her and thought of how he'd almost lost her.

Thankfully, that was behind them.

"Did you get the pictures?" She set aside her work.

He held up the bag. "Right here. Walgreen's was delighted to print out a bazillion digital pictures for us. I haven't even cheated and gone through them yet."

He went and sat beside her, his arms automatically going around her as he gave her a lingering kiss.

"Mmm," she sighed. "With your looks and the way you kiss? You could be Jake."

He raised an eyebrow. "Your lead character? I'll consider that high praise."

Nick kissed her again, inhaling the familiar honeysuckle scent on her skin. It went to his head every time. He needed to watch it or they'd be in the bedroom within the next thirty seconds. He really needed to share the news he'd just received with her.

Callie reached for the sack and pulled out the envelopes with their pictures from Mexico. Nick decided to let her enjoy those for a few minutes. Her delight at retracing their spontaneous trip after her wrist and his ribs healed gave him immense satisfaction.

She paused at one of them on the beach, the sun beginning to set behind them as they sealed their wedding vows with a kiss.

"I think we did the right thing. Getting married with no fuss. Just us. No *paparazzi*."

"Works for me every time," he said as he nuzzled her neck.

"I'm glad Aunt C understood."

"Well, she gave us one hell of a party after we returned so I don't think she's holding a grudge against us."

Nick took the pictures from her hands and placed them on the coffee table in front of them. He took her hands in his.

"I need to tell you something," he said softly.

She tensed. "It's about him, isn't it. Raymond Morris."

He nodded. "After I stopped in for the pictures, I ran into Eric. He was going to come over and talk to both of us but once I saw the look on his face, I pretty much forced it out of him."

"Eric did always give away what he was thinking." She took a deep breath. "What is it, Nick?"

"He's dead. He won't ever bother us again."

Her eyes widened. "What do you mean? Dead? His trial isn't even—"

"An inmate killed him, Callie. And in an ironic turn, he turns out to be a huge fan of Jessica's."

"What?"

Nick shook his head, still hardly believing the story. "You said you have your prison groupies who tune in to watch you. Well, Jimbo Fineman claims he's your biggest fan. He's even a member of your fan club. Has your pictures all over his cell's walls.

"When Jimbo found out that Morris is the one who tried to kill you? Let's just say he took justice into his own hands. Eric said it happened early this morning. Supposedly, Mr. Fineman has been crowned a hero by his fellow prisoners."

She shuddered. "I can't believe someone... *killed* for me. That's so weird."

Nick squeezed her hands. "Weird or not, it's over. It's behind us, babe. We can sleep better tonight, knowing Morris will never trouble us again."

A grin crossed Callie's face. "Who said anything about sleeping?

Also by Alexa Aston

HOLLYWOOD NAME GAME:

Hollywood Heartbreaker

Hollywood Flirt

Hollywood Player

Hollywood Double

Hollywood Enigma

LAWMEN OF THE WEST:

Runaway Hearts

Blind Faith

Love and the Lawman

Ballad Beauty

SAGEBRUSH BRIDES:

A Game of Chance

Written in the Cards

Outlaw Muse

KNIGHTS OF REDEMPTION:

A Bit of Heaven on Earth

A Knight for Kallen

SECOND SONS OF LONDON:

Educated by the Earl

Debating with the Duke

DUKES DONE WRONG:

Discouraging the Duke

Deflecting the Duke

Disrupting the Duke

Delighting the Duke

Destiny with a Duke

DUKES OF DISTINCTION:

Duke of Renown

Duke of Charm

Duke of Disrepute

Duke of Arrogance

Duke of Honor

MEDIEVAL RUNAWAY WIVES:

Song of the Heart

A Promise of Tomorrow

Destined for Love

SOLDIERS AND SOULMATES:

To Heal an Earl

To Tame a Rogue

To Trust a Duke

To Save a Love

To Win a Widow

THE ST. CLAIRS:

Devoted to the Duke

Midnight with the Marquess

Embracing the Earl

Defending the Duke

Suddenly a St. Clair

THE KING'S COUSINS:

God of the Seas

The Pawn

The Heir

The Bastard

THE KNIGHTS OF HONOR:

Rise of de Wolfe

Word of Honor

Marked by Honor

Code of Honor

Journey to Honor

Heart of Honor

Bold in Honor

Love and Honor

Gift of Honor

Path to Honor

Return to Honor

Season of Honor

NOVELLAS:

Diana

Derek

Thea

The Lyon's Lady Love

About the Author

A native Texan and former history teacher, award-winning and internationally bestselling author Alexa Aston lives with her husband in a Dallas suburb, where she eats her fair share of dark chocolate and plots out stories while she walks every morning. She enjoys travel, sports, and binge-watching—and never misses an episode of *Survivor*.

Alexa brings her characters to life in steamy historicals, contemporary romances, and romantic suspense novels that resonate with passion, intensity, and heart.

KEEP UP WITH ALEXA
Visit her website
Newsletter Sign-Up

MORE WAYS TO CONNECT WITH ALEXA

CPSIA information can be obtained
at www.ICGtesting.com
Printed in the USA
LVHW041756230322
714085LV00008B/1048

9 781648 39